ELUDE

Eagle Elite Book 6

by

Rachel Van Dyken

Elude
by Rachel Van Dyken
www.rachelvandykenauthor.com

ELUDE

ISBN 13: 978-1514210666
ISBN: 1514210665
Cover Art Designed by P.S. Cover Design

EAGLE ELITE SERIES

Elite
Elect
Entice
Elicit
Ember
Elude

NOVELLAS

Enchant
Evoke
Enamor

Elude: *To evade, get away from. Throw off the scent. The process of slipping through someone's fingers.* Example: *I never knew that in eluding death — I'd be faced with hers.*

PROLOGUE

Sergio

THE FLUORESCENT LIGHTS BURNED my eyes. I blinked them rapidly — thinking it would make the stinging go away, but it only made everything worse. The pain was indescribable, like someone had broken my body in half, repaired it, and then repeated the process.

"He's not going to make it." I recognized the voice. It was Nixon's. Why the hell was Nixon there? Wasn't he dead? No wait, that was me. I'd taken that bullet.

Memories of the past few days flashed across my line of vision, causing a searing headache to build at my temples.

The fight.

The gunshots.

The agreement.

My wife.

Tears burned the back of my eyes.

Wife…

"I'll do it. I'm a match." I gripped her hand firmly in mine.

"You'll die," Tex whispered. "Your body… it's too weak from everything else."

"We're running out of time!" I screamed, my voice hoarse, eyes frantic. "Do it now!"

"No." She wrapped her frail arms around my neck. "No."

"Yes." I pushed her away. "If I don't — you could die. The doctor says it needs to be now, so operate."

Her eyes were sad.

Both Tex and Phoenix looked down at the blue and white tile floor, faces pale. I knew what they were thinking. I'd already lost too much blood, my kidneys were barely working, and I wanted to give her part of my life.

I'd known going in I would most likely die.

But I'd do everything within my power to save her.

It's odd, when you face death every day, when you elude it, when you finally come to terms with the fact that you won't be on earth for forever — that's when you think you're at peace.

I thought I was okay with dying.

Until I met her.

And then I was faced with someone else's death every damn day — it's harder. People don't tell you that. It's one thing to come to terms with your own mortality; it's quite another to stare down death of the one you love, knowing there is nothing in this world that will stop it.

My vision blurred again.

"He's flatlining," a voice said in the distance.

I tried to keep my eyes open. I saw white-blond hair, big brown eyes, and that tender smile. I reached for it and held onto it, held onto the memory of her. The girl who'd changed my world from darkness to light.

The girl I never wanted.

But desperately needed.

"Tell her I'll love her…" I didn't recognize my own

gravelly voice. "…forever."

With a gasp, I felt my heart stutter to a stop.

And welcomed the shade of night that overtook me.

CHAPTER ONE

Six weeks earlier

Sergio

LONELINESS TASTED LIKE HELL. It also, lucky for me, tasted like a fifth of whiskey and what would most likely be a throbbing headache come tomorrow morning.

I brought the bottle to my lips and tilted it back, my eyes trained on the fire in front of me, the flames licking higher and higher, reminding me that I wasn't exactly in any position to ask God for any favors…it may as well have been hell waving back at me and confirming my suspicions.

I'd killed too much.

I'd lied even more.

And I was officially out of favor within my family — within my world.

I hissed as a drip of whiskey landed on my blood-caked knuckles. Beating the shit out of the wall hadn't even stopped the anger.

Ah anger, that was something I could talk about,

something I could tangibly feel as it pulsed through my body. It had been my mistress for so long that I knew if I actually let it go — I'd be even more lonely than I already was.

I tried to take a deep breath, to calm myself down, but air wouldn't go into my lungs, I felt paralyzed and on an adrenaline high all at once.

Maybe that was another part of my punishment. I had exactly twenty-four hours before I had to marry a Russian.

And not just any Russian.

An enemy, a double agent who had worked for both the FBI and, apparently, the Nicolasi family. She had sold out her own crime family, the Petrovs, and now… she was under the protection of the Italians.

How messed up was that?

I took another swig of whiskey and eyed the clock. Make that twenty-three hours and fifty-eight minutes.

I wasn't drunk enough.

I wasn't even close.

Marrying someone for protection I could do. Marrying someone and even killing them afterwards? Piece of cake. After all, that was my MO. I was a killer, a ghost, whatever the family wanted me to be.

But marrying someone, keeping them safe, only to watch them die within six months?

No. Hell no.

She had leukemia.

So why keep her alive this long?

I snorted and took another sip of whiskey. "I'd be doing her a favor by killing her."

"Ouch," a light airy voice said from somewhere in the room, causing all my hair to stand on end. "So as far as pep talks go, yours officially needs work."

I carefully set down the whiskey, not trusting myself not to throw it in her direction in an anger-filled rage. "I was talking to myself."

"Another sign you need to get laid." She laughed.

I didn't.

"Go away, Arabella."

"My name's Andi."

"Your legal name is Arabella Anderson Petrov. Care to know your social security number and credit score as well?"

"Romance is lost on you." I felt her move around the room. The air seized with electricity; she'd always had a presence about her, and right now I was five seconds away from losing my shit and ramming my head into the fireplace just so I could escape it all.

"Don't I know it," I huffed and reached for the bottle again.

Small warm hands clasped around mine before I could get there. I jerked away, causing her to stumble in front of me.

White-blond hair covered her soft features. Big brown eyes blinked back at me. I hissed in a breath and cursed. "You should go."

"We need to talk."

"Oh goody. Is this the part where you tell me I have to give up my virginity on my wedding night?"

"What?" She blinked like a startled deer, then a weak smile pulled her lips upward.

I ignored the way my body reacted and rolled my eyes in irritation.

"Aw, he has jokes now. At least, I hope it's a joke. You're not, are you? A virgin, I mean."

I snorted and eyed the bottle, calculating my odds on reaching it before she stopped me, then gave up. "Fine." I huffed. "Hurry up and get to talking so I can get drunk."

Andi sat opposite me in the leather chair and tucked her feet under her body. She was small, around five-one, but she packed a punch, knew how to use every automatic weapon on the market, and I was pretty sure I had once overheard that she was well-versed in torture. Looking at her, you'd think she was just graduating high school and getting ready to go shopping for her favorite pair of shoes with Daddy's credit card.

"You're upset," she finally said.

"No." I licked my lips and leaned forward. "I'm enraged. There's a difference."

Her eyes narrowed. "You know you can talk to me – since you're stuck with me for the next... while. That is, unless you kill me first... like you did that FBI agent."

My blood ran cold. No one knew about what I'd done last week. When I'd gained intel from another agent. "Her cover was blown. I did her a favor."

"Did you?" Her eyebrows arched.

"Have you ever been shot, Andi?"

She sighed and leaned her head back against the lush cushion. "No, why? Are you going to educate me on what it feels like?"

I exhaled and popped my knuckles; the sound reverberated through the empty room. "It happens in three stages."

"What does?"

"Getting shot."

"You mean you don't just pull the trigger?" she joked.

Ignoring her, I continued. "Shock. It's always the first emotion because the human brain hasn't yet caught up with the fact that you've been wounded. So your body starts going into shock, and then the pain happens, but it's not the type of pain you'd think. It burns, but it's more of an empty, hollow pain, that starts to spread from the wound throughout the rest of your body until a slow chill starts to descend. When the chill descends, the shock wears off and confusion sets in. Why was I shot? Why me? What have I done? As humans, our brains aren't meant to understand violence, so we have to logically explain it away. I had to have done something wrong to get shot. Or maybe I was in the wrong place at the wrong time. The minute your brain finds something that makes sense you move onto the last stage."

Andi barely moved a muscle. "Death?"

"Worse." I reached for the bottle and took a long swig. "Denial."

"Why is denial worse?"

"You tell me."

Her eyes closed briefly before she offered a shrug. "Because it means you aren't ready."

"Look who just earned an A in class," I mocked. "And you're right. Denial happens when you realize it shouldn't be you, that even if your brain connected the dots, it isn't yet your time. The lovely little memories of your life start to play on repeat in your head — the moments you should have done something but didn't, the things you'll never say, the things you'll never do. And then… you either get lucky or, if I'm the one who pulled the trigger, your memories will click off after about one minute, and you'll be no more."

The fire crackled.

Andi refused to look at me.

"I'd make it fast, Andi."

"Are we seriously doing this?"

"What?" I shrugged.

"Having a conversation in what should be a nice cozy room, about you killing me?"

"It would be a kindness."

"Go to hell!"

"Already there, Andi. Already there. Don't you know? I belong nowhere. My family's punishing me, the FBI's investigating me for the murder of my superior, and now I have to marry a Russian whore."

"So…" She stood. "…you'd rather kill me than marry me?"

"Was I not clear? I thought I was… Allow me to say it slower, perhaps in Russian? If that's all you people understand." I stood, meeting her chest to chest. "I'd rather kill you than see you suffer… I'd offer a dog the same kindness."

"I'm not a dog."

"You're Russian."

"Stop saying that."

"What?" I sneered. "The truth? Well, sweetheart, it doesn't get any truer than your reality. Allow me to kill you before your family or cancer does, and at least you can own your own death rather than fearing it."

She reached for me, touched my shoulders, and then cupped my face. I hated it because I liked it; my body leaned without me telling it to. She was so warm. "And what makes you think I fear my own death?"

"Everyone is afraid of dying. The hardest part is never admitting we're mortal, but coming to terms with the fact that we have no control over how long we're given. You do."

"No… I don't… You're trying to take that control."

"Say the word." My hand moved to the Glock strapped to my thigh.

"I'm not afraid." Her lips trembled. "At least not of death… but I am afraid of something."

"Oh yeah?" I hissed. "What's that?"

"Yours."

Confused, I stepped back, immediately looking for a weapon. "I don't understand."

"You wouldn't." She shrugged. "Because you, Sergio Abandonato, are already dead." She moved gracefully across the room. "You're dead inside… and you don't even know it. Forget cancer — and take a long hard look in the mirror — that's what death looks like."

CHAPTER TWO

Andi

MY ALARM CLOCK WENT OFF at seven a.m.

Not that I needed it. I'd been waking up early my entire life. Call me paranoid, but it seemed sleep was the only time someone could actually hurt me. If I was sleeping, then I was vulnerable, even if I had packed a semi-automatic under my bed, a pistol in my nightstand, plus two ninja stars under the pillow just in case.

I groaned, placing my hand against my clammy skin. You'd think after years of having chronic leukemia I'd be used to the symptoms, but who in her right mind would ever get used to waking up in a pool of her own clammy sweat?

I blew out air between my teeth and stood on shaky legs. I needed a shower, and my room — the room I'd chosen at Sergio's house last night after he'd all but offered to kill me — didn't have a bathroom attached, meaning I had to go searching for one.

Stupid, stupid, Andi.

I'd listened to Frank, the Alfero boss, when he'd dropped

me off last night. His words had been, *"He'll be fine, just give him time."*

I'd felt like a kid getting dropped off on her first day of school. The house was impressive, daunting even, but I'd been around scary all my life, so I didn't think anything of it. Not when the lights were all turned down, not when I heard what I could have sworn was a ghost floating through the halls, and not when I happened to overhear my future husband say aloud that killing me would be a kindness.

I had been half-tempted to say, *"Not if I kill you first."*

But that would only have been out of anger.

In the end, he would be doing me a favor, loath as I was to admit it. Honest moment? I felt sorry for him. I might be marching toward my death, but that guy was in way worse shape than I. Did he even appreciate life? I highly doubted it.

I managed to throw on the smallest sweatshirt I had and tightened my black pajama shorts. I was losing more weight.

I refused to look in the mirror because it would only confirm my suspicions… the symptoms were worse… I'd need a bone marrow transplant, or I'd die.

And all the money in the world wouldn't put me high on that list.

Especially considering my connections, my birth father, my reputation. I shook the negativity from my head and opened my bedroom door. The hallway was silent.

Which was really unfortunate, considering my new roommate had decided to drink all the alcohol in the entire house.

With a smirk, I ran back into my room, grabbed the baseball bat from the corner — yet another weapon I kept around just in case — and ran down to the kitchen.

Where I found a large enough pot.

I started walking through the long upstairs hallway.

Banging it to hell.

Bang. Bang. Bang. "Sergio?" *Bang. Bang. Bang.*

A groaning that sounded a lot like an animal either dying or attempting to give birth erupted from the farthest bedroom down the hall.

I hit the pan harder.

"Son of a bitch!" The groaning turned into yelling, and, sure enough, the door flew open and a crappy looking Sergio turned his murderous chocolate eyes in my direction.

Did I say chocolate?

I meant possessed.

No way was I allowed to find him attractive. It would be weird, my wanna-be killer being sexy.

Wasn't there a term for that? Stockholm syndrome or something?

"What." His voice was deep and gravelly. Oh, what the heck, he was sexy. "The. Hell." He wiped his face with his hands, his fingers pressed against his temples. "Is. That."

I held up the bat. "Not a fan of sports?"

He glared then stomped toward me, jerked the metal slugger out of my hands, and threw it down the stairs. "Can't say that I am."

I tapped my fingernails against the stainless steel pot and grinned.

"You have a death wish."

"I believe we established that last night."

His lips pressed together in a fine, angry-looking line as his hands reached for the pot and pulled.

I didn't let go.

He jerked harder.

I smiled.

"Let go."

I gritted my teeth. "You first."

His smile was pure evil as he slapped my forearms down. The pot made a loud clang as it slammed against the Spanish tile floor.

Sergio tilted his head and leaned in, his lips brushing

against my ear. "I could break you in half by sneezing, Russia. Don't."

I opened my mouth, but he slammed his hand across it and shook his head. "I said. Don't." He removed his hand. "Don't speak, don't scream, don't yell, don't hum. Silence. I have a hell of a headache, I haven't had any coffee, and I'm pretty sure a train ran over my face last night. The least you could do is get the hell out of my way before I make good on my promise."

"Promise?"

"To put you down."

I rolled my eyes. "I'm not an animal."

His eyebrows shot up. "Banging a pot with a baseball bat at seven in the damn morning? I'll believe it when I see it. Now step aside before I physically remove you."

"I'd like to see you try." I poked him in the chest.

"Fine." He smiled. I wasn't sure if I liked that smile; it threw me off course, made my stomach get little butterflies, while at the same time telling me that he was dangerous.

The next minute I was in his arms, getting carried down the stairs toward the kitchen.

I was saved by the ringing doorbell, but instead of setting me down, he simply hefted me higher over his shoulder and opened the door.

His brother Ax stood on the other side. His amused grin made me want to go back and search for the bat. "Carrying the wife over the threshold already, huh, bro?"

"Eat shit."

I waved at Ax. "He always this cheerful in the morning?"

Tex, the Cappo suddenly appeared behind Ax and smiled. "Having never been one of Serg's one-night stands, I can't actually say yes or no, but if I was a betting man, I'd say many a woman leaves *un*satisfied."

Sergio growled.

I giggled at Tex's wink. I'd liked him the minute I'd met

him.

Heck, I liked all the mob bosses. The five families were like royalty in the mafia world and ever since they'd been taken over by the younger, better-looking sons, they'd basically thrown organized crime into a tailspin.

My own biological father was even singing their praises — which basically meant he just wanted to be the one taking credit for killing them all.

The mob world was weird.

Sadly, it was the only thing that made sense to me. So maybe I was just as off-kilter.

"Put her down, Sergio..." Ax shoved past us. "...before you hurt her."

"You heard him." I slapped Sergio on the ass. "Put me down. Wouldn't want to hurt me."

Sergio slowly, methodically hoisted me forward and slid my body down his. I felt every hard plane of muscle and noticed the fiery need burning in his eyes — to throttle my ass.

"Thanks…" I licked my lips then rose up on my tiptoes, grabbing his face at the same time and kissing his cheek. "You'll be such a good husband."

He paled.

Tex burst out laughing.

All in all, it was a typical mob morning… a little bit of violence, some sexual tension, some laughter, and a loud wakeup call.

"Andi…" Tex cleared his throat. "…before everyone gets here I—"

"Everyone?" Sergio repeated, his voice laced with dread. "What do you mean everyone?"

"It's a wedding," Ax answered for Tex and slapped Sergio on the back. "Come on. I'll make coffee."

I followed the guys into the kitchen. Tex shot me curious glances while Sergio avoided all eye contact, making sure we were very aware that he was all but molesting the kitchen counter with his eyes. Well, to each his own.

"Everyone," Sergio said again, while Ax sighed aloud and passed me a hot cup of coffee.

"The girls." Tex reached for a mug while Ax poured the dark liquid into it. "The women, I should say."

"And why are they coming?" Sergio tapped his fingers against the counter, the sound causing my nerves to leap into action.

Most men I could figure out — Sergio, on the other hand, was too cool, calculated. He rarely showed his emotions, and when he did, you realized you were wrong about wanting to see them in the first place. He was scary, too controlled, too everything, and the minute he let you see that, you wanted to nail Pandora's box to the bottom of the ocean and put a giant ass whale in charge of guarding it.

Tex eyed me carefully. Ah, I knew that look. With a sigh, I brought the coffee to my lips and blew. "Just say it, boss man."

He cursed. "I suck at this."

"Me thinks you suck at many things." I winked.

"Russians." His grin was teasing, friendly. "Serg, she's dying."

"Elephant!" I coughed and then raised my hand for a high five.

Tex met it with a weak slap of his oversized hand. "Hey, if you can't joke about it…"

"Don't." Sergio's voice was chilling. "Never joke about death."

"Says the man who offered to put me down this morning." I winked.

Tex's nostrils flared. "What? YOU WHAT?"

"So, back to the wedding…" Ax said in a strategically calm voice. "Andi's only getting married once. It should be special, so the girls…"

Tex's chest was taking in more and more air as he glared

at Sergio.

"Damn, make the sick girl run interference."

I set my coffee down and held my hands between the two of them. "Chill, you're both pretty, now adjust your balls, scratch your ass, and burp so we can get back to dresses and champagne."

"You're not drinking," Sergio snapped.

"Who died and made him my dad? Because I refuse to marry my father. It's just weird."

"She can't drink!" Sergio clearly wasn't listening to me or anyone else in the room. "She's sick! It will make it—"

"What?" I interrupted. "Worse? Trust me. There is no worse where I'm concerned."

Ax whistled from the corner. "Off topic."

"Ax…" I held up my hands. "..Please, stop interfering. If we're lucky, they'll get into a catfight, take off their shirts, and then mud will get involved and rolling around in it and—"

Tex smirked while Sergio cursed under his breath.

"Oh, sorry. Did I say that daydream out loud?" I snickered into my coffee. "No, but seriously, do continue talking about my impending death with me standing right here, Sergio. It's good uplifting pre-wedding talk."

"Girl has a point." Ax nodded in encouragement.

"Fine." Sergio slammed his hands against the granite countertop. "Do whatever you want. I just wasn't aware that the Make-A-Wish Foundation had all but thrown up on our yard this morning."

Tex's jaw actually cracked. I heard it. Like a bolt of thunder dropping into the kitchen and bouncing off the walls. "You're an ass."

"I second," Ax added.

All eyes fell to me, all but Sergio's that was; he was still engaged in his weird love affair with the countertop.

"Oh, I have to side with my husband." I shrugged. "It's Biblical."

"Do Russians own Bibles?" Ax asked aloud.

"Hmm…" I tapped my chin. "I don't know. Do Sicilians even know how to read?"

Ax winked then gave me one solitary clap. "Andi one, Axton zero."

"Then you marry her!" Sergio yelled, slamming his fist against the granite again. "Why don't you guys just kill me? Wouldn't that be easier for everyone?"

"Ignore him." I waved my hand in the air. "Last night he offered to kill me too. And look. Still standing. He's all smoke and mirrors. Just give him a bottle with a nipple full of whiskey and put baby in the corner where he can pout."

"Nobody puts baby in a corner." Ax met my gaze.

"You… you and I are officially friends."

"He doesn't need any more friends." Sergio's face went purple as he clenched his teeth and leaned toward me. "Can we talk? Alone?"

"Are you armed?" I peered around his body. "Because when I learned about gun safety in school, they specifically warned me not to be alone with criminals."

"She got you there." Tex laughed. "Pull out your badge, Sergio."

"Sore subject." Ax coughed.

Sergio looked up to the ceiling and groaned. "Andi… now."

"Later, boys." I waved to the guys. "Just let the girls in when they get here. Then we can pop champagne and have a pillow fight. I always wanted a bachelorette party!"

Sergio jerked my arm, pulling me outside into the cold winter air. It was late January, not exactly my favorite time of year for Chicago. Then again, Russians apparently have ice in their veins, so whatever.

"Andi…" Sergio's eyes were hard and black. "Don't make me do this."

"What? Stand outside in the cold."

"Marry you."

"It's not forever, Sergio."

"That's the problem."

"I'm sorry, what? You want to be with me forever."

"No... I..." He ran his fingers through his wavy dark hair. "Damn it, I just... I want to marry someone once... someone I love. I don't want to have something arranged. It's just another thing the mafia has taken away from me. Can't you see that?"

"Make me see it," I said softly. "Make me understand."

His eyes were hollow, his gaze distant. "I don't... I can't... I just—"

"GIRLS are here!" I heard a female voice yell. Male voices joined in, and then music started.

"Later." Sergio pulled away, his footsteps already drawing back. "We'll talk later, but we will talk. Before we say vows, we're talking, Andi."

"Where are you going?"

He shook his head and kept walking. "One minute, Andi. I just need one damn minute to myself. Go inside."

CHAPTER THREE

Sergio

IT WAS AN OUT-OF-BODY experience… watching someone talk so callously about her own death and smile at the same time. Every single moment I was with her, I wanted to puke. Not because she wasn't pretty.

She was beautiful.

Gorgeous, actually.

Which made it so wrong.

How could someone so full of life be dying? And how could she be so okay with it? The whiskey had worn off, leaving me with too many confusing questions and not enough answers to suffice.

Laughter bubbled out of the house. I could hear it all the way out in the field, meaning, the girls had really brought champagne and were most likely getting Andi drunk.

I didn't want to be an ass.

Just like I had never planned on being a killer.

It's not like I woke up one day and thought, *I'm going to work for the FBI and the mafia as a double agent then threaten to kill everyone I love and hold dear, and then, just for kicks I'm going to marry a girl who's dying… and hell, why not add salt to the wound and drown a litter of kittens?*

"Shit." I kicked the ground with my boot and wiped my face with my hands.

I needed to get back to the house.

I knew there was no way to get out of my predicament. I just wished I wasn't so stuck — I wished the mafia didn't control me, I wished my family would actually listen to me, and for the first time since I'd taken that first step into the bureau… I wished for a second chance.

A do-over.

I would never have walked in.

I would never in a million years have thought to double-cross my family in order to save them…

People would have died.

But my conscience would have been clear.

The jaded feeling that choked me every waking hour would be gone, and I'd be free.

Instead, I was getting married, not to someone I loved, even if I was capable of love, but to a family enemy who probably deserved life more than I did.

"Hell," I whispered under my breath and marched back toward the house. As long as I didn't let her in… I'd be okay. As long as I looked at her like a victim, like one of my victims, she wouldn't get in.

The truth terrified me.

Because the truth was… I liked her enough to mourn her — and when you liked someone enough to mourn, you were in danger of love.

And I knew if I loved her, if I ever let myself feel; it would destroy me.

So I grabbed onto every shred of hate and resentment I could find in my body and armored myself with it.

I would not let her in.

Ever.

"Let's talk wedding night," Bee, Phoenix's wife, announced from the bedroom, loud enough for the entire house and possibly the outskirts of Chicago to hear.

"Wed-ding night, wed-ding night," the girls chanted in unison while I searched for alcohol like a crazed man.

"Right here." Nixon seemed to appear out of nowhere and handed me a stiff glass of vodka.

"What?" I snorted. "No wine? Are we even Sicilian anymore, or are we letting Russian tradition crap all over the place?"

"Remember when you used to be the easy one to be around?" Nixon asked, ignoring my outburst. "I do. You used to be all calm, collected, semi-happy. What happened to that person?"

"Apparently, according to Andi, that is, he died... and now my corpse is staring back at me through the mirror. I imagine I'm going to turn into a zombie any day now."

Nixon chuckled; his blue eyes matched mine almost perfectly. We were, after all, cousins, even though it was a distant fourth or fifth down the line. For some reason, we looked more alike than Ax and I did, probably because Ax refused to grow his hair longer than an inch now, and he'd had his nose broken more times than he could remember.

"She's dying," said Nixon, interrupting my thoughts.

"Why the hell do people keep reminding me of that?" I threw back my entire glass and held it out for more. "Do I have a sign on my face that says stupid?"

"Don't leave yourself open to that one, Serg." Phoenix walked up to us, water bottle in hand. "That's just begging Tex to take advantage."

Phoenix was the newest leader of the Nicolasi family, and

it showed in the way he carried himself. Once a rapist and the worst of the worst. You wouldn't know it if you saw him now. No more dark circles under his eyes, and he was wearing dark jeans and a shirt with a tailored jacket; the guy looked like he'd just stepped out of a magazine. His wife probably had more to do with that than he did, but still, it was an improvement from his haunted look of a few weeks ago.

At least then, my misery had enjoyed company, even if we had barely tolerated one another.

Chase approached us, his eyebrows raised. "Are we at a wedding or a funeral, Serg?"

"Both." I tilted more vodka back while the guys' expressions froze on their faces.

Slowly, I turned and cursed under my breath. Andi was standing in the doorway of the living room, her face pale, her smile weak.

"Hi, guys." She waved. "I was just wanting to ask Sergio's opinion on shoes."

Chase choked on his drink while I fought to regain my composure. Had she heard? And why the hell did I care if she was upset? That was the plan: upset her, don't let her in.

"Wear them." I shrugged. "Or go barefoot. Why the hell should I care?"

"Ass," Phoenix hissed, while Nixon nudged me from behind.

"So…" Andi poked her feet out from her long white skirt. "…do you like the silver or the tan?"

I licked my lips and stared at the shoes. Of course I had an opinion. Before my fall into the depths of hell, I'd probably been the most well-dressed of all the guys. I'd always loved clothes — the way they felt, the way they looked, the way they commanded a room.

"Andi, listen very carefully." I set my glass down on the table and folded my arms. "I couldn't give a rat's ass what shoes you wear."

I could feel the guys shooting daggers at my back. I ignored it. Maybe they'd lose their tempers and kill me — wouldn't that be a kindness?

"Barefoot, it is." She smiled brightly and started walking out of the room, then quickly turned around and skipped toward me. "Also, if we're planning a dual funeral and wedding, can you give my eulogy? It's only fair since you're going to be my husband and all. I could even write your speech for you. It should include how sexy I was, how much vodka I could drink, and the fact that I had the ability to kick your ass if I so chose."

I rolled my eyes.

And then suddenly, I was on my back. With no recollection of how I got there, just a view of the ceiling peering down at me with amusement, and my back feeling like I'd just gotten hit by a two by four.

"Holy shit." Chase burst out laughing. "I choose Andi for team captain when we go to war against the Russians."

"What…" My lungs seized as I wheezed out a breath. "…was that for?"

As Andi glanced down at me, her indifference was alarming. "You were being an ass, so I did you a favor by not only handing your ass to you, but making sure you landed on it, just in case there were any questions." She looked around the room. "This is what happens when I get treated like less than I deserve on my only wedding day… any questions?"

"Nope." Nixon chuckled.

"Hell no…" said Tex and Phoenix in unison.

"Just one." Chase's easy grin had me on edge.

The guys groaned. "What?"

He shrugged. "I just want to know how she did that so fast."

"If you're lucky I'll teach you." She winked and waltzed back through the door while I stayed on the floor, my pride bruised, my anger boiling.

The guys slowly, one by one, moved to stand over me. No hands were offered. They simply stared and, by their expressions, wanted me to try to get up just so they could set me back on my ass again.

Finally, Ax stepped through and offered his hand. When I took it, he released it then kicked me hard in the ribs. "Don't make me kick your ass too. Go pick out some damn shoes."

"She's going barefoot," I argued.

Another foot kicked me in the ribs, not hard, but it was firm enough to cause a sharp pain to throb down my side.

Nixon grunted. "Go, before I pull my gun."

"He'd do it too." Chase nodded somberly. "We've all seen enough gunshot wounds between us to prove it. Don't make Tex or Phoenix lift their shirts. Just go make it better."

With a grunt, I moved first to my knees, and then to my feet, rubbing my back as I slowly made my way down the hall. I knocked twice.

Trace answered, her glare murderous.

I sighed and leaned against the doorframe. "Is Jackie Chan available?"

"Depends." She crossed her arms. "Are you still an ass?"

I shifted on my feet. "Probably."

"At least he's honest," Andi called from somewhere in the room.

"Trace…" My voice cracked. "…just let me through so I can apologize."

"Amazing you know that word," Mo said, immediately joining Trace's side.

"Let him through," Andi called in her sing-song voice. "I want his opinion on the dress."

"It's bad luck," Mil said from the bed. "But then again, you are marrying Sergio, so..."

"Hilarious." I flipped her off and walked farther into the room. It looked like a dress store had puked all over the place. Lace, ribbons, and veils were scattered all over the bed, the floor, and the desk. Makeup was set up on one counter, while the other one was lined with shoes from every single color of the rainbow and then some.

It was enough to send me into a seizure.

I turned around, trying to remember why I was in that specific hell in the first place, when Andi came out of the closet and held out her hands. "You like?"

My mouth dropped open before I could stop it.

Her dress was all lace. No straps, just lace around her breasts, covering what needed to be covered, leaving little to the imagination and a feast for my eyes. The lace met with heavier silky looking fabric that kissed her hips and then fell in ruffles all the way to her ankles.

I wasn't sure how long I stared.

It was probably an embarrassing five minutes before I was able to actually form words. "It's… nice…" I coughed into my hand. "…for a dress."

"Wow, write me some poetry, why don't ya?" Andi winked then twirled in front of me.

I was just about to say something mean when I noticed her steps falter. Her face paled, and she collapsed directly at my feet.

"Andi!" I grabbed her lightweight body and lifted her into my arms then walked over to the bed and set her down amidst the fluffy dresses. "Andi, can you hear me?"

Her eyes fluttered open. "Oh… sorry." Her face reddened. "Just a bit dizzy."

"Then don't spin," I said through clenched teeth.

"But it's one of those dresses," she argued, lifting her arms into the air. "A twirling dress. You have to twirl or you may as well not wear it."

"Don't twirl if you're going to get dizzy and pass out."

"But I must."

"One twirl."

"Two!" she argued, leaning up on her elbows so that our

faces were nearly touching. "Please?"

We were so close I could see the flecks of gold in her brown eyes. I tried to ignore the hypnotic pull I felt just by staring and blinked away.

"Fine." I licked my lips, my gaze entirely too focused on her mouth, considering I was trying not to stare into her eyes. "Two twirls but go slow, no passing out."

"Careful, Sicily, your true colors are showing." She leaned up and whispered in my ear, "Don't want people thinking you actually care."

"I don't." Even I wasn't convinced with the lack of passion behind my words.

"Sure." She nodded and patted my shoulder. "And thanks… I think I'll pick this dress. Your reaction was perfect."

"But I didn't react."

"My point exactly."

I kept staring at her, trying to figure her out, while at the same time irritated that she seemed to see right through everything I threw at her. Big brown eyes stared right back at me, knowing me, seeing me.

I jerked back.

Having forgotten there were other women in the room, I nearly collided with both Mo and Mil while I made my escape.

I slammed the door behind me then leaned back against it, my hands clenched into clammy tight fists as I closed my eyes and muttered a curse.

"Wow, the dress was that nice, huh?" Nixon was leaning against the wall, his eyes missing nothing. Damn him.

"For a dress," I said in a weak and completely unconvincing voice.

Nixon smirked, his silver lip ring caught the light filtering in from the high windows. "You know it doesn't have to be a punishment."

"Ha." I pushed away from the wall. "But it is. You're forcing my hand, and why? That's what I want to know. What makes that girl—" I pointed at the closed door. "—in that room so damn important? Say her father finds her... What then? I protect her with my life."

Nixon sighed. "I'm disappointed you would even need to ask that question. A husband always protects his wife, regardless of his feelings. Once you're married, you're blood. You share something precious, something eternal. Protect her with your life? Damn right, you better. Because if you don't, if you hesitate, if you fail us one more time..." His expression didn't waver. The man wasn't even flinching as his words dealt physical blows to my body. "...I'll kill you myself."

"So die or marry." I exhaled and put my hands on my hips, willing my mouth to shut the hell up.

"You could try to enjoy yourself. She's beautiful." Nixon turned on his heel and started walking back down the hall. "Or you could just continue being an asshole and let me shoot you."

"Good talk, cousin," I muttered under my breath.

"Yeah well," Nixon called over his shoulder. "You're lucky I don't do worse. You deserve worse and you know it."

Yeah, I did.

Guilt gnawed at me from the inside out. I deserved worse than what was getting handed to me. Then again, I couldn't actually comprehend what was worse than being forced into a marriage with a bloodthirsty Russian only to be told to keep her alive while her equally bloodthirsty father hunts her like a dog, only to have that same Russian die a few months later.

Death had always surrounded me, always.

I thought after I confessed my involvement in the FBI to the families they'd at least kill me — silence the whispers and screams of all the people I'd killed — and put me out of my misery.

Instead, the voices were louder than ever. And I knew it was only a matter of time before it got worse, before all I saw was death, and I would be powerless to stop it.

That's the thing about killing, about dying. When you're the one dealing it, you think less and less about it until it's as normal as reading the morning paper.

But when you lose your grasp on it, when for one second, you lose control… it turns into a monster again.

And chases your every waking nightmare.

Andi was death – but she was also life, and I didn't know how to fuse the two. I wasn't even sure I wanted to.

CHAPTER FOUR

Andi

THE DRESS WAS PERFECT. I'd never been one of those girls who got overly emotional about anything. My pet bird died when I was six. Instead of crying, I'd simply made it a gravestone, written a eulogy, then asked my father for a new one.

He'd said yes. And so the circle of life continued. My adopted father, the one I'd lived with my entire life, made sure to give me everything I could ever hope for, while never lying to me about where I'd come from or why I'd been given to him.

I was blood money, plain and simple.

My real father, Petrov, as I so lovingly called him, had given me to the head of the FBI organized crime unit as a bribe when he discovered Smith wasn't able to have children.

Smith, overjoyed he wouldn't have to adopt — considering it was expensive and his salary was crap — had said yes.

But Petrov had one condition.

Train me in all ways Russian.

I'd gone to a Russian boarding school.

I'd only spoken Russian in the house.

I'd only been allowed to eat Russian food until I threw a knife at the wall on my sixteenth birthday.

I knew my adopted father loved me as best he could, but the longer I stayed in his home, the more he pushed me away. Probably because he slowly started to realize the danger in keeping me, the danger in knowing that the Russian mob always kept good on their promises, and that my father would one day ask for a favor in return.

I twirled in front of the mirror, lost in my thoughts.

Luca Nicolasi — now dead — the old boss of the Nicolasi family, he'd rescued me. Naturally, it happened after I'd been sent to kill him.

I'd been eighteen.

He'd laughed in my face, then offered me a different job, one I could really bite into.

Spy on my fathers. Both of them.

Get revenge.

And forget about the fact that I had chronic leukemia.

"You… " Luca pulled the knife from his thigh. "Clearly have a death wish."

"Why be afraid of death when you're already dying?" I shrugged and pulled out another knife.

"Ah…" He held up his hand. "Why indeed?"

My eyebrows rose. "Why aren't you trying to attack me?"

"Because…" He took a seat at the kitchen table. The house was dark except for the two of us; his men had no idea I'd even infiltrated. Luca tipped back a glass of wine and cleared his throat. "You only come to kill so you may feel."

"Bullshit." I held up my gun again.

"You want to feel alive… because your body is dying… you feel it every day when you wake up and are a little bit weaker, you see it in your father's eyes, and you know it's only a matter of time

before your use to your real father is lost."

He had me there.

"Control..." Luca patted the chair next to him. "What you want is more control over how you live, yes?"

How could he see right through me? My father hadn't; nobody had. Maybe because I kept walls up so high even I couldn't see over them.

"I can help you."

"I don't need help."

"You reek of the desire to belong… of the desire to control your own destiny…" He chuckled. "Let me help you, and I'll make you a promise you can't turn down."

"Oh yeah?" I snorted. "What's that?"

"I'll save your life."

My heartbeat picked up. "There is no cure for cancer."

"No," Luca said with sadness in his voice. "But when the time comes, when you need out of the FBI's grasp, when you want away from your Russian father, I'll offer protection the only way I know how."

I lowered my gun. "How?"

"My name."

I burst out laughing. "If you think I'm going to marry you, you've got another thing coming."

"Not me." He licked his lips. "My son."

"Andi!" Trace shouted from the other side of the door. "It's time to get started! We need you downstairs — oh, and who do you want to walk you down the aisle? Tex is arguing it should be him. Frank says he's older and wiser. Nixon just punched Chase, and I don't think—"

"Coming!" I interrupted and shook my head.

I took one last look in the mirror and whispered, "Thanks, Luca." I might not be marrying his son, but I was marrying into the Abandonato crime family. Not even my father could touch me now.

Because next to the Campisis, I was officially marrying into mafia royalty.

I just wished Luca would have lived long enough so see it. To walk me down the aisle and pat my hand.

He'd always told me everything would work out.

It had.

It was.

But I missed him, desperately.

And I still didn't know where his son was — or why I was the only one who even knew about his existence.

"Take it to your grave," he'd whispered one night. "If something happens, you take it to your grave."

Well, something had happened.

"Love you, old man," I said at my reflection in the mirror. "Thank you."

CHAPTER FIVE

Sergio

"A TUX?" I SAID IT LIKE A SWEAR WORD because, well… it was white, and looked like something out of *Saturday Night Fever*.

Tex wrapped a muscled arm around me. "It's what the bride wants."

I stepped away from him and examined the giant white piece of ugly. "This? This is what she wants? Are we all wearing costumes?"

"Just you." Tex grinned.

I shot Tex a glare out of the corner of my eyes. "You're enjoying this way too much."

"I was going to bring popcorn, but Mo said no."

I could have sworn the eyesore of a tux was starting to glow. "Thank God for Mo."

"You don't get to thank God for my wife," Tex hissed, his eyebrows doing that thing again that made them look like they were going to shoot off his forehead and dive into his reddish brown hair.

I lifted my hands up in surrender. "Whatever. Are you

going to watch me undress, or can I get a bit of privacy?"

He crossed his arms.

"You've got to be shitting me." I jerked my shirt off and tossed it at his face. "Do you really think I'm going to blow off the wedding?"

"Yes," Tex said in an amused voice. "Because you're chicken shit. That's what you do. You bail."

"That's it." The door to my bedroom opened just as I was contemplating lunging for him and punching him in the jugular.

"Tex." Chase wore a perplexed expression as he scratched his head. "A Nicolai Blazi—"

"—On it." Tex eyed me one last time. "You bail, I chase, and we both know how much I enjoy hunting."

"Oh, go to hell, Tex." I continued undressing, not caring that the door was wide open, and started the painful process of putting on what looked like cheap polyester and wool.

It was official. Andi was dying, and she wanted to take me with her, death by sweating. As if I wasn't already freaking out over saying my vows in less than a few hours.

I buttoned up the pants, irritated that they fit and that I couldn't use that as an excuse to throw on something Italian.

At least we knew how to make clothes.

"Oooo, sexy," Andi's chipper voice said from the doorway just as I was starting to button up the painfully uncomfortable white shirt.

I glared at her through the mirror. "Your idea, I take it?"

Her eyebrows crooked as she bit her lip to suppress a grin. "What? You don't like?"

"I don't."

"Not a fan of the arts? I mean, come on, the movie's a classic!"

I sighed and continued buttoning the shirt. "I get it. This is my punishment for last night."

"And what exactly happened last night?" She pulled her

hands behind her back and moved farther into the room, her dress swishing with each movement.

"I threatened to off you..." I smiled into the mirror. "...like a family pet."

She clapped. "Bravo, he can be trained."

"So... you're either going to torture me or kick my ass the whole time we're married? This what I have to look forward to? Horribly made clothing and sneak attacks where I land on my ass?"

"The attack wasn't sneak." She rolled her eyes. "You're just pissed I got you on your ass."

"Was there something you needed?" I jerked at the necktie and nearly hung myself in the process.

She rolled her eyes "Here let me."

"I don't need your help," I said through clenched teeth.

"You almost committed accidental suicide." She grabbed the tie and pulled my body closer to hers. "The least I could do is assist."

"Ha."

We were nearly chest-to-chest. I could smell her perfume; it was flowery but not overbearing. If I wasn't so pissed, I'd be tempted to lean in farther, but she was the enemy, she was the reason for everything going so horribly wrong.

Her soft hands glided against the fabric of the tie; my body jumped in response. I had to tell myself it was only because I hadn't been with a girl in so long.

Days had turned into months.

Months had turned into a damn year.

It was a hell of a dry spell.

At first, I'd blamed Mo Abandonato... the girl I'd wanted but lost to Tex... and then I couldn't use that excuse anymore; it progressed into just not feeling anything for anyone at any time.

It was like I had lost the ability to care.

The ability to even lust.

So the fact that my body responded to her? Just pissed me off all the more.

I jerked away once she was finished and snorted as I gazed at my ridiculous reflection in the mirror. "How is it fair that you look like a princess and I look like the punchline of a joke?"

Andi's smile faltered. She hung her head. "You really think I look like a princess?"

"Yes," a foreign-sounding voice said from the door. "I'd say you do."

I quickly turned around, ready to defend her, ready to fight because I knew we hadn't invited anyone outside the family, but Andi was already walking toward him, and then she was running, and then she was in his damn arms.

"Absolutely stunning." He kissed her cheek.

I damn near bit my tongue. "Who the hell are you?"

The man set Andi down and glared at me. We were matched for strength and height. He was around six foot two and had dark features. His eyes almost looked black, his hair just as dark, but his teeth were so white it was nearly blinding, and he had dimples.

I officially wanted to end his life.

And cut the dimples from his cheeks.

Andi rescued him from certain death when she moved in front of him, still holding his hand. "This is Nicolai Blazik."

"Shit." I rubbed the back of my head. "The Doctor?"

"The famous doctor," she said, emphasizing famous a bit too much for my liking.

The guy was a freaking celebrity. Women wanted him, men wanted to be him, and I was pretty sure that he owned half of the United States, or at least that's what the rumor was.

"Pleasure," he crooned from behind her.

"Likewise," I hissed.

"This—" Andi moved over to my side and grabbed my arm. "—is my fiancé, Sergio."

"Cute name." Nicolai chuckled.

Shit, he was just asking for me to shoot him. Did he have any idea what I did for a living? What I would do to him if he pushed me too far?

I gripped Andi harder then wrapped my arm around her. "I would say thank you, but I'm pretty sure you didn't mean it as a compliment."

"I didn't."

"If you don't mind Nicolai…" I turned to Andi and kissed the top of her head. "…my future wife and I were in the middle of something."

His eyes flashed. "Fine. Andi, I'll see you downstairs. And Sergio?"

I tilted my head.

"You hurt her, I cut out your heart."

I burst out laughing. "Oh, doc, I'd love to see you try."

He bit out a curse before walking out of the room.

"Pissing match, party of two," Andi said under her breath.

I hadn't realized I was still holding onto her, and I wasn't sure if I wanted to let go.

Slowly, she lifted her gaze to mine. "So… you were saying I looked like a princess."

"How do you know that's what I was going to say?"

"You already said it. I was just waiting for you to confirm it."

I sighed.

"Confirm it, and I'll let you change out of your suit."

"Really?" I blurted.

"Ha!" She poked me in the chest. "I knew you had a weakness for clothing and shoes… Imagine my disappointment when my future husband couldn't even take the time to tell me if I looked nice. Your real suit is in the closet. This was left over from Halloween. Apparently, Trace made Nixon dress up last year after losing a bet."

"Thank God." I looked heavenward.

"Ahem." She elbowed me. "The words. Please."

I sighed then forced out the words. "You look pretty…"

She tilted her head.

"…like a princess," I finished.

Andi's megawatt smile nearly toppled me over. I didn't have a chance to fight it off or to put up any walls so it wouldn't spear me directly through the heart. Instead, I was defenseless as the smile wreaked havoc on my heart rate as well as the rest of my body — not having a physical reaction to the girl would mean I was basically dead. Then again, she'd said as much to me, so there was that.

Her smile was like seeing something beautiful for the first time, only to not believe it even existed for your pleasure of staring at it in the first place.

"Sergio…" Andi reached up for my face and brought it down to hers, then placed a soft kiss on my lips. "Thank you."

I lingered. Unaware that I was lingering… until she jerked back, breaking the moment, then skipped out of the room.

I stared after her for a few minutes, unsure of how to proceed. I'd been in her presence less than twenty-four hours and already she was winning.

At everything.

Huh, and up until now I hadn't even realized I was in a game.

Andi one, Sergio zero.

CHAPTER SIX

Andi

MY HANDS WERE STILL SHAKING AFTER my run-in with Sergio. I wasn't sure if it was the cancer or the nerves at being so close to him.

Regardless of how horrible he'd been to me…

One thing was absolutely true about the man — he was absolutely stunning.

Like a mythical knight in a romance novel, his features were chiseled so perfectly that you almost wanted to get a closer look just so you could find a flaw. His strong jawline accentuated a near perfect mouth with full lips and straight white teeth that, when he wasn't hissing at his prey, framed a breathtaking smile.

His hair had been recently cut, but it was starting to grow out past his ears, giving it a wavy luscious look that screamed rock star with bad boy habits and a similar sexual appetite. It had to drive women crazy. In fact, it was shocking that he was even single.

Then again, he did have a high body count attached to his

name. Killing didn't exactly scream commitment, and I already knew he kept his secrets close to him.

I wasn't sure if he was just playing off the tortured and wronged hero, or if he really was in a dark place.

Either way.

He was stuck with me.

So he needed to man up and do something about it rather than pout and scream empty threats in my direction.

People like that pissed me off — ones who couldn't see past their own misery to actually see that they were gifted with another day.

Luca had taught me that.

He'd taught me that each sunrise was a new promise, a new beginning, a new chance at extraordinary.

I gathered my thoughts and made my way downstairs. It was a flurry of excitement. The girls were yelling at the guys to hurry up with the food while the guys were sweating bullets, pun intended, while trying to tie their ties and move tables at the same time.

"Hurry!" Mo whistled then started clapping her hands in a cadence that reminded me of my old piano teacher.

Trace let out a laugh as Chase tripped over his feet then yelled at Tex to move the napkins. A lot of cursing was going down on my wedding day. That much was certain.

"You sure you want to marry into this?" Nicolai said from his spot in the corner.

Ah, of course he was in the corner. The man brooded well. He had it down to an art form. Arms crossed, shoulders straight back, amused smirk firmly in place while pieces of dark hair fell across his forehead. If Sergio was dark, Nicolai was darker, and that was saying a lot. I wouldn't exactly trust him with my first born… or a goldfish for that matter.

"Two Russians in my home, God save us all." Phoenix smirked as he made his way over to us from the other side of the room. He held out his hand. "Nicolai, always a pleasure."

Nicolai shook his hand and nodded. "Business is good."

I knew that question. It was a typical mafia question. *"Business is good"* was always said as a statement, never a question, because if it wasn't, it typically meant you were the reason it wasn't going good. This was usually followed by a gunshot or getting messed up.

Phoenix's face didn't give way to any emotion. He simply shrugged and said, "As always."

"Can we trust him?"

Nicolai asked the question I hadn't wanted to even acknowledge needed answering. I wanted to inch closer but knew it would give me away. Instead, I perked my ears and pretended to be interested in the commotion around me.

Phoenix glanced at me out of the corner of his eye before answering. "Yes. And if something goes wrong. I'll simply pull the trigger, so you won't have to get on a plane."

"Generous of you." Nicolai laughed and patted Phoenix on the shoulder. "I'll be leaving soon after this, but I was wondering about that favor?"

Both men shared a look with one another before turning to me. That was my cue.

"Loud and clear boys." I pointed behind me. "I'll just go make myself scarce."

I walked away from them but not before I heard the word *sister*. Yeah, they were talking about my family. I only hoped that meant that Phoenix was going to work hard to keep me safe from them.

The last thing I needed was to be captured and used as collateral against the Abandonatos. Then again, Sergio hated me so much I highly doubted he would actually go to war just to bring me back. He'd probably be relieved he didn't have to kill me himself.

Or watch me die.

Death.

Death.

Death.

Wow, I needed to stop thinking so much about it at my wedding. I was supposed to be happy. I deserved happy. I'd never been one of those people who sat around depressed, wondering why the world wasn't doing me any favors. We had free will; therefore, I imagined I had the power to change anything about my circumstances. All it took was a step, one choice, and the universe shifted. It was a simple equation of cause and effect. Nothing changed in your world if you didn't will it to happen.

I wanted happy.

And I was going to get happy.

Even if it meant my ending was going to be a bit more tragic and dramatic than most. Then again, I'd come from a crime family, so who was to say I wasn't going to die young anyway? Odds weren't exactly in the favor of a Petrov living to fifty, just saying.

The sound of a dish crashing onto the floor had me nearly colliding with the wall. A hand gripped my shoulder and steadied me on my feet.

"You drunk already?" Sergio teased, or at least I thought he was teasing me; his mouth wasn't exactly forming a scowl, and I could see a bit of light in his eyes. Then again, I could be hallucinating the whole thing, considering the man had no soul and ate small children for breakfast.

"No." I jerked away. "Sorry, just... woolgathering."

"Wool what?" His blue eyes narrowed. "Is that English."

"It sure as hell isn't Russian," I said in a sweet voice.

"I may regret this later..." He crossed his arms. "...but I'll bite. What's woolgathering?"

"Reading, Italy. You should try it." I tapped my head with my finger and winked.

"I read."

"Romance." I said it slowly. Heck, I would have spelled it too, but by the look on his face, I imagined it wouldn't earn me any points toward wife of the year.

"Ha!" This time he did crack a smile. "Ridiculous fiction at its finest. Romance, the kind I'm sure you're reading, doesn't exist in the real world. They even have to make up words."

"Real word, dude." Chase came up behind him. "Mil read it in some Dukes of Horny London story a few weeks back."

"Now that's a fake title," I pointed out. "Though I can see why it would sell really well."

"Woolgathering." Chase cleared his throat. "To be lost in one's thoughts."

"Don't say *one's*." Sergio shook his head. "Ever."

"Nice British accent." I held up my hand for a high five.

Chase winked and slapped it. "I have my uses."

Sergio smirked. "Yeah, you can cook better than your wife, read historical romance, and, oh wait, I'm sorry. Do you even remember where you left your balls? Or did you even have them in the first place."

"He's just nervous about the wedding night," Chase said to me, ignoring Sergio completely. He leaned in and whispered, "Virgins always are."

"I'm not a virgin!" Sergio shouted, his face red with what I hoped was rage rather than embarrassment at Chase telling the truth. Then again, Sergio hadn't really answered when I'd teased him about it the night before.

All activity in the kitchen stopped.

And silence.

Chase bit down on his lip, smiling so hard I was afraid he was going to crack his face or something.

"Uh, Sergio..." Tex scratched the back of his head. "...something you need to tell us, man?"

"No judgment." Chase held up his hands in mock innocence. "I mean, you gotta get on that horse sometime."

I raised my hand. "Can I not be the horse?"

"Damn, I think you just lost your chance." Tex burst into laughter.

Sergio bit back a curse. "Could you just stop? For once?"

"What?" I laughed. "Stop what?"

"This!" He sneered. "The happy act. Grow up!" We were chest-to-chest; his breathing was ragged. "Newsflash, Andi. You're dying! What the hell do you have to be so happy about?"

I kept my smile in place, though I felt the edges of it trembling. "Life, Sergio. I can smile about life."

"Yeah, well." He bared his teeth. "I guess that's what happens when you only have a little bit of it left, huh? Take what you can get? Use who you can use? Me included? My whole damn family is getting put on the line for your protection. Hell…" He rubbed his face with his hands. "…your life isn't even worth anything. Why would I risk mine? To save it? You're already dead."

My smile was officially gone, replaced by what felt like a face that was going to crumple into a sob in an instant. He wasn't just soulless. He sucked the life out of everything — even me — and I had to admit that was a hard thing to do. I was optimistic by nature. I couldn't help it.

His darkness was choking.

I had to get away.

Without thinking, I pushed at his chest, giving me enough space to walk away.

"Andi!" Chase called after me. Right, Chase, not my soon-to-be husband.

"May as well shoot him now," Nicolai said in a gruff voice. "Put the bastard out of his misery."

The voices stopped.

Because I was suddenly outside… running, running as fast as my legs could take me. Running through a giant muddy field with my wedding dress on.

Pieces of grass stuck to my legs.

The wind was chilly.

Freezing actually.

I wrapped my arms around my chest and let out a little sob — not because of what Sergio had said, but because of what he represented — because of who he was.

I pitied him.

And maybe a small part of me pitied myself a bit too. I allowed myself a few selfish seconds where I felt sorry for my short life.

I closed my eyes and imagined walking down the aisle of a large church. I'd have a huge bouquet of white roses — they'd always been my favorite. My veil would trail a few feet behind me *Sound-of-Music*-style, and the groom would be the love of my life. His smile would be so full of life that the effects of it would heal me from the inside out.

No more cancer.

Only his smile.

And it would be enough to fix everything.

He'd open his arms to me, I'd walk into them, and he'd tell me I was the most beautiful girl in the world.

I'd vow to stay with him forever.

And he'd promise to love me for longer.

I giggled at the thought and did a little twirl in the field. Then, just because Sergio had said I could only do one twirl in a two-twirl dress, I did another turn and another.

"Thought I said only one twirl." The voice was harsh and totally ruined my special field moment.

"You weren't here..." I didn't open my eyes. "...so I decided to live on the wild side."

"Hmm."

I could feel him behind me. Slowly, I opened one eye, then the other. Sergio was standing next to me, hands shoved in the pockets of his black trousers. He opened his mouth.

I held up my hand. "Don't apologize."

"Wasn't going to."

"Oh, this is new." I nodded. "So you chased after the bride to what? Yell some more? See if you can make me any less enthusiastic about my only wedding day?"

The wind picked up, causing Sergio's hair to blow across his forehead. Damn, even his forehead was nice. I briefly contemplated giving him a black eye just so I could stare at least one flaw on his perfectly shaped face.

Maybe I'd just bite him when they said *"kiss the bride…"* At least then, by drawing blood, I'd feel like we were on even ground. He hadn't beaten me, at least not physically, but emotionally? Well I felt pretty bruised.

"Can we not do this?" He looked at me, his blue eyes flashing. "I can't be what you need me to be. I won't be. It's not in my makeup. I'll do my duty, which is marrying you. There will be no kissing. No sex. No date nights. Nothing. I'll protect you with my life, but don't expect anything more."

"How about human decency? Can I expect that?"

Sergio hung his head, lifting his hand to pinch the bridge of his nose. "You deserve that… but I can't promise I won't fly off the handle. I'm not perfect."

"Gee, could have fooled me, and here I was just getting ready to build an *I–heart-Sergio* altar in my closet and light some incense. Damn, thanks for killing that dream."

"I take you more for a voodoo-doll type of girl."

"And the dream's reborn!" I smiled. "Look at that. You are good for something."

"I'm not," he whispered. "Not really good for anything anymore."

Cue awkward silence.

"Wanna talk about it?"

"I'll talk about it the day I grow tits."

I frowned. "To be fair, you already have tits."

Sergio sighed.

"All animals do."

"Heart-to-heart time is done now." Sergio shoved his

hands back into his pockets.

"Oh wow, that was a heart-to-heart? You didn't even cry!"

"I've cried twice in my life. Believe me, I won't cry over you. Ever."

That I could work with. In fact, he had no way of knowing — but that was a promise I needed him to keep. I didn't want to be the cause of more pain in his life, regardless of how he treated me. I wasn't sure I could live with it.

"Promise." The word was out of my mouth before I could stop it.

"What?" His perfect eyebrows knit together in confusion. "Promise you what?"

I licked my suddenly dry lips. "Promise me you won't cry over me."

"That's a really strange request."

"Think of it as my wedding gift."

He exhaled. "Fine. I promise I won't cry over you."

It felt like a thousand-pound weight had been lifted from my chest. "Awesome." I held out my hand. "Now let's go get hitched."

"That's it?"

"Huh?" I chewed my lower lip, pondering how I was going to get some of the dirt out of my perfect dress.

Sergio, to his credit, gripped my arm and helped me walk across the field. "You just forgive me like that?"

I shrugged. "Forgiveness is never given in order to make peace with the offender. It's given to make peace with yourself. Besides, I can't hate you for being honest."

"Yes, actually you can."

"But I don't." I stepped over a large rock and leaned heavier on him. "But I am curious…"

"I knew it couldn't be that easy."

"Did they get chocolate or white cake for the reception?"

"Huh?"

"Well, I like both, but if I had to choose, it would be a type of swirl concoction… ohh… with amaretto. You know, I could have totally been a baker in another life."

"Who are you?"

"Andi, your soon-to-be wife and future baker."

Sergio stopped walking and stared at me, his blue eyes blazing a fiery trail all the way up and down my body. "I'm never at a loss for words."

"Shock." I winked. "Now hurry up. I want cake."

We walked in silence the rest of the way to the house. But sometimes you don't need words. And with Sergio, I was beginning to realize he might say one thing… but his body language said quite another.

Case in point?

His hand never left my back the entire way to the house, and when I took the stairs, he gripped my hand — hard.

His words said he hated me.

His body said he wanted to keep me safe.

I wondered… in that moment… if he was going to be able to keep his promise after all.

Because I *was* dying.

And the last thing I wanted was to take the remaining pieces of his humanity with me to the grave.

CHAPTER SEVEN

Sergio

NUMBERS.

Numbers made sense.

Code.

Computers.

There was a certain kind of beauty about numbers, about their certainty and meaning. Writing code was no different. It was just numbers, letters, mixing together, creating, evolving. It made sense. It was my comfort. It was my life.

Women, however, made no sense at all.

I expected Andi to be pissed. Hell, after seeing how all the wives treated their husbands I fully expected her to pull a semi-automatic out from underneath her dress and point it at my face.

And I honestly wouldn't have been angry had she pulled the trigger.

I deserved it.

See, that was the thing about anger. It allowed you to act out — to react, even though you knew it was wrong. It was like jumping off a cliff without a parachute, you thought the air would somehow slow you down, but it didn't, and you eventually went faster and faster until you hit the ground so hard you were almost broken.

But the pain?

The pain of hitting?

For a brief second, it makes everything else go away.

It makes the jump worth it.

So you climb back up the cliff.

And repeat the process.

Yeah, I was an idiot.

I braced my hands against the sink in the bathroom, my knuckles going completely white as I gripped harder and harder, willing the visions of Andi's face to stop torturing me.

So maybe I did have a heart, because I felt like shit for what I'd said to her.

Two loud knocks sounded at the door. "Dipshit, it's time to say your vows!"

Leave it to Tex to completely ruin any sort of emotional breakdown I was having in that small bathroom.

I stared at myself in the mirror. "Give me a minute."

"One minute," he yelled. "I don't care if you're taking a shit, I'm breaking down the door and forcing you at gunpoint down that aisle if I have to."

"Fine," I snapped.

"Fine!" He banged the door again.

At this rate, I was going to have to replace it. Damn Sicilians with their uncontrollable tempers.

The mirror revealed too much. Dark circles framed beneath my eyes revealed how tired I really was.

I hadn't actually slept since I had been confronted by the family. Since they'd told me I had no choice but to marry Andi and figure my shit out.

Sleep only came if it was induced by alcohol. Which sucked because I really hated hangovers, and I'd never been one to drink that much.

Great start to a marriage!

My messy dark brown hair looked like I'd just hung my head out the window while driving top speed through a field.

I tucked the pieces back behind my ears in vain, knowing that in seconds the hair would fall forward, covering part of my face.

I'd cut it off so I looked the part of professor for my short stint at Eagle Elite, and now that it was growing back, I felt like I resembled more of a drunken pirate than teacher.

Luckily, the minute my time in the FBI had ended, my time at the school had as well.

Leaving me… jobless.

Because, if I was really honest with myself, the FBI wouldn't want any loose ends. They wouldn't want someone they couldn't trust, and, in the end, they'd have to find me in order to interrogate me in the first place.

And I was extremely good at not being found.

I'd spent years as a ghost.

I could do it again.

Except… Andi.

I had to wonder if by keeping her alive, I was signing my own death sentence. What was to keep the FBI from silencing me completely?

If I couldn't disappear… I groaned into my hands. "Focus, Sergio. Marry the girl, say I do, and power through." I chanted it into the mirror. "Six months. Only six months."

Damn, I was a callous bastard.

But I had to be, especially when it came to her.

I took a few deep breaths then jerked open the bathroom door just as Tex was starting to knock. He wasn't looking, so his hand collided with my forehead before I reared back and slammed that same hand against the door, crushing his fingers against the wall.

He let out a howl then scowled. "Was that necessary?"

"Completely," I said in a cold voice. "Let's go."

"Oh, so now you're in a hurry," he grumbled behind me. "Damn it, that hurt. What the hell type of karate you been practicing, Serg?"

I rolled my eyes.

"Huh, remember the days you used to threaten me?"

"Are you under the impression they're over or something?"

"You're more quiet than you used to be."

I sighed. "I'm a lot of things now that I never used to be."

"Guess that's what happens... when you sell your soul to the government, huh?"

I stopped walking.

Tex grinned menacingly. "The rest of the guys may be on your side... but remember this. We aren't blood. We've never been blood. If you take one misstep... I'll beat Phoenix to the punch by shooting you myself."

"So now there's a line?" I nodded. "Good to know."

"I'd kill him so I could get first shot." Tex popped his knuckles.

"Save your aggression for the bedroom, Cappo." I shoved past him. "I'm clean... no more FBI, unless they kill me, that is, and no more working for the family. Now I just exist."

I didn't stay back to listen to whatever bullshit he was going to throw at me; instead I marched into the large banquet room. It was at least two thousand square feet with huge windows lining the entire backside overlooking the rose gardens.

There was a time when my family used to host parties there.

They'd been huge, epic, something my family had done in order to show the world how much money they had — and how many government officials they had in their pockets. That was all before my father was arrested along with a few other family members, who, lucky for me, were also outlaws. They'd been released on probation just last year. None of us had heard from them since. But I knew, he was always lurking, especially since the FBI had forced me to cut off ties with them, freezing their accounts.

I'd danced my first dance with my ma in that ballroom.

I'd also experienced my first kiss there.

Then again, the first time I'd seen someone shot had been in front of the middle window. The bullet had shattered it. I remembered my mom being pissed because it had been unnecessary. My father's response? War was unnecessary, yet it existed, didn't it?

I shook the memory away. And now… now I was saying my vows.

Without my father… thanks to him being an outlaw.

Without my mother… on account of her being dead.

And with my brother who looked at me like a stranger and my cousin who'd all but disowned me a few days ago, along with the rest of the four crime families.

"Hell," I muttered, making my way slowly down the improvised aisle and standing at the end by Ax.

Everyone was seated.

Tex stomped into the room and pulled out a chair. It made a screeching sound across the marble floor before he plopped into it, pulling Mo nearly into his lap and then kissing her forehead.

I got it. She was his.

Damn, that man irritated me.

Classical music trickled into the room.

I closed my eyes, preparing myself for the worst. For the moment when I'd see Andi and really see her.

When her joy would cloud my better judgment and make me want to reach out to her.

When her smile would be so damn beautiful and inviting that I'd beg her to be my wife and live.

Just live.

It was like fighting two parts of myself.

I didn't want to be the good guy — not now, not anymore.

The good guy rarely won.

The good guy rarely even got a fighting chance.

The good guy got his heart slaughtered.

The good guy… sacrificed everything for family and still got shit on.

I was no longer good.

I wasn't bad either.

I was just… existing. Like I'd told Tex.

The music became louder and louder. My hands started to get clammy as the anticipation became more unbearable as the music continued.

And finally… the door opened, and Andi stepped through.

I had prepared myself for her smile. My body stiffened as she walked happily down the aisle with Nicolai escorting her.

She even threw her own damn rose petals.

The girls joined in the soft laughter as she continued tossing them out of a small basket.

When she was at the end of the aisle, Nicolai kissed her on the top of the head and took his seat up front.

She turned.

I glanced at her smiling mouth. I didn't allow myself to feel anything. I simply stared at it and thought to myself, *Wow pretty smile, full of life, marrying, contract, done deal.*

"Pssst." She gripped my hand. "You're forgetting something."

"Um…" Was it normal to talk during the ceremony? I leaned forward and whispered. "What?"

"My veil," she mouthed.

"Oh." Feeling stupid I quickly pulled the veil back from her face and froze.

Pure joy met my gaze.

Stunned, I continued to stare, my hands trembling.

"You… uh, you can put it down now." She winked.

I'd prepared myself for her smile.

But I hadn't prepared myself for her eyes, for their inviting warmth, for the adoration I didn't deserve.

She looked at me like I was her hero.

And for one brief moment I wanted more than anything to storm the castle, rescue the girl, and ride off into the sunset.

"Shit," I muttered, releasing the veil and turning toward the minister.

"Romantic." She elbowed me in the ribs.

I would not smile.

I would not fall.

I would not, could not allow it… I just couldn't.

I told my body to stay straight; I told my head not to turn to the side; I told myself not to lean in and smell her.

But no matter what I told myself…

I didn't listen.

She smelled like lilacs; her skin was perfection; her laugh was warmth.

And I was screwed.

CHAPTER EIGHT

Andi

THE CEREMONY WASN'T MY DREAM COME true. I'd be lying if I said it was.

But it was… interesting. Especially during that brief half-second when Sergio had actually looked at me like I was pretty — like I was desirable — like he wanted to be there.

The moment quickly dissipated.

Replaced by the word *shit* and the sinking feeling he was referring to the fact he was about ready to commit his life to me.

I tried to keep the smile on my face during the reception. And to my utter delight, I had two different flavors of cake; meaning, I was going to kiss Mo on the mouth next time I saw her.

But now… everyone was gone.

And I was exhausted.

My body wasn't what it once was, and I hated acknowledging the fact that I couldn't just stay up all night and party with my new family.

I couldn't even keep my eyes open.

One minute I'd been sipping champagne and leaning heavily on the table. The next I'd felt strong arms lift me up and carry me to bed.

I thought it had been Tex or one of the guys. I mean, all of them were basically muscular bad asses in their own right, so it would be easy for me to confuse which chest was which.

But the smell.

The smell of expensive cologne tipped me off.

Sergio, with all his anger issues, always had a tell. He wore *Versace* and he had a weakness for expensive everything.

I'd never been the type of girl to like cologne. It seemed overpowering and fake. It reminded me of stuffy overweight men in suits, smoking cigars and talking about crime.

But on Sergio?

Well, let's just say I had a brief fantasy where we starred in our very own cologne commercial, jet-setting across the world in fast cars and yachts.

Oh, and my bathing suit was black and awesome.

And I wasn't sick.

I was healthy and swimming in the ocean.

Damn. I missed the ocean.

I blinked against the darkness blanketing the room and held tight to Sergio as he slowly lowered me to the mattress.

My teeth chattered, not because I was cold, but because I wasn't sure what to expect. Would he try anything with me? Or would the idea actually repulse him?

I tucked my knees up or at least tried to, but Sergio jerked my legs back down.

"What?" I tried to get up on my elbows but was too weak.

"Lie down, Andi. Sleep."

"But you—"

"Sleep," he said in a gruff voice as he removed my shoes then very slowly turned me on my side and began unzipping my dress.

"Are you—"

"Going to take advantage of a sick tired girl?" He finished. "No, Andi. I'm not that guy."

"Bummer," I joked.

I could have sworn I heard him laugh; then again, I was teetering on the edge of passing out from exhaustion. So, in my weakened state, I probably thought Ryan Gosling was taking his place.

The cool air bit at my skin as he slowly pulled it down over my feet. I shivered and reached for the blankets, but was once again lifted into the air.

"Warning, next time a warning," I gasped as my cold skin met his heat.

For a second his eyes met mine. It felt important, that moment, like he wanted to say something but wasn't sure how.

I blinked. I had to. I mean, people blinked in real life. But, because I blinked, we broke eye contact. And the moment disappeared like it hadn't happened in the first place.

He carefully set me in between the satin sheets and pulled the down comforter over me.

"Thank you," I whispered.

"Here." He set a brand new cell phone on the nightstand. "Text me if you need anything…"

"Are you leaving?"

"I'm going to go… downstairs," he said in a hard voice. "Don't text me unless you're dying."

"Ha ha." I yawned. "Not yet, Sergio. You're not that lucky."

"No…" he said in a low voice. "I'm really not."

Something told me we weren't talking about my death anymore, but I couldn't stay awake any longer. I succumbed to sleep and dreamed of my faceless knight with dark hair.

At least in my dreams.

He was real.

CHAPTER NINE

Sergio

I SAT AT THE KITCHEN TABLE, tapping my fingers against the tumbler full of whiskey, irritated that my thoughts kept straying to the girl upstairs lying in my bed.

Her white-blond hair had looked like spun silver in the moonlight, and I'd wanted to tangle my hands in it just to see if it felt as soft as it looked, but the minute I'd leaned down, it was like my mind went into shutdown mode, telling me, yet again, that it would be a bad idea.

So I'd jerked back, and nearly pulled her off the bed in my attempt to get her dress off.

Not how I pictured a wedding night going.

I wasn't tired — I was exhausted. But my eyes refused to give in to sleep; instead, I tilted the tumbler back and drank deeply.

"This how all Sicilians celebrate?" a dark voice echoed in the kitchen.

I bit back a snarl. "Nicolai… I don't think we've formally met."

"No." He pulled out a barstool next to me then reached for a glass and poured himself a double. "I don't believe the honor of my handshake has been bestowed upon you just yet."

I rolled my eyes.

"Saw that."

"Wasn't trying to hide my disdain."

Out of the corner of my eye, I noticed a small sickle tattoo on his left wrist Disgust rolled throughout my body. I knew what it meant. Knew what it represented. The Russian mafia marked its men in plain sight, unlike my family; we marked ourselves where only we could see. It was a humility thing.

There was nothing humble about the Russians.

It was laughable to even think about it. Then again, sitting at the table with a Russian was just as hilarious. Hell, I'd married one. Damn me.

"You'll protect her..." He licked his lips and turned his dark menacing eyes toward me. "...or I'll cut you from belly to chin."

"Doctors and their toys," I muttered.

"I'm excellent at hiding bodies — even better at causing pain but not allowing you to scream it out. I like my victims to suffer in silence."

"How..." I arched an eyebrow. "...utterly poetic."

"Sometimes I listen to classical music while doing it." He smirked.

"That's very Hollywood of you."

"Makes it feel less horrific."

We sat in silence for a few more minutes, both sipping our drinks, refusing to make eye contact.

Finally, when I couldn't take it anymore, I asked the question I'd been dreading all night. "Why are you really here? Clearly, her father isn't aware you're helping us — and I saw you talking to Phoenix earlier."

"I wasn't trying to hide the fact that I need a favor."

"We've already done enough for you," I spat.

"No." He shrugged. "This is more... personal."

My eyes narrowed. "How so?"

"Andi's safe." He frowned. "At least as safe as she's going to be with the likes of you. But others in her family? They're still in danger. I just need the right kind of information in order to save them."

"And when you say them?"

"I mean her."

"Her is who?"

"I keep my secrets well." He grinned. "Do I have your word?"

"You haven't told me anything."

"About Andi," he said slower this time, methodical, as if I was a slow learner.

Then again the booze was starting to do the trick. Already my hands felt heavy, my eyes burned with the need to close off the world and succumb to the darkness of sleep.

"I'll protect her."

"Good." Nicolai let out a breath. "Because her father won't be happy she's disappeared. She's no longer useful to him now that Director Smith is dead, now that her brother is dead. She's...." He sighed.

"A very loose end," I finished.

"She's as good as dead if she gets into the wrong hands."

I fought the urge to bang my head against the granite. "She's already dying."

"A fact you keep reminding her of." He tilted his head. "I wonder why?"

"Because." That was all I had. Because. Weeks ago, I could have talked the guy under the table and convinced him he was an escaped ostrich from the zoo. Now? All I had was *because*. Damn, I was broken.

Nicolai stood, a smile forming across his lips. "You're not trying to convince her." He tilted his head. "You're trying to convince you."

"What?" I snapped.

"Keep saying it, then maybe one day you'll believe it enough to keep your distance, to keep your hands off of her. But my guess?" He chuckled darkly. "You've already followed the rabbit. Careful when you jump. There won't be anyone there but Andi to break your fall, and something tells me that's exactly what you don't want."

"Go to hell." My voice was hoarse, unsteady, basically telling him exactly what he claimed he already knew.

She could be a potential weakness for me.

And I hated weakness.

I hated it in others, but I especially hated it in myself.

"Good talk." Nicolai stood and pulled out a business card. "If you ever find yourself in Seattle, or if you need good surgeon."

I glanced at the white card with the red embossed letters.

"JR? What's that stand for?"

He shrugged. "Family crest." Without another word, his light footsteps echoed across the floor. He made it to the hall then turned, his expression one of pity. "You know… when this is all over… I can make you forget it even happened."

My eyes narrowed as dread trickled down my spine. "You'll have to be more straight-up with me. I don't speak doctor."

"When she dies…" He said it softly. "…which she will… have no doubt about it… call me if you… find that that stony heart of yours actually cares about that girl upstairs. The least I can do is help you forget the pain, help you forget everything."

My hand trembled against the glass. "Is that what you really do? Brainwash people? Break them? Make them forget?"

He inclined his dark head. "Have a good night, Sergio. And remember my promise. Sometimes pain, especially that of a broken heart, is best forgotten."

"Thanks, but my heart's just fine."

His eyes said he knew otherwise.

My damn erratic heartbeat concurred.

I wanted to smash my hand into his face.

Instead, I saluted him with my middle finger and ripped his card in half.

With one last dark chuckle, he moved down the hall. Finally, the sound of the front door clicking shut gave way to absolute, blissful silence.

The exhaustion that had earlier been creeping in was gone. And in its place, extreme paranoia that Nicolai saw me better than I saw me — that he knew my secrets, he knew my fears, and in the end, he knew I'd come calling. Because the very last thing I wanted…

Was to break.

I'd already lost so much.

It seemed unfair that she'd be the final catalyst of my downfall.

Rubbing my eyes with the backs of my hands, I moved away from the bar and padded down to my office.

I clicked on the lamp at my desk and went to work.

I'd just married someone who I needed to make disappear. With a sigh, I cracked my neck and placed my hands on the keyboard.

Passport first.

License second.

Marriage license third.

And I went to town. This, I could lose myself in. Numbers, I could do. Hacking was something I could probably do with my eyes closed.

I fixed, and I fixed, and I fixed.

When I was finished, I should have felt better. Instead, I felt worse, because the whole time I'd been creating a new identity for her, I'd felt, somewhere in the back of my exhausted brain, that I was simultaneously losing my own.

Who was I anymore?

What was my purpose outside of paying back my family for all my secrets? My lies?

I glanced down at the black folder Phoenix had placed on my desk a few days ago…

"Read it," he ordered slamming it onto my desk.

"I'll pass." I pushed it away with one of my pens, and for a brief minute contemplated throwing it into the fire. "There's nothing in there I don't already know about myself."

"Ha!" Phoenix chuckled "You have no freaking clue, Sergio. No clue."

"Maybe I like it that way." The black folder seemed to elevate toward me, tempting me, taunting me. "Being in the dark."

"Trust me, you won't. You don't." He nodded toward the folder. "Everyone has secrets… how do you know this isn't so much about yours… but someone else's entirely?"

That piqued my interest. "I thought it was my folder? The one that Luca kept on me in order to keep my balls within his grasp."

"I didn't say it wasn't."

"Phoenix." I said his name like a curse. "How about you just tell me what's in it so I don't have to read."

"It's better it come from him."

"He's dead!" I yelled.

Phoenix hung his head. "I'm well aware that Luca, one of the greatest men I've ever known, is no longer breathing, but that doesn't mean he still can't reach his creepy ass hand out of the grave and give us a bit of a… surprise."

"I freaking hate surprises," I muttered.

Phoenix laughed. "Well put your party hat on, my friend, because it's about to get real."

"And it's been what?" I leaned back in my chair. "A cakewalk all up until now? Do you even realize how many times we've almost gone to war with other families in the past two years? How many lives have been lost? How many lies I've told?" My voice was

getting louder and louder. I couldn't help myself, I was pissed. It wasn't Phoenix's fault. Hell, the guy had more of a reason to be pissed than I did, and there he was, passing out top-secret folders and smiling.

Jackass.

His wife probably had something to do with it; well that, and they had a baby on the way. Lucky bastard.

"Read the folder," he said again, then tapped his knuckles against my desk. "And try to get some sleep. You look like hell."

"You do realize I used to say the same thing to you not so long ago."

"Karma's a bitch." His snarky reply as he slammed the door to my office, leaving me alone with the folder.

I reached for it, but something stopped me, something that felt a hell of a lot like fear.

Fear that Luca had known things that I'd done — things I still hadn't 'fessed up about.

The bodies I'd hidden for the FBI. The ones I'd hidden from them.

The people I'd killed, all because it had been my damn job.

And the families I'd destroyed all in order to save my own ass.

I knew I was a selfish bastard; I just didn't want others to know how deep that selfishness went.

Deciding against it, I pushed away from my desk and got out of my office before I did something stupid.

Taking the stairs two at a time, I hurried into my room then froze. Shit. Andi was sleeping in my bed.

I had at least twenty-two other rooms I could sleep in — I lived in a mansion, for shit's sake.

But my bed.

She was in my bed.

FML. Seriously.

I had two choices. I could get my head out of my ass and walk backward, slowly out of the room, and crash somewhere else.

Or I could watch her sleep like the creepy son of a bitch I was… no way I would actually be able to succumb to sleep if I was next to her.

She was too…

Everything.

The decision was made when she made a little moan, not one out of pleasure, but something that sounded fearful, like she was afraid of the dark and needed a teddy bear.

Shit, had I really just thought *teddy bear?*

And unfortunately my body reacted — responded, one foot after another — and suddenly I was pulling my shirt off and lying down on the soft mattress.

Like a pubescent high-schooler, I stayed on my side of the bed, careful not to touch any area she'd been on.

It worked for about ten minutes.

And then an arm plopped onto my chest, followed by a leg covering my leg, and then, I was getting used as a giant ass pillow.

My teeth clenched. My body tightened with awareness, and just when I was getting ready to get the hell out of there, she whispered.

"Safe."

I was anything but safe. But, in that moment, I vowed never to let her feel fear again, even if it meant I had to kill every son of a bitch in my way.

Safe I could do.

Safe I could promise.

CHAPTER TEN

Andi

I KNEW BEFORE I EVEN OPENED my eyes that I had molested poor Sergio in his sleep.

I only felt sorry for him because I knew my sleeping habits. I wasn't one of those girls who slept quietly with their arms folded across their chests, their hair softly lying across the pillow, lips glossy, makeup still on.

Um, no. Sleep for me was a full contact sport — one I embarked on with my mattress nightly.

It wasn't rare to find me on my ass on the floor, because somehow during the night I'd decided that my sheets were trying to strangle me alive, and in order to protect myself, I'd had to pull them from my bed and create a makeshift fort on the floor.

My favorite position usually consisted of my feet being where my head should be and my head nearly teetering off the bed, hands hanging in front of me, just ready for someone to pull me the rest of the way off and onto the floor.

Needless to say, I was a bit cautious when I opened my

eyes.

First off, I'd feel horrible if I'd accidentally punched him in the eye or something. Heck, I wouldn't put it past me to knee him in the balls a few times just because I wasn't used to men sleeping with me.

They were never welcome.

The few times I'd had one-night stands, it had been to gain intel for dear old Dad. Love had had nothing to do with it.

Survival – did.

Sergio's chest rose and fell with a slow rhythm. He was still sleeping, or I assumed as much, so I stared like a raging lunatic.

I took inventory of his abs, noting that they were, in fact, as cut as I suspected; my fingers itched to trace the hard edges, and when my eyes drifted lower, I fought this insane temptation to see if the rest of him was that impressive.

Unfortunately, he'd kept his pants on from the night before; meaning, if I wanted to explore, I'd need to actually unbutton said pants, and that set me up for risk of exposure.

Ha! Exposure.

I held in a giggle at my own joke.

He let out a little moan and shifted closer to me.

And like a complete idiot – I let him. Because he was warm, and sexy, and had I mentioned sexy?

At least with his mouth closed, I could finally see what all the fuss was about. It was hard to look past his cruel nature when he was constantly speaking or, you know, breathing.

His chiseled jaw was clenched tight. His eyebrows furrowed a bit as if he was concentrating extremely hard on whatever type of dreams invaded that head of his. I imagined he probably dreamt of death.

Lots and lots of death.

I reached out and briefly touched his silky dark hair. It should be a sin to have such soft hair and be a man.

He already had long enough eyelashes to make me green with envy.

I sighed and tucked a strand behind his hear. My hand hovered near his temple.

Holy crap.

He had a scar.

I kind of wanted to throw a party. The man wasn't perfect. Thank God. I needed to see a flaw because things were looking pretty uneven at that point. He didn't snore, he smelt like heaven, and even his eyebrows had a perfect arch.

But that scar? Yeah, I could work with that.

It was small, barely noticeable. A pinkish white line trailed from his right ear down the back of his neck, his hair covering it perfectly. Hmm, I fought the urge to trace it with my finger.

Or my tongue.

But that was inappropriate, almost as inappropriate as raping him with my eyes, but hey, I at least deserved some eye candy after the way he'd treated me in the field.

It was a sort of payback.

My eyes receive a treat after my ears receive a scolding. Plus, he really wasn't in any position to get mad at me.

He let out another moan then turned toward me. Uh-oh. I tried to slide away, but his left arm snaked out and pulled me close while his right hand found.

My breast.

I ignored my hormones, or at least tried to, and shifted away. Then the man squeezed.

I closed my eyes and muttered a curse.

He started massaging.

Okay, so maybe he wasn't dreaming about death.

I knew the minute he woke up…

Because his hand froze.

I wasn't sure if I should pretend to be sleeping, yell at him, or simply stare.

I chose the latter.

Hoping my expression wasn't one of lust but of mild curiosity, as in *why the heck did you grab my boob?* and not *will you please touch the other one too?*

"Shhi-i-it." He drew out the word, his eyes focusing on the hand currently holding my boob captive. "I umm…"

"Why don't you have morning breath?" I asked, truly curious as to why he didn't smell. It would have been a mercy had he been remotely human. But no, apparently he was some sort of Sicilian god.

"Huh?" He shook his head, his long eyelashes fluttering against his cheeks. "How am I even supposed to answer that?"

"Well…" I licked my lips. "…you could start by taking your hand off my boob."

He looked down again.

"Or you could keep it there if that's how you start all your mornings, but then it begs the question… do you grab your own, or do you simply imagine someone else's?"

He jerked his hand away. "Sorry. I didn't mean to…" He sighed. "Just, sorry."

"It's okay. I liked it." I winked.

Did he just growl?

"So, morning breath…" I pushed up onto my elbows. "…not something you're plagued with, huh?"

"Too early," he grumbled, reaching for his cell.

"Warts?"

"What?" He dropped the phone and turned his hazy gaze to me. "You have warts?"

"No." I made a face. "Do you?"

"No." Again with his slow one word answers.

"Zits? Tell me you had zits when you were a teen, and your parents tried everything, and nobody would be your friend, so you made up an invisible friend and named him, then had to see a shrink for three years because you were thought to be mentally unstable."

Sergio stared at me for a few minutes then asked. "Are you always this weird in the mornings?"

I threw my hands into the air. "Flaws, Sergio, I'm trying to find flaws." I shrugged. "You know, other than the fact that you tend to be a giant ass-hat most the time."

"That's a flaw."

"An epic flaw. Poor me." I smiled. "I'm stuck with your ass-iness."

"Not a word."

"Is now."

"Can we at least have coffee before you continue assaulting my ears with your voice?"

I rose from the bed. "Fine, fine. You win."

Sergio's mouth dropped open, his eyes flashing with something I couldn't really decipher.

"What?" I put my hands on my hips — and panicked. I was in my wedding lingerie. A cute white corset that had gone perfect with my wedding dress and white lacy boy shorts.

He opened his mouth then closed it. But didn't look away. No, that wasn't Sergio's style; he didn't do embarrassed or guilty. He wasn't that guy, the good guy that even turned around when you dressed.

He stared.

And I liked it.

Because it made me feel wanted — desirable, so I did what any sane woman would do when she had a hot man who just so happened to be her husband in her bed.

I took off my bra. "You said my words assaulted you. I figured I'd attack your eyes too."

He swallowed, his Adam's apple bobbing slowly down before he spoke. "You should probably put clothes on."

"Nah, I think I'll go naked all day. Never done that before, and you only live once." I winked.

"Clothes," he croaked.

"Naked."

"Andi—"His voice held a warning tone. "—put some damn clothes on before I do it for you."

"Now that I'd like to see... you'd really dress me? Kind of reminds me of the song "Barbie Girl." Have you heard it?"

"If you start singing it, I'm going to spank you, and it's not going to be the type of sexy spank you're expecting."

"Try it," I smirked. "I'll just kick your ass again."

"Shit, you're annoying."

"'I'm a Barbie Girl...'" I started, "'in a Barbie world...'"

Sergio launched himself from the bed and pulled me over his shoulder, then very angrily stomped out of the room and into mine, which was farther down the hall. He set me on my feet then started rummaging through my drawers. A T-shirt flew by my face and then a pair of skinny jeans.

I ducked when my favorite pair of riding boots nearly collided with my nose.

The socks I actually caught one-handed.

When he was done, he didn't turn around, didn't say one word to me, just slammed the door behind him. I continue singing the Barbie song, while echoes of his curses joined my voice in harmony.

All in all? Not a bad start to my first day of marriage.

Because for the first time in a while — I felt really alive. And it was all because he was an ass. Who knew?

CHAPTER ELEVEN

Sergio

I DIDN'T FEEL GUILTY. NOT WHEN it was her own damn fault that I'd even seen her topless. I wasn't one of those guys, the kind that looked away.

I think she knew that too.

Which is why I felt like I was in some sort of warped version of chicken. She wanted me to look, but she also wanted me to get embarrassed.

I didn't do embarrassed.

So she was going to have to do a hell of a lot better than trying to flash me in nothing but a smile.

Hands shaking, I braced myself against the dresser and tried to wipe my memory of her naked body.

And when that didn't work…

I focused in on every delicious curve that had teased and taunted me. She was gorgeous. A petite little thing with curves in all the right places.

I white-knuckled the dresser a bit longer than necessary, nearly breaking the damn thing in half, then pulled out clothes and shakily put them on.

It was going to be a long day — and something told me it was going to get worse if she was in one of her taunting little moods.

With a sigh, I took one last look in the mirror then reached for the door. My cell phone went off.

Not my usual cell — the one the guys used — but the one given to me by the agency.

Cursing, I went over to my nightstand and slid my finger across the screen. "Yes?"

"Agent..." The voice was low, mechanical. "...we've come to a decision."

"Fine."

"The report states you had no direct involvement in Director Smith's death."

"No shit." I rolled my eyes and stared at the ceiling. "What? Did you guys think I was a double agent? Working for the mafia while still working for you?" I added in a laugh because, hell, that's exactly what I'd been doing, but I'd learned the hard way. Always beat them to the punch. Say the truth to their face, and they would take it as truth; they had no choice. Guilty people tended to cover up with a lie. Instead, I stated exactly what they were thinking and made them feel stupid for even coming up with the thought in the first place.

"No. Of course not." He cleared his throat. "But it doesn't change our decision."

I'd known it before he'd even said the words. Bracing myself for impact, I simply waited while the line cracked.

"Your services are no longer needed, Agent."

"My services are no longer needed," I repeated. "Should I expect a visit from another agent, or are you guys simply cutting me off without trying to kill me this time?"

No response.

I sighed. "Fine. I understand."

"No need to clean out your desk. It's been done for you.

Someone will be by to collect your badge and security clearance."

"And by someone, do you mean someone with a gun?"

"Goodbye, Agent."

The line went dead.

What else had I expected? I ran my hands through my hair and quickly reached for my badge, gun, and clearance. I didn't want to take any chances that they were going to send someone to eliminate me.

So I called the only person that I figured wouldn't want me dead — at least not yet.

"Nixon?" I hissed into the phone.

"What?" he barked back, sounding less than pleased that I was calling him at seven in the morning.

"The agency's sending a guy over to collect my things."

"Ha." Nixon let out a snort. "So they're going to try to kill you?"

"It's the FBI not the CIA." I sighed. "But I don't want to take any chances, not with Andi here."

He was silent and then, "Are you asking for a favor?"

"Damn straight, I'm asking for a favor. I need men. ASAP."

"Fine." He sighed heavily into the phone. "I'll be over in a few minutes."

"Wait…" I held up my hand even though he couldn't see me. "…I need men. You don't have to make it personal."

"You made it freaking personal the minute you signed on with a government agency, cousin. Therefore, as your boss, I'm going to drive my ass over to your house with enough men to cover, and I'll wait until we see the taillights from the bastard's car. Got it?"

"Yeah." I wanted to add in a thank you but figured it would only get me cussed out, and, considering I was already at my limit for emotional stress for the day, I kept my mouth shut.

The phone went dead.

What the hell was with people hanging up on me lately?

"Shit," I muttered and smashed the phone against the ground. It spread into three pieces. Knees cracked as I bent down to retrieve the battery and sim card. It had been a cheap phone. Most agency phones were, because — newsflash — they aren't as easy to hack as an iPhone or any other phone that was basically like a computer.

Listening devices, my ass.

They couldn't do shit with crap track phones.

To be safe, I separated the pieces then put them in my burn pile just in case.

My life, or the life I'd led for so many years, was over. There had to be some poetic justice in that. I was married, and now I was turning over a new leaf, one that included taking care of a Russian lunatic.

As if on cue, I heard Andi singing "Barbie Girl" at the top of her lungs. Damn, I already missed the agency.

Slowly, I made my way out of the room and down into the kitchen.

Andi was wearing the outfit I'd thrown at her. In my haste, I hadn't really paid attention to the clothes I'd chosen.

I really should have paid attention.

The white T-shirt rose just above her hips.

The jeans had holes right below her ass and on her thighs.

And the combat boots just made her look — shit. They made her look bad ass and completely screwable.

"Sunshine of my life," Andi said in a singsong voice. "What's the plan for today?"

"The plan?" I grabbed some OJ from the fridge. "I'm sorry, were you under the impression I was your cruise director? I don't make a daily itinerary for you, Andi. You're an adult. Pretty sure you don't need me to write shit down."

She put her hands on her hips.

I ignored the jolt of electricity that went through my body

while I blatantly stared at her trim waist and curvy body.

"What? No honeymoon trip?" Her lower lip folded down into a pout. "And here I was so excited about wearing a bathing suit."

"Here's a thought." I put the OJ back and slammed the fridge door. "How about I turn on a sprinkler outside, and you can run through it?"

She smirked. "But it's cold outside. What's the fun in that?"

"I'll put a heater next to the sprinkler. Think of it this way. You can run back and forth until your hearts content. Isn't that what dogs do anyway? Until they tucker themselves out and take a lazy afternoon nap?"

"I don't know. You're the bitch here. You tell me." She said it in such a sweet little voice I nearly choked on my tongue. Nothing sweet about the words coming out of that mouth.

"Good one." I rolled my eyes.

"Husband." She skipped up to me then steadied herself by putting her hands on my shoulders. "Whoa, sorry, kinda dizzy."

I jerked back. Not because I wanted her to fall on her ass, but because it made me feel like a complete asshole that she couldn't even skip without getting dizzy, and I hated that she made me feel worse than I already did on a daily basis.

"Woo!" She took a deep breath. "Okay, so this is what I think."

"Wow, I don't recall asking for any of those deep thoughts about shoes and lipstick."

Andi got a starry look in her eyes. "I do love shoes. And before you start being an ass again, don't think I didn't see those Prada loafers in your closet."

"Why the hell were you in my closet?" I shouted.

She waved me away. "Besides, you like clothes the way I like chocolate."

I snorted. "How do you figure?"

With a saucy grin, she trailed her fingertips down my chest. "You love the way they feel against your skin, just like I love the way chocolate feels against my tongue. All lush, sweet, deep."

My body twitched on cue.

"As I was saying."

What? What were we talking about?

"I think we should do a honeymoon. After all, I only get one, and I think you owe it to me to make it bad ass."

"I owe you?" My thoughts were too jumbled by talk of chocolate and licking it off her body to actually form a better sentence or comeback than that.

"Yup." She shoved her hands in her pockets, drawing my attention back down to the skin peeking through her jeans. My mouth. Right. There. I could almost taste her. "I've even compiled a list!"

"Why does that not surprise me?"

She held up her finger then reached into her back pocket. I peeked around her body and received a smack on the chest when I checked out her ass a little longer than necessary.

"No looking if you don't intend on tasting." She winked.

"Wait, what?" Did she just say taste?

"You can look…" She nodded slowly. "…but only if you intend on following through. Otherwise, off limits."

"Don't you have that backward?"

"No." She shook her head, a perplexed look crossing her cute features. "I don't think so."

"So I can look, but I have to touch?"

Andi answered my lame-ass question by quickly grabbing my hand and placing it on her ass. "Any questions?"

I wasn't easy to shock. Hell, it was damn near impossible. So the fact that she'd managed to do that in under twenty-four hours was pretty impressive.

Clearly, my body agreed with me, considering my hand

plastered against her ass, then squeezed. Blood quickly rushed into all the wrong places.

She let out a little huff as her cheeks tinged with red. Anger replaced the lust. I hated that she wanted me almost as much as I hated how much I wanted her.

I jerked her against my body. "Don't get yourself too excited, Russia. I don't screw corpses."

"Oh thank God, I'm still alive then." She fanned herself. "You should probably work on your game though, because I'm not going to make it easy for you when you do eventually want to partake."

"Partake? What is this? One of your historical romance novels?"

"You'd be a sexy Duke." She winked and let out a light laugh. "Now, the list."

A piece of crinkled paper was smashed into my free hand.

"You can take your hand off my ass now." She smirked.

I pinched, just because I could.

She let out a little yelp then narrowed her eyes. "Play fair."

"Never." I chuckled then started reading the list.

My stomach clenched tighter and tighter as I mentally checked off all the things she wanted to do for our honeymoon.

"There's like a hundred things on here," I pointed out.

"Ninety-nine, but hey, it's okay that math isn't your strong suit."

"The hell it isn't!"

"Ah, he doesn't like to be the less smarter one in the room. Gotcha." She smacked my check. "You're super smart, Italy. Swear."

I muttered a curse and shoved the list into my pocket. "Fine, we'll do some of these things, but that's only because it's a better alternative than jumping out of my window —

something I was actually pondering after the FBI decided to—"

What the hell was I doing?

Confessing?

Andi's body froze, and then she slumped a bit, as if the energy from before had completely drained out of her. "Is it because of me? That they fired you?"

"Firing would have been a nicer word to use." I sat on the barstool and eyed the eggs she had been busy sprinkling with cheese. "And no, it's not because of you. It's because of me."

"They gonna try to kill you now?" she asked, her face serious.

"Ha, now wouldn't that be convenient for you." I was lashing out, trying to make her feel bad because I felt bad, and because I hated that she looked like she pitied me.

"Actually, no." Andi grabbed two plates and started piling food on both of them. "It's convenient that I have my own sexy bodyguard who's going to dress up as a duke later. I mean, if I didn't have you, I'd have to go hire someone."

"I never said I'd dress up."

"And I already bought the costume so…"

"Costume?" I repeated.

Her answer was to hand me a fork and a plate. "Besides…" She shoveled food into her mouth. "…I like your muscles."

"What?" I choked out a bit of egg; it fell onto my plate. Embarrassing. Huh, and I didn't do embarrassed. Always a first time for everything.

Andi smiled, mouth full of eggs, cheeks stuffed to the brim. On anyone else, it would have looked messy — slothlike. On her? It may or may not have been slightly endearing.

I looked down, breaking eye contact.

"Muscles. For when I can't walk anymore." She said it in a happy voice, but I could tell there was a bit of sadness there. How could she not be sad?

"So not only am I your husband-turned-protector-turned-duke, but now I'm your damn nurse too?"

"Ask me if I got an outfit for that too."

"Almost afraid to." I sighed. The doorbell rang, and then the door slammed shut.

"Are we expecting company on our first day of wedded bliss?" Andi's voice sounded hurt.

I looked into her eyes and cursed.

They were pooling with tears.

What the hell?

"Russia…" I wasn't sure why I felt the need to explain myself. "…Nixon's stopping by to add some backup, just in case the FBI decides to tie up a loose end."

"Me?"

I shook my head. "Me."

"Don't worry." She placed her hand on mine. "I'll protect you, Italy."

I bit back a smile. "I wouldn't will you on anyone."

"Aw." She took that same hand and put it on her heart. "You and your compliments. Don't make me blush."

I was about to say something in response when Nixon waltzed in.

"How's wedded bliss, Andi?"

"Great." Andi shoved more eggs into her face and shrugged. "We're going to play dress-up later."

Nixon bit down on his lip, probably to keep from laughing his ass off. "Oh really?"

"Yup." Andi smiled. "Want me to record and upload to YouTube?"

"Hell yes," Nixon said at the same time I said, "Hell no."

"Andi…" I was already exhausted. She ran conversational laps around my typical mornings where I didn't even speak until two hours after waking up. "…why don't you clean up while Nixon and I check out the perimeter."

"I'll come with," she said cheerfully.

"No." I laughed. "Sorry, Andi, but this is guy business."

Her eyes narrowed. In an instant, she had pulled open one of the kitchen drawers, pulled out a gun I'd never seen before in my house, loaded it, then pointed it in my direction. "Dude, I got your back. I told you this. Why don't you listen?" She turned to Nixon. "He always this dense?"

This time Nixon did laugh. "So, married life seems to be going well."

"Bite me," I muttered.

"Andi..." Nixon nodded toward the door. "...feel free to help us out. We could always use an extra set of eyes."

"Awesome."

I rolled my eyes. "Don't forget to duct tape her mouth — it's a dead giveaway to the bad guys."

"Ooo, say bad guys again, only this time make your voice lower and whisper in my ear," Andi said in an excited voice.

"Russians." I looked heavenward.

"Thought they didn't smile," Nixon said more to himself than to me. "And she hasn't stopped since I got here."

"And she probably won't," Andi said triumphantly. "I've got a lot to be excited about."

She was kidding, right? And this is why I kept reminding her of death, because she seemed to forget every damn second! Why the hell was I the logical one in this situation? Newsflash. Dying. Death. The End. Do not pass go. She had to realize that.

Yet she smiled.

Yet she lived.

Damn, she pissed me off.

Because she was one puzzle I honestly couldn't figure out. The numbers didn't match. They certainly didn't compute.

CHAPTER TWELVE

Andi

I LOVED SHOOTING THINGS.

It was a strange obsession I never could quite figure out. I loved the feel of the heavy gun in my hand. The way my finger hovered over the trigger and squeezed when I found my target. I'd never really been scared of guns, maybe because I'd grown up around them, and knew they served a purpose. The minute you started to fear something was the minute you gave it power.

Just like cancer.

If I feared it – suddenly it was bigger than me, something I couldn't conquer, something that could choke the life out of me.

Without fear, it was just a word.

And the power behind the word was meaningless unless I chose to give it power, which I didn't.

I could never understand why people allowed themselves to become overpowered by things they had no control over.

Control was a façade. A word people used in order to feel better about life. When really, the word in and of itself was a fabrication.

People thought they could control cars, but really? Cars controlled them; they were mechanical; the tires could go flat; the brakes could stop working.

Even remote controls were fallible — everything in our life had the potential for error.

Which meant there would never be a situation or thing you would have real control over.

Maybe it was because I'd lived a life outside my control for so long — it was easier for me to swallow.

I shot a sideways glance at Sergio. He was in mafia mode, his sharp eyes taking in every detail around the perimeter of his house as he barked orders to the men.

Surprisingly, Nixon let him.

More surprisingly? Had I been in Nixon's position, I would have too. There was a scary awareness about Sergio. Like he saw everything, even the dust particles in the air, and was able to measure just how fast the bullet would go if it was shot against the wind.

Man had skills.

I knew that.

I just didn't want him to know I knew that, lest he get a big head. Already I felt the need to bring him down a peg — or ten. He was cocky as sin; then again, he had the looks, body, and intelligence to basically make his smug attitude understandable.

I licked my lips and looked around the house. Nixon had brought ten men with him.

All of them armed to the hilt.

I'd been around organized crime my whole life, but it surprised me how loyal the men seemed to Nixon.

In the Russian mafia? Sometimes it seemed like every man was out for himself. With the Italians? Well, a part of me wondered if it was more than just a job to them, more than even a lifestyle, but a belief system.

Almost a religion.

Protect blood.

Luca had said that a handful of times, and I was beginning to see it play out before my very eyes.

Regardless of what Sergio had done to the family, he was still blood, Nixon would die for him.

And Sergio would return the favor.

Neither of them would hesitate.

My chest clenched a bit. What would it feel like to have that type of real loyalty? Or even that type of love?

I was Sergio's punishment.

I wasn't blood. Not even really a wife other than on a piece of paper.

Whatever. I wasn't going to go there because I knew if I went down that road, it would only lead to selfishness and a stupid pity party that would only leave me depressed about life.

My vision clouded a bit.

I sighed, irritated that the dizziness was getting worse. How the hell was I supposed to shoot things if I was dizzy?

I stopped walking, waiting for the moment to pass.

Sergio turned around. His expression showed concern for about one second before it turned to irritation, his mouth forming a thin irritated line. "Tired already?"

I swallowed back a snappy retort and blew him a kiss instead.

His bewildered expression told me that it was the right thing to do. Keep him on his toes — I kind of thought of myself as his entertainment. Clearly, he needed more happy in his life if I was the one cheering him up.

Maybe I'd be sainted when I went to heaven for putting up with his crabby attitude and all around gloomy outlook on life.

Was the sun shining? Yes.

Was he alive? Yes.

So why be grumpy?

The man lived in a mansion, and so what if I'd snuck into his room the night I moved in while he'd been passed out on the couch from drinking too much?

His closet was ridiculous.

Like something out of a movie.

There were still tags on some of the suits. And the suits weren't just expensive — they *screamed* money. I'd probably sleep better in one of his suit piles than I had in his bed.

The fabric was that rich.

His shoes were a completely different story. Even I was jealous, and I'd been spoiled my whole life.

Prada, Valentino, Versace — there was so much Italian leather in that boy's closet that I half-expected him to have cows out back or something.

"Andi!" Sergio barked. "Did you hear me?"

"Er..." I scratched the back of my head with the tip of my gun. My shirt rose above my hips.

Sergio's eyes dipped to the exposed skin.

When all else fails, distract him. "Yes?"

Sergio slowly lifted his gaze to my face. "I said, the gates just opened. Make yourself scarce."

I pouted.

"Andi..." He stomped toward me. "...they don't know you're here. According to the agency, you're still attending Eagle Elite and dating the star quarterback."

Wait, what?

He swore. "I'll explain later, for now. Hide in the bushes."

"You're serious?"

"No time for you to go back in the house, so yeah, I'm serious. Go."

I glanced over my shoulder. The black sedan pulled into

the circular driveway.

"Fine." I skipped over to the bushes and ducked while Sergio made his way to the front of the house.

The large water fountain made it hard to hear any sort of conversation, but I could tell it wasn't a fun one.

Sergio's hands were in the air making gestures, while the agent's hands were in defensive mode.

Finally, Sergio threw a badge and a few other things onto the ground then emptied his gun and handed it over.

He was defenseless. Why would he do that?

The agent took the gun and leaned down to pick up the rest of the things Sergio had thrown. He hung his head, almost like he was sad, and then the strangest thing happened.

The agent wrapped his arms around Sergio's stiff body and hugged.

"His old partner," Nixon said from behind me, scaring the crap out of me.

I nearly fell over.

"Sorry."

"It's fine." I pressed a hand to my chest, my heartbeat was erratic. "I didn't know he had a partner."

"Apparently they were close — though he never knew Sergio's true involvement with us."

I frowned and continued to watch the exchange.

"Will he hurt him?"

"Who?" Nixon asked in a calm voice.

"Will the partner hurt Sergio?"

"Doubt it," Nixon whispered. "Regardless of the information the feds have on us, they still know that Sergio's part of our family. Retaliation would be expected. If they bite, we bite back only harder. Kill one of us, we kill ten of them. It's kind of how these things work. In the end, it's not worth the effort on their part."

"So why the precaution?"

Nixon stood as the FBI agent walked around his car and

got in, slamming the door behind him.

"I never said the feds were smart." Nixon shrugged. "Sometimes their balls get too big, and we have to cut them down to size."

"Sounds painful."

"Killing always is." Nixon's icy stare met mine. "Then again, you know that all too well, don't you?"

I licked my lips and shrugged.

"Don't hurt him."

I jerked my head up. "Who?"

"You know who," Nixon said in a deathly cold voice. "I know how bad it really is. Sergio may not know, but I do. Don't hurt him, Andi."

"Sergio should know." I sighed. "I keep telling him I'm dying."

"Don't put it past him to try to save you." Nixon's eyes were sad.

I choked out a laugh. "Believe me, that's the last thing he wants."

Eyes narrowed, Nixon opened his mouth but was interrupted by Sergio walking around the corner.

"I hate today."

Nixon sighed, sharing a look with me before putting his gun back in its holster. "Maybe you should take a honeymoon with the wife? Might cheer you up."

"Hey!" I jumped to my feet. "That's what I said."

"Don't encourage the communist." Sergio pointed at me.

"Hey!" I put my hand on my hips. "I'm a US citizen, ass-hat!"

Sergio grinned; it was actually, a really nice smile, the type that made me feel warm inside. "Whatever you say, Russia."

"Alright then." Nixon patted Sergio on the back. "You kids have fun. No killing each other."

"No promises." I winked at Sergio.

He smirked. "I'd like to see you try."

"I could dig that." I nodded. "First one with a flesh wound loses?"

Nixon cursed. "Don't make me come back and referee you two. I mean it. Play nice." He waved at us and walked around the corner, leaving me and Sergio alone.

"You look like you could use a drink." I took in his pale appearance and dark demeanor.

"It's eight in the morning," Sergio said dumbly.

"So? It's five o'clock somewhere!"

He closed his eyes, probably in irritation, or maybe just so he could take a time out. "Andi—"

"Come on." I grabbed his hand before he could jerk it back. "I'll spike your coffee, and then we can knock some things off that list."

"That damn list had sex written on it like fifteen times," Sergio grumbled.

"I'm sorry, were you just complaining? And so what? You don't have to cross those items off, though it would be kind of nice to get some aggression out. I bet you'd feel better."

"If I screwed you?"

I nodded. "You're really tense."

"Ha." He popped his knuckles. "You have no idea."

"Clearly I do, since I listed it fifteen times."

"Anyone ever told you that you aren't normal?" He held open the back door for me and placed his hand on the small of my back, ushering me back inside.

"All the time." My face cracked into an uncontrollable grin. "Are you complaining?" I reached my hand into his front pocket and slowly pulled the piece of paper from it, my fingertips lingering around the top of his jeans as I moved him closer to me until we were hip to hip.

"Andi," his voice wavered. "What are you doing?"

I shrugged. "Grabbing my list."

I was semi-pissed that his expression was relieved. So, to keep him on his toes, I grabbed his head and jerked it down so our mouths touched.

He didn't kiss me back for a few seconds.

And then somehow I ended up on the counter, my legs wrapped around his body as he tugged my lower lip between his teeth and smashed his mouth against mine in an almost painful kiss.

I dug my fingers into his hair as he lifted me off the counter and slammed me against the wall, our mouths still fused together.

His kisses didn't give — they took, they stole little parts of me I didn't even know I was keeping close until they were gone. I couldn't control my breathing as his tongue tasted mine. Sergio wasn't about asking permission for anything, just like I highly doubted he'd apologize after this kiss once he came to his senses.

His hands moved to my jeans.

I thought he'd stop.

Instead, he started pulling them off my body. At eight in the morning. In the middle of the kitchen — against a wall.

By the weird cow magnet that said *Wyoming*.

I moaned as he retreated, only to come at the kiss from a different angle. His lips were soft; they didn't coax. It was like his mouth was making love to me. I'd never been kissed the way he was kissing me.

"Ahem." Someone's throat cleared.

Sergio jerked back but kept me pinned against the wall. Slowly we both turned our heads to see Nixon standing in the doorway. His grin was huge.

"I almost forgot. Trace wanted me to drop off your wedding present, but I'm pretty sure you're on your way to opening a different one, cousin… so I'll just leave you to it." He placed a large box on the counter and laughed as he walked out of the room.

I expected Sergio to drop me on my ass.

Instead, he eyed the present, his grip tightening on my body.

Swallowing, I waited for his logic to kick in. It had to, right? I mean, he despised me.

But nothing kicked in.

Instead, Sergio kissed me again.

And again.

And again.

I was lost in his kiss, lost in the sensation of his mouth pressed against mine; the way he tasted could easily become my favorite addiction.

I didn't have to like the guy to appreciate the fact that his kiss was sinful, his hands weapons in their own right.

"This means nothing," he whispered against my mouth. "Don't fall in love with me just because I'm good in bed, Andi."

I laughed against his mouth. "Yeah, I'll be the judge of that, Italy."

He kissed me savagely. His lips quirked into a playful smile. "Oh really?"

Who was this guy? Was that all I needed to do? Seduce him and suddenly he was going to play nice?

His fingers dug into my skin.

Or rough.

I let out a little yelp as he trailed hot open-mouthed kisses down the side of my neck.

"I won't," I finally answered.

"Won't what?" he said in between kisses.

"Fall in love with you."

"Mm-kay." He dragged his lips across my collarbone, his teeth nipping my skin.

"But maybe you shouldn't keep kissing me like that if you want me to keep my promise."

A dark chuckle was his only response.

I liked this side of him.

But a part of me felt… a bit used.

Almost like I wanted to be able to have a normal conversation with the guy before he saw me naked.

Then again, he'd already seen the goods, but…

I froze.

And in return — so did he.

Meaning, I had officially killed the moment.

Slowly, he released me, my body sliding down his until my feet touched the floor. His lips were a bit swollen, his blue eyes piercing. "Second thoughts?"

"No," I lied.

His grin was almost mean as he leaned forward, pressing his hands against the wall on either side of my head. "Liar."

I met his gaze, licking my lips, tasting him everywhere. "I just… I didn't want you to drop me, and I panicked."

His eyebrows shot up. "Is that right?"

I nodded.

"Hmm…" He backed up. "…next time you offer your body, make sure you can follow through on it."

"I can!" I argued. "I mean I want to." I reached for his face, but he moved out of the way.

"No, you're right." He continued to back away from me. "It's best this way. Getting physically involved with you will only make it harder."

"Make what harder?"

"Shooting you later when the pain gets too intense… when the days get too dark."

Stunned, I could only stare at him.

"What?" He shrugged. "I figure that's also part of my job… as your husband. I may not kill you, but I'll happily pull the trigger once you're begging for it. Wouldn't be the first time."

And just like that, I wanted to hate him all over again. "You're a real piece of work, you know that?"

"Oh, I know." He chuckled. "I know."

He left the room.

A door slammed.

And I didn't see him the rest of the day.

So much for a honeymoon.

CHAPTER THIRTEEN

Sergio

I HOLED UP IN MY OFFICE like I was guilty of something.

Which sucked, considering the last time I'd felt real guilt was when I'd stolen cookies out of the cookie jar at age eight.

I expected Andi to knock on my door or break it down, considering breaking things was more her style.

But she left me in peace the entire day.

I worked for hours making sure she had a cover at the university and also keeping tabs on her father.

It was busywork. The type of work a person did to keep his mind off more pressing matters.

Like the way her body felt against mine.

The way her mouth tasted.

"Shit." I slammed my hands against the desk and reached for my phone. The text messages hadn't stopped for hours.

First a message from Tex saying I was an asshole.

Nothing new in that department.

Then several emojis from Nixon — of presents.

Hilarious.

Phoenix had called a few times too, but I'd ignored those as well.

Just like I'd ignored the seven invitations to family dinner. It was a tradition, one I didn't want Andi to be a part of. Because I knew there would come a night when her seat would be empty.

My stomach lurched at the thought.

I picked up my phone and checked my voicemail.

"Hey, man, it's Phoenix."

I rolled my eyes.

"Answer your damn phone. I can't get hold of your wife."

I deleted the message. Asshole. She was my wife, not his.

The next message was the same thing.

Finally, around the fourth message, I started to get a bit concerned.

"Dude, if you don't answer I'm going to break down your freaking door! Andi's not answering and she missed her doctor's appointment."

Wait, what?

Doctor's appointment. /?

I pulled out the list that she'd made earlier that day. Sure enough, on the corner it said, *And don't forget to take me to the doctor like a good husband!*

She'd drawn a heart next to it.

The appointment had been three hours ago.

I told myself not to worry. She'd probably fallen asleep or left her phone in the house or something.

I quickly ran out of the office and started calling her name.

"Andi?"

No answer.

I went into the kitchen.

Nothing.

Panic swelled in my chest as I took the stairs two at a time. I burst into her bedroom. It was empty.

Shit!

I moved down the hall. "Andi?"

A soft whimper sounded. I called out her name again.

The bathroom door closest to her bedroom was shut.

I tried the handle.

It was locked.

With a curse, I slammed my body into it. The door broke free, revealing a crumpled Andi near the toilet.

She was pale.

Her eyes were closed.

And a part of me died inside.

How long had she been here?

"Andi?" I got on my knees and pulled her into my lap. "Andi, can you hear me?"

I lifted her head, but it only fell back, lifeless. Her skin was so pale it was almost translucent. "Andi?"

Her eyes fluttered open.

"Thatta girl," I encouraged.

"Not dog," she whispered, the fight so completely out of her words that the panic worsened until I felt like I was going to be sick.

"Do we need to go to the hospital?"

She frowned. "Aren't we at the hospital?"

"No—" Frantic, I felt her forehead. "Shit, you're burning up. We need to go to the ER."

"Hate doctors. Hospital smells." She scrunched up her nose then pressed her face against my chest. "You don't though. You smell like dirty sex."

My voice felt shaky. "Oh yeah?" I pushed to my feet and heaved her into my arms. "Pretty sure you're going to regret that compliment when you're lucid."

"Lucid?" she repeated. "Like ice cream? I think I want vanilla. What are you going to have, Sergio?"

I took one look at her pretty face and answered honestly — maybe the most honest answer I'd had since being with her.

"Chocolate."

Her smile was weak. "I love chocolate."

"Me too, Andi."

"You were mean."

I carried her down the stairs. "I'm sorry."

"I'm sick." Andi tucked her head underneath my chin. "I think… fever."

"We'll get you better." I was saying it for both of us, because I wasn't sure I could handle her getting sicker. It did something to me. I felt powerless — I hated that feeling. I opened the door to my Escalade with one hand and gently put her down, pulled the seatbelt tight, and buckled it.

"Don't make me go." A big fat tear slid down her cheek. "Please."

I swallowed the tightness in my throat. "Tell you what… after we visit the hospital, how about I take you to get some chocolate ice cream?"

She closed her eyes; another tear slid, then another. "Promise?"

"Yeah, Andi." I wiped her tears away. "I promise, but right now we need to get you to the hospital, okay?"

She gave a weak nod.

The minute I got into the SUV, I gripped the steering wheel and cursed. It was too close to home.

She didn't know that.

I wasn't even sure anyone else knew — other than Ax and Nixon.

I didn't push her away because I hated her.

I was terrified of her.

The fear choked me the entire way to the hospital. I didn't need to MapQuest it, didn't even need to check my phone for the closest one.

I knew this hospital by heart.

Just like I knew the cancer wing by heart.

Because my mom had died of the very same thing.

I'd lived through it once.

I wasn't sure I'd actually survive it twice.

Every move was mechanical. I tried to detach myself emotionally as I lifted Andi out of the car and walked into the ER.

But memories assaulted me.

The smell was the same.

"Let her go, she wants to go," the nurse said. "Say goodbye."

"No!" I yelled. "If I say goodbye, she'll leave!"

"Son," my father said in a gruff voice. "Don't make a scene."

My mom reached for me, her hand outstretched. I tasted blood in my mouth. Maybe I'd bitten my tongue. Maybe my heart had broken, and that was what happened when hearts broke inside the body. They bled from the inside out.

Our fingertips touched, just briefly before my father ripped me from the room and told me to stop crying.

Ax was in the corner, his face haunted.

And it was Nixon who finally held me before I collapsed onto the floor. "She's gone, she's gone, Nixon she's—"

"She's in heaven," Nixon said simply.

"No," my father said behind me. "People like us don't go to heaven… we go to hell."

I jerked away from Nixon and lunged for my father. I pulled the gun from his own holster and pointed it at his face.

He laughed. The bastard laughed. "What? Are you going to shoot me in the hospital? When you're the guilty one?"

The gun shook in my hand. "Guilty one?"

"Remember this." My dad sneered. "You killed her. You killed your mother – not the cancer. You did this. And you know why. Such a disappointment."

"Don't listen to him, Sergio," Nixon said behind me. "He's a bastard."

"He may be a bastard, but he's right." I was fifteen but not stupid. I knew the truth.

It was my fault my mom had died. I had no one to blame but myself.

CHAPTER FOURTEEN

Andi

My mouth was dry as a desert. I'd always hated that expression — what was worse? Actually being able to use it and know that it seriously didn't do my situation any justice.

Water.

I opened my mouth to ask for it.

And suddenly, like magic, a cup appeared, and the cool liquid trickled down my throat.

I opened my eyes.

Sergio was sitting on my bed.

Not next to it, but on it.

I blinked. "What are you doing?"

His expression wasn't readable. Damn him. He truly kept his emotions on lockdown. "Giving you water."

"No, I mean on my bed."

He held the water to my lips.

I sipped deeply then pushed the cup back. "Th-thanks."

"I went to med school." The information was offered freely.

And since he didn't tend to share anything about himself, I chose not to speak, hoping my silence would help the moment.

Sergio's jaw flexed as he clenched his teeth together. "I never finished. My involvement with the feds and the family… well, it made things difficult. But that's not the point. The point is this." He reached for something in the chair. When he pulled back, I felt myself get sick to my stomach. He had my chart in his hands. I tried to reach for it, so I could jerk it away and throw it across the room, but he held it out of my reach.

"So…" I licked my lips and looked down at the scratchy hospital blanket. "…you really can read. Good for you."

"I can read." His voice was calm. "Why didn't you tell me?"

I rolled my eyes. "Look, I told you I was sick. I told you I had cancer. I told you I was dying in six months. What more was there to tell?"

"You're a coward."

I gasped.

"And no I won't apologize for telling you the damn truth. You're a coward, and you know it."

"Get out!" I yelled.

"No." He bared his teeth. "Why the hell didn't you tell me you could get a bone marrow transplant?"

I sighed and leaned back against the pillows. "Because I can't."

"You've tried everything but the transplant."

"I know."

"Why?"

"Just because you're my husband doesn't mean you have the right to demand answers out of me."

"Like hell it doesn't!" He slammed the chart onto the chair and faced me, his hands bracing the side of my bed. "Tell me why."

I felt my body hunch, almost like I was trying to crawl into myself. I hated feeling small, and in that moment with that large Italian man hovering over me, his face menacing, I felt small, not afraid, but small. Like maybe I did deserve his anger.

"Because it won't work," I whispered.

"And you know that how?"

"Because nothing else has!" I yelled. "Alright? Nothing has helped. I've had leukemia for years, Sergio, years! Doctors appointments, chemotherapy, radiation, pills, pills, and more pills. Nothing has worked. Nothing. Besides, I'm too far gone, the odds of a bone marrow transplant, the odds of someone else's blood working in my body? Slim to none."

"But there's still a chance."

"There's always a chance."

"So take it."

"You don't get it.

"Try me," he growled. "This isn't you, this scared little girl. It's not you."

"Oh, and you know me so well." I rolled my eyes. "Besides, this isn't your style, Sergio, you don't worry about people in hospitals. You freaking put them there!"

"You don't know shit!" His voice rose.

"I know you don't care!" I fired back. "So why start now?"

His eyes filled with tears. What the hell was wrong with him? "It's stupid, not to take a chance, regardless of how slim that chance, at life."

"What? So now you're preaching to me about living when a few days ago you wanted to put a bullet in my head?"

His eyes were shuttered again, no emotion showing through. "Not everyone gets the chance you're getting."

"Why can't you let me die happy?"

"So that's it? You're going to selfishly let yourself die when you could live, because you're afraid of something not working? So what? It doesn't work, then you still die, Andi. At least you tried. Not everyone who has cancer has options. You do."

"I've made my choice."

"Like I said…" He rose from the bed. "Coward."

"Get out!" I yelled, my voice hoarse.

"Like I would stay!" He basically stomped out of my room.

It wasn't more than three seconds before Nixon was in my doorway.

I glanced at him guiltily. "You heard?"

"Pretty sure the whole floor heard." He winced. "Kinda harsh, Andi."

"Not you too." I was too weak to argue more than I already had. "He doesn't get it."

"I think you'd be surprised what he does and doesn't get, especially when it comes to cancer."

My eyes narrowed. "What do you mean?"

"Look…" Nixon sat on the edge of my bed. "…I'm only telling you this so you don't hate him more than you already do, or more than he already hates himself. His mom died of cancer. In this hospital. On this floor."

My stomach sunk.

"It was aggressive, so aggressive she literally had no options. It was like, one day she was fine and the next the doctors were telling the family she had weeks to live."

Tears welled in my eyes.

"So…" Nixon stood, his movements jerky. I could tell he wasn't used to talking about himself or about anything personal. Nixon was a lot like Sergio in that way; he kept pieces of himself hidden. "…Sergio was here every damn day. And in the end, when his mom died, he took the blame."

"But…" I shivered and pulled up the blankets. "..It's not his fault she got cancer."

Nixon let out a bitter chuckle. "His father thought

otherwise… had Sergio been a better son, his mom wouldn't have been stressed, and the cancer wouldn't have been able to spread so quickly. Had Sergio watched his mother more carefully while his father was away doing business, they would have caught it in time. Really, take your pick. It was all Sergio's fault. What's worse? I think a part of Sergio believed him—Hell, I think he still believes him. His dad was a real piece of work. My father despised him, and that's really saying something, since my father considered torturing me an extracurricular activity."

"Nixon…" I blinked back tears. "…get my husband and send him back in here?"

"No." Nixon shook his head. "He doesn't deserve your pity, just like you don't deserve his. He hates it. He'll know I told you. And I didn't tell you so that you'd feel sorry for him. I told you so you'd understand why he's so pissed at you."

"It's my choice."

"Right." Nixon nodded. "And I get that, believe me, but sometimes our choices aren't just about us — but the people that love us, the people that have to stand by and watch us suffer."

"He doesn't love me."

Nixon said nothing.

I squinted, waiting for him to agree with me.

Instead he shrugged and walked out.

Well, that was helpful.

Two hours went by.

And then three.

Around eight that night, Sergio finally returned. He held two small cups in his hand.

No words were exchanged. Instead, he put both cups on the tray and moved it to where I could reach then sat in the chair.

He handed me a spoon.

And dug into his own cup.

Ice cream.

I vaguely remembered him promising me ice cream.

Guilt slammed into me as I grabbed my spoon and then my cup and started eating.

The hum of the TV and the beeping heart monitor were the only sounds emitting from the room. It may as well have been nails on a chalk board.

"So," I said finishing my ice cream. "You were gone a while."

"Yup." He eyed the TV.

"Thanks for the ice cream."

"I keep my promises." His gaze still didn't leave the TV.

"Look." I took a deep breath.

Sergio held up his hand, finally turning toward me. "Let's not do this."

"But—"

"No." Sadness filled his eyes. "I know what you're going to say."

"Oh yeah?"

"Yup… you have that look. May as well paint guilty across your face. It's the same look I saw on Nixon earlier. He told you. Now you know. Whatever."

"That's not what I was thinking." I lifted my chin in defiance.

Sergio's mouth tilted into a small smile. "Oh? Enlighten me."

"I was thinking about the kiss," I blurted.

Sergio's smile quickly turned into a cocky grin. "Were you now?"

"It's probably why I got dizzy and passed out," I pointed. "Your fault."

"So…" Smile gone. "…my kiss makes you sick?"

"That backfired," I grumbled.

He let out a humorless chuckle. "Andi, what do you want?"

Loaded question.

I wanted so many things.

I wanted to live. I wanted to hope that a transplant would work. I wanted to see what this thing was between us. This attraction that neither of us were actually admitting to.

I wanted to kiss him again.

I wanted him to want to kiss me.

"It's not rocket science, Andi. Just tell me right now, in this moment. What do you want? More than anything."

"You know how long it's been since anyone has actually asked me that?"

Sergio moved until he was sitting next to me on the bed.

I acted on instinct and reached for him.

"I want to hold your hand." The scary words were out before I could stop them. I always expected an irritated reaction out of Sergio.

But this time, he reached for my hand and interlocked his fingers, then brought my hand to his lips, kissing it gently. "That, I can do, Andi."

CHAPTER FIFTEEN

Sergio

SEX REMINDED ME OF NUMBERS. It was mechanical; no love needed to be present. It simply existed to bring pleasure, and once the pleasure was done, you parted ways.

It was easy.

Not hard.

It made sense to me, a simple cause and effect; your body physically reacted; therefore, your hormones demanded you respond.

This whole time, out of sheer paranoia, I'd been avoiding sex with her, avoiding something that would bond us physically, something that would tie us together even more than we were already bound.

What I hadn't realized…

What I hadn't factored in…

Was the simple gesture of holding her hand.

The minute our palms pressed together, our fingers linked, something snapped inside of me.

I'd later come to realize it was that moment.

Not just any moment.

But the moment I fell for Andi.

And as our hands clenched, something inside of me shifted, my heart pounded a little faster, my breathing was a little quicker, and I realized, Nicolai, had been right.

Because my heart was invested.

And I knew it was only a matter of time before that investment turned on me.

Before the simple act of holding her hand would bring about a chaotic destruction I wouldn't be able to protect myself from.

He 'd been right.

The Russian bastard had been right.

Because I knew, without a shadow of a doubt, that at the end of our time together, I was going to ask him — no, I was going to beg, on my hands and knees if necessary — to take the pain away.

To take the searing loss I'd feel.

When she left this life.

When she left me.

When I was without the sun — without her.

I glanced at her sleeping form. We had to stay in the hospital overnight. I knew the doctors wanted to monitor her. I also knew firsthand what their expressions meant. They were grim, hopeless, the same look my mom's doctor had had.

Unable to sleep, I picked up her chart and read through it again. She was on a list, but I knew unless a miracle occurred, she wasn't going to be getting any transplants soon.

A perfect match.

That's what she needed.

The odds of that happening were slim.

But I wanted her to try. It was stupid. I mean, I barely knew her, but the thought of her just… giving up? It destroyed me.

I quickly made a call — one I wasn't sure I was going to

regret come morning.

She could never find out.

If she did, I'd be the one dead.

But maybe, even if it meant I died — it would be worth it. She'd been right before, when she said it was a two-twirl dress. She'd been gorgeous on her wedding day, and she deserved more than one twirl.

She deserved a hundred.

A thousand.

The least I could do was try to get her to that place where she could run without getting dizzy. Where she could twirl and truly experience life.

My fingers slid across the numbers on the screen.

"Yeah?" Tex barked into the phone. "How's our girl?"

"My girl's fine." I sighed. "Look, I need a favor."

"I'm not killing the doctors. They're the best money can buy and—"

"Not that kind of favor."

Tex paused. "This surprises me. Okay, you have my attention."

When I was done explaining, I was met with complete silence. I started to break out into a cold sweat.

"No promises," he finally croaked out. The line went dead.

Andi was discharged two days later. The doctors wanted to make sure she didn't have an infection. It turned out she'd just had a minor case of walking pneumonia. Though any sickness could potentially kill her — they'd given us the green light.

And she was back to her chipper ways.

Which included waking me up at dawn with her bat and pan.

And then singing at the top of her lungs while making eggs with extra ketchup… the ketchup she said represented blood, and, since I'd killed so many people, she wanted to remind me of my sins every day.

Her words. Not mine.

I continued holding her hand whenever she asked me to, and honestly, each time our fingers touched, it felt more and more like I was losing a part of myself.

I knew she was getting bored; you couldn't simply keep a girl like Andi cooped up in a house, but it terrified me that she would get sicker if we went somewhere, and as much as I hated to admit my own terror, well, there it was.

Finally after five days at home, something gave.

It happened when I was in the shower — because naturally Andi didn't do anything like a normal human being; her timing was always off, her ideas harebrained.

I was just putting shampoo in my hair when the door to the bathroom opened.

"Hey, sailor," Andi called.

"What the—" I dropped the shampoo onto my foot and turned. I wasn't in one of those showers, you know, the types that hid every part of you.

I lived in a freaking mansion. My shower was glass on every side and gave the impression that I was in a monsoon rather than a bathroom.

"Andi?" I licked my lips, not bothering to cover myself up. "Can this wait until I'm out of the shower."

"Nope." She heaved herself up onto the counter and smiled. "You're more vulnerable this way."

"No shit," I muttered then grabbed some body wash and continued trying to shower while her eyes drank me in.

"So…" She yawned.

I was slightly offended at her reaction. Could she at least stare wide-eyed and in absolute wonderment?

The woman did amazing things to my ego.

"I was thinking."

"That's unfortunate for me." I faced her again. "So? What were you thinking, Andi?"

"You like holding my hand."

I quickly turned back around lest she see the effect even thinking about holding her hand had on my body. "Yeah?" I croaked out. "So?"

"So, you like spending time with me even if you won't admit it."

"Get there faster, Andi."

"The list," Andi called out. "I think we should do some list-like activities. I wrote down all the honeymoon things I'd want to do if we were able to leave the country without going to prison."

I sighed. "Andi, we wouldn't go to prison."

"I would die in prison. I'm too pretty."

"And I'm what? The Hunchback of Notre Dame?"

I met her gaze again.

She tilted her head. A small smile formed across her lips. "You do have horrible posture."

"Do not," I argued, straightening my back.

"Do too." Her grin widened. "You'll probably be one of those crotchety old men that can't look past a woman's breasts because he can't lift his head. I can see it now. *'Bring me more pasta!'*"

"Wait, what?" I turned off the shower. "Why am I yelling for pasta?"

She shrugged. "Just seems like something your grumpy ass would say."

"Your opinion of me needs work."

"Maybe you should be nicer, and my opinion would be higher."

"I bought you ice cream."

"After yelling at me." She tossed me a white fluffy towel then pointed at my side tattoo. "Hey, what's that?"

I slapped her hand away and turned so she couldn't see the markings then wrapped the towel around my waist. "Okay, so you want to… what? Have sex fifteen times?"

She was still trying to peer around me. "I wrote it fifteen times because I figured we'd be on a honeymoon for seven days — that's sex twice a day plus a bonus round."

I walked past her, steam billowing off my body. "Sweetheart, you don't plan sex."

"Well…" She crossed her arms. "…I do."

I leaned against the countertop. "So that's it? You're propositioning me?"

"Nope, I picked out a few other things on the list." She slid it across the granite counter and leaned her hip next to my body. "Read."

"So demanding."

"I'll go get my pot and wood stick."

"Reading," I grumbled.

"Pet a giraffe?" I said aloud. "What the hell?"

Andi shrugged and examined her fingers. "Sergio, if we were going on an African safari, I'd get to see a damn giraffe."

"And you want to see a giraffe because?"

"They're tall."

I fought for control over my temper. "That's it? Because they're tall?"

She nodded.

"Fine, can we just paint Tex to look like a giraffe and give you a paintball gun so it's like a real safari?"

Andi tapped her chin. "That may work. Hey, you're useful after all!"

I kept reading. "I hate hippos."

"Well, that's unfair." Andi started wiping off the mirror with a fresh towel then tossed me my deodorant. "Have you ever even met a hippo?"

"If I had, I wouldn't be standing here."

"Oh, please," She waved me off. "You'd be fine, flesh

wound, nothing more."

"They drown people!" My voice rose an octave. "Because they can!"

"Details."

I huffed while I applied the deodorant, then tossed it back at her and walked toward my large closet.

"Next!" She clapped her hands and shoved past me into the closet and began frantically looking through my designer jeans.

I paused and looked at the honeymoon wish list. "Sharks? You want to swim with sharks?"

She nodded but didn't turn around; instead, a pair of jeans went flying through the air, nearly hitting me in the face.

I caught them just in time. "How about I take you fishing, and we can pretend there are sharks, or better yet, I get a blow-up shark toy and put it in the pool out back?"

"Hmm…" A sweater sailed over my head. "…I may agree to those terms as long as you put on the *Jaws* theme song."

"I'll hum it."

She stood to her full height and laughed. "Such a good sport."

"Right. That's what I'm being — a good sport. I figure if I don't at least try to make you happy, you're going to make my life hell then shoot me in my sleep."

"The idea has merit."

"See?"

"Wear those." She pointed to the clothes she'd tossed onto the floor. "And I really like the new boots you bought online a few days ago."

"You read my mail, don't you?"

"Can I have a credit card with no limit?" she asked, ignoring my question but actually answering it, considering she'd probably seen my credit card statement.

"Sure… can you stop waking me up with your pot-and-pan trick?"

"Ohh... he drives a tough bargain."

"I'll give if you do." I picked the clothes off the floor and approached her. "What do you say?"

"I say..." She eyed the list in my hand. "...give me one thing on the list today, and you have a deal."

I glanced back down at the list. She wanted to go on a foxhunt, whatever the hell that was. An idea popped into my head. "Fine, go change into something you can move in."

"Really?" She squealed.

Her excitement was this tangible real thing, almost like I could taste it in the air. I fought to keep myself from catching her enthusiasm. "Really."

"You're the best husband ever!" Her hand reached for my towel. She tugged. The towel fell.

I scowled but had nothing to hide.

Her hand moved to my hip, and then her fingertips grazed my abs. "You sure you don't want to work on those other fifteen options?"

My body said yes.

Her eyebrows arched in... ah, there it was, not necessarily wonderment, but I could tell she was at least semi-impressed by the way she licked her lips.

My body was on board, but every other part of me said no — that it would be the final straw, that I'd fall and have no hope of ever being the same again. I took a step back.

She pouted, but her eyes drank their fill. "Fine, but one day I'm going to stop asking, and where's that going to leave you?"

"Rhetorical question?"

"Food for thought." She winked. "I'm going to get ready. Hurry up! Don't want to be late for our first adventure."

She skipped out of the room.

Leaving me in silence, in my giant closet.

Her presence was like the sun, making everything seem

brighter, happier. I hadn't realized until that day how boring and dark my life had become.

But that was what happened when you actually experienced life through someone else; you realized what you've been doing wasn't living, but existing.

And I had a sinking feeling that my existence would miss hers even now… after only knowing her for a week.

It was a scary thought.

Terrifying actually, to imagine a world where people like Andi — where Andi herself — didn't exist.

CHAPTER SIXTEEN

Andi

I LOOKED UP AT THE HUGE BUILDING and grinned. "You, my dear husband, are a brilliant, scary man."

Sergio gripped my hand tighter. I let out a breathy sigh because, well, he was wearing the tight jeans I'd picked out for him and the black long-sleeved sweater that hugged every single muscle he possessed.

It helped that he'd finished the look with a pair of D&G aviators.

They should be illegal on a guy that sexy.

He looked like a walking sexy-man commercial. You know, if those existed.

"You ready to do this?" He released my hand and moved his fingertips to the small of my back. "I mean, if you're scared we can go back."

I took a deep breath. "But we're already here."

"True."

"And it's important that I face my fears."

"Also true." He chuckled. "So what will it be, little

Russia? You gonna run home with your tail between your legs? Or are you gonna play?"

"I may get hurt."

"Yup."

"You could get hurt."

"Yup."

"We could die trying."

"Yup."

"Are you just going to keep saying yup?"

He paused then shrugged. "Yup."

I rolled my eyes. "Okay, we're doing this."

He checked his watch. "We've got two hours to burn before family dinner."

"And if we show up all bloody and sweaty?"

Sergio took off his sunglasses and winked. "It's family dinner. How else do you think we show up? Holding hands and singing 'Kumbaya?'"

"Valid point."

"You first." He gently pushed me forward.

"But—"

"Come on, Andi," He tugged my body back against his ripped stomach. "Where's your sense of adventure, oh hippo trainer?"

"I said I wanted to meet a hippo not train one."

"Chickening out?"

"No." I kept staring at the entrance to the building. "Okay, fine. But how is this even possible if I've never been trained?"

Sergio gripped my hand again. "You haven't been trained. I have." With that, he tugged me toward the door.

I tried to dig my heels into the cement. It didn't work.

Fifteen minutes later, I was signing a consent form that basically said if I died, I couldn't sue the company.

I felt the need to point out that if I was dead, I wouldn't be able to sue in the first place.

Sergio coughed up a laugh then slid our papers forward to the old man, who may or may not have been blind. I couldn't tell on account he refused to take off his sunglasses and hadn't uttered one word to me other than "Name, date, sign."

"You taking her?" The old man sniffed loudly. "Or you want me to get one of the guys?"

I wasn't at all comfortable with the way Sergio grinned in my direction. "I think I'll take her."

"Think?" I repeated weakly.

"Come on." He tugged me back outside.

A guy who looked about my age waltzed toward us. "Been a long time, Sergio."

"Oh gosh." I was going to puke. "You're taking me, and it's been a long time?"

"Chill." The guy laughed. "It's not like you forget how to jump out of a plane. Just make sure to check your equipment so you don't go splat. Clean up's a bitch."

I felt all blood drain from my face.

"We're on our honeymoon." Sergio wrapped his arm around me and squeezed tightly. "Aren't we, sugar pants?"

Oh? Little Italy wanted to play? I could dig that. "Sure are…" I pinched his ass. "…Mr. Big."

Sergio let out a strangled cough while I placed my hand on his chest. "He's a huge *Sex and the City* fan. Refuses to let me call him anything other than that… for…" I looked down at his tight jeans then cupped him with my hand. "…obvious reasons, though it seems just about anything excites him these days, huh, baby?"

Sergio gritted his teeth. "Whatever you say, baby."

I fought back a laugh, removing my hand.

He squeezed my ass, nearly bruising me in the process.

"Whoa, you guys have one of those… fifty-shades relationships?" The guy took a step back and nodded admiringly.

"What can I say?" I shrugged. "My man likes whips."

"Okay." Sergio gripped me by the shoulders and steered me toward the plane. "Get everything ready, Tom. I'm just going to go over the basics with her before we take off."

"Cool." He walked off.

I watched him, my brow furrowing the more I watched. "He's like ten years old."

"Twenty-three."

"He's flying a plane."

"That's typically what pilots do."

I pointed at him. "He can't even grow facial hair."

Sergio rolled his eyes. "And you know that how?"

"I bet he still drinks milk before bed."

"Andi, stop stalling, and follow me. We have to pack the chutes."

I needed a paper bag or something to breathe into.

"You know…" My knees felt weak, and this time it wasn't because I was having dizzy spells or my cancer was being a bitch; it was because real live fear was beginning to boil in my chest. "…we don't have to do this. When I wrote down that I wanted to jump out of something scary, I meant like… a car."

"A car?" Sergio turned, his smile mocking. "Really?"

"Yeah, like a really old car, one that was perhaps missing an engine and a steering wheel, making it so we had to roll it down a hill and just take our chances by hopping out."

"You're doing this." Sergio grabbed one large, black pack-thing and pulled a chute out of it. "I always fold my own chute. Never trust someone else to keep you safe."

"Good life lesson."

"You pack your own chute even if the person swears they did it right because you know you the best. Got it?"

I nodded numbly, watching as he took special care in making sure the chute wasn't torn. His fingers ran over every part of the material. I shivered.

He had nice hands.

They were soft, strong, not too rough, but really masculine at the same time.

"You cold?" Sergio asked without looking up.

"Um, no."

"Mm-kay." My eyes followed his hands as they moved the parachute, folding it, and then shoving it into the pack. "We're good to go."

"But I haven't learned anything."

Sergio glanced up at me, his eyes clear, so bright and blue that I let out a little gasp. "Do you trust me?"

Yeah. I really did. He may not particularly like me, but he'd protect me, he'd said as much. He would never let anything happen to me. So I gripped his outstretched hand and managed a weak "Yes."

"Great." His smile was easygoing — not dark or irritated. "Then all the training you need is to trust me and hold on tight while I take care of us and give you one of your honeymoon wishes."

It felt like mere minutes before we were up in the air, and I was in some sort of weird suit, getting strapped to Sergio.

I was shaking so hard I thought I was going to puke.

"You're Russian," Sergio whispered hotly in my ear. "Don't embarrass your country."

"Easy for you to say." My teeth chattered. "You've actually done this before."

"No, he hasn't," the pilot called back.

My eyes widened.

Sergio burst out laughing. I hadn't heard his laugh often, but it was deep, sensual. I leaned closer to his body. "He's kidding."

"Hilarious." I flipped off the pilot behind my back. He probably didn't see me, but I felt a lot better knowing I'd shown my irritation.

"At altitude," the pilot called.

Sergio pulled the goggles over my face.

My back was pressed against his front. Everything was snug. I could feel his body heat. I wondered if he could feel my heart rate going off the charts.

"You ready?" Sergio yelled above the noise as the door to the airplane opened.

"No." My teeth chattered.

"Trust me," Sergio called. "Alright?"

I had no choice but to nod my head back.

"Jump when you're ready, Andi."

"But…" I couldn't turn around. "…shouldn't you jump?"

"I'm attached to you. Jump, Andi."

"But—"

"It's your choice… to jump. It has to be your choice, Andi."

I was empowered in that moment. I'd never been in control of anything in my life, and he was offering me a small part of it.

A small part.

But it was there.

All I had to do was jump.

So I did.

My breath rushed out of me as air hit my face, making it hard to breathe and think all at once.

It was loud.

So loud that I knew even if Sergio was saying something to me, I probably wouldn't be able to hear him.

I tried to enjoy the scenery of Chicago.

I closed my eyes and then spread my arms out wide, like I was flying. My face broke out into a grin as I opened my eyes and felt, for maybe the first time in my life, completely free.

We fell.

My smile turned into laughter.

And then I felt movement behind me. The chute was pulled; it tugged our bodies hard, nearly hanging me in the process.

The rest of the ride was smooth. Sergio didn't say anything as I continued flapping my arms like a crazy person. Laughter bubbled out of me once we hit the ground.

And it was like, in that moment, reality came crashing down.

I wasn't free.

I wouldn't be free until I was dead.

In those brief moments, Sergio had given me all I'd ever wanted — but had never been brave enough to admit.

Freedom from the thoughts of sickness.

Freedom from the thoughts of death.

Freedom from my physical body reminding me that it was soon.

My laughs quickly turned into sobs as Sergio unhooked us. I fell to my knees, tears dripping onto the ground, mixing with the dirt and grass.

Sergio didn't yell at me.

He didn't tell me to get up.

No, my husband, the man I wasn't even sure I liked most of the time, sat with me in the dirt, and pulled my body into the protection of his chest and let me cry.

We sat there for at least fifteen minutes.

He didn't say anything — then again, he didn't need to. He held me, he let me cry, and when I didn't think I had any tears left, Sergio tilted my chin toward his face and whispered, "You're the bravest person I know."

Nobody had ever called me brave before.

He may as well have said he loved me for the impact his words had on my life, on my very soul. I tried to avert my eyes.

He didn't let me.

Sergio brought his mouth to mine. And kissed me.

Not because he was pissed.

Or because it was on my stupid honeymoon list.

But… I think… because he wanted to.

And I let him — because in that moment I realized one thing. I more than liked him. I was on my way to loving him — the way he fought with me, the way he teased, the way he let me be me without any judgment.

The way we lived — in a constant battleground.

"You did good, Russia," he said when he pulled back.

"The kiss?" I teased.

"The jump…" He rolled his eyes then kissed me again. "But for the record… this was good too." His tongue licked the seam of my lips before pulling back. "Family dinner?"

I nodded, my face felt sticky from crying.

We held hands the entire walk back to the building.

CHAPTER SEVENTEEN

Sergio

HER TEARS SCARED ME.

Because they represented what I already knew. She hadn't fully grieved or come to terms with what was happening to her — what was going to happen.

I respected her positivity.

Hell, I respected her in general.

But I knew, as the days progressed, I'd probably see more tears as life continued to spin out of control for both of us.

I was on the same ride as her. Selfishly, it felt more painful because I was powerless to stop anything.

I could hold her hand.

Kiss her tears.

But in the end that's all I had, and it sucked.

My mind went back to the phone call in the hospital. Tex had yet to get back to me, but that didn't necessarily mean anything good or bad.

Family dinner would at least take my mind off the emotional day. By the time we arrived at Nixon's, Andi was back to her usual self. She even had a marker and was going through the list that she'd somehow confiscated from its hiding place in my office.

Just thinking about my office made my vision flash to the black folder. What if she read it? What if she found out secrets about me even I didn't want to know? And why the hell did I care?

"Origami," she announced. "That's next."

"The hell it is!" I shouted. "How is that even honeymoon-related?"

"You're rich," she stated. "Therefore, our honeymoon wouldn't have stopped at the African safari."

"Oh?" Her reasoning was exhausting. I pulled into the driveway and shut off the car.

"Japan." She nodded confidently. "You would have taken me to Japan, and how can you go to Japan and not learn the art of origami?"

"I'm not folding paper."

"You are."

"Not."

"Are…" Andi unbuckled her seatbelt and leaned across the console. She unbuckled mine and trailed her fingers slowly up my stomach.

"Seduction?" My eyebrows arched. "Isn't that a bit above your usual tactics?"

"You kissed me, therefore I figured it would probably work this time…"

Damn her. "You may have a point."

"After origami, we can bake."

"I hate to ask…" I groaned. "…but why the hell do we have to bake a cake?"

"Because when I did my Internet search, almost every single honeymoon couple goes to those all-inclusive resorts where they teach you how to bake, but learning how to grill a fish is stupid. Who doesn't know how to make salmon?"

I wanted to point out that I'd probably have to look it up online but kept my mouth shut, knowing Andi she'd just add it to the list of honeymoon activities.

"But cakes? Muffins? Chocolate? Come on, that's way more fun. Besides, I've always wanted to be a cake boss."

"How about you just pick one or the other?"

Her fingers gripped the front of my shirt; she gave a little tug. Our mouths nearly collided. "Well, we do have fifteen other activities that come to mind."

My eyes focused on her mouth. "True."

A loud horn honking interrupted our little discussion and then banging on my side of the window startled me.

Slowly, I looked over my shoulder.

Tex was waving a gun around and grinning like an idiot. I was going to shoot him.

We didn't have the best of relationships — not that either of us actually tried to be nice to one another.

"Family dinner!" he shouted against the window.

"Why is his gun out?" Andi asked.

"Guns to Tex are like water to fish."

"Both need it in order to survive?"

"It wouldn't surprise me at all if his skin was starting to actually grow around the trigger."

Andi scooted out of the car and met me on the other side. She took one look at Tex and then in seconds had the gun out of his hand.

One minute it was in his hand…

The next it was in hers.

I stared dumbstruck.

Tex's mouth dropped open. "What the hell, Andi?"

I think I fell in love with her a little bit right then. I patted Tex on the back and whispered. "Remember, she's on my team."

"Damn straight I am, partner," Andi said in a southern accent then handed Tex his gun. "Let me know if you need pointers later."

Tex's eye narrowed. "I wasn't prepared."

"Well maybe you should be… next time." Andi gripped my hand in hers. "After all, terror comes in all sizes."

"Don't I know it," I grumbled under my breath.

Tex laughed softly and followed us inside. "You're alright, Andi."

"I'm more than alright. I'm amazing," she announced.

Nixon was at the head of the table pouring wine. His eyes met mine briefly before he looked back at Andi. His lips curled into a mocking grin.

Whatever, shit face. Yes, we were getting along. No need to go and celebrate or anything.

He looked about five seconds away from patting himself on the back like he was the one responsible for fixing things, when really it was…

Well, I don't know. Maybe insanity… or just time.

She was growing on me — like a freaking weed I couldn't get rid of, only prettier and funnier. Damn it!

"Sergio's doing honeymoon activities with me on account that we can't travel out of the country without getting shot at by the FBI or my father," Andi blurted out to the entire group

All talking ceased.

I briefly contemplated crawling underneath the table and rocking back and forth; maybe then they'd think I'd gone insane and stop staring at me like I was the freaking Grinch who'd finally managed to grow a heart.

"That's so sweet!" Trace was the first to talk. "What did you guys do today?"

"I know what they did a few days ago," Nixon said into his wine glass.

I kicked him under the table.

He didn't even wince, the bastard.

"Oh, did you like my present?" Trace asked, her eyes alight with excitement. I'd always liked Trace, but yeah, not the best question to ask right then.

"Yeah." Nixon leaned forward. "Did you have any trouble unwrapping it."

I kicked him again.

But this time Chase yelped. "What the hell, Sergio? Why'd you kick me?"

"The present was… unexpected."

My eyes narrowed. Not exactly a glowing review of my seduction skills.

"I mean, at first I was…" Andi's gaze met mine. "…surprised."

"I knew you would be." Trace nodded encouragingly. What the hell had she given us? A dog? Shit, I hoped not, because it would be a dead dog by now.

"And then, I don't know, it just felt natural," Andi continued. "And perfect."

It was getting hard to breathe. The air was thinning by the second.

"Oh, um…" Trace shared a confused look with Nixon. "…I'm glad?"

"Me too." Andi blushed brightly before looking away and shrugging. "Monogram towels were really so thoughtful. I especially liked that Sergio's had little mustaches on them."

"Ah-ha!" I slammed my hand onto the table. Not meaning to do that out loud. Towels! Of course. I'd used one already.

All eyes turned to me.

"Forgive him, he really likes the towels." Andi nodded. "Gets him all excited in the shower. I would know."

I choked on my wine while I received curious stares from every single one of my family members.

"I'm happy for you… guys," Bee interjected, rubbing her still-flat stomach. She was only in her first trimester. "You both look so happy."

Could we not be the center of attention?

A knock sounded, and then Frank waltzed in. Thank God. He was always late to family dinner. I finally felt like I was out of the hot seat.

"Grandpa." Trace rose up from her chair and kissed him on the nose.

He blushed and took his seat at the head of the table.

"Sorry for being late. I had a few things to collect."

"Did you find them?" Nixon asked, his gaze cool and indifferent.

Frank's eyes darted around the table then finally settled on me. "I did."

"No better time than the present."

"What?" Trace touched Frank's arm. "What's Nixon talking about?"

Frank poured a shaky glass of wine. "I guess it's best to get things out before dinner. It's hard enough as it is."

Dread filled my stomach. This couldn't be good, whatever it was. Frank rarely just announced things at family dinner.

"Trace…" His gaze was loving, adoring even as he tilted her chin toward him and flicked her nose with a chuckle. "…I am old."

"No shit," Tex said under his breath.

I held in my laugh.

"And the rest of you — you are so young. So… alive with ideas for your own families. Luca left the Nicolasi family to Phoenix. He has a small child on the way. Trace, you and Nixon have the Abandonatos to deal with. Mil and Chase, the handful that is the De Langes."

"Here, here." Chase lifted his wine glass into the air. I knew they were still giving Mil hell since she was one of the only female bosses in existence; then again, Chase was a trained assassin, so they didn't fight it much.

"The Campisis..." Frank motioned to Tex. "…a tighter run family I've never seen."

Tex did a little bow.

Frank let out a breath. "And my family… the Alferos, while I trust my men, I want to leave my family to blood." His eyes fell to Trace. "You do not need the added stress of leading two families. I want you and Nixon to have beautiful grandchildren, I want you to laugh, to enjoy life as much as possible, which is why I need to do this."

His speech was making me more and more uncomfortable. Andi shifted in her seat, her eyes downcast like she knew something. But how?

Frank pulled out a black folder. "It's Luca's."

Wow, not what I expected.

Andi's gaze met mine; she was so pale she looked like she was going to be sick. What was going on?

Frank set the folder on the table and opened the first page. A picture of a guy and girl around my age stared back.

Trace frowned. "I don't understand."

"More secrets…" Frank sighed. "Trace, your grandmother and I were not entirely honest with you."

Nixon pulled Trace closer. Bastard knew what was coming; I could see it in his eyes.

"Before we went into hiding — three years before to be exact — your grandmother had an affair."

The table was completely silent.

"With Luca," he whispered. "She was ten years younger than me, still in her early forties."

My mind tried to do the math, tried to put the puzzle together.

Andi was looking sicker by the minute, and Trace was well on her way to joining her.

"They had twins," Frank continued. "A boy and a girl. They both went to live with Luca, though his lifestyle at the time wasn't exactly child-friendly. He put them in the best schools, but when he discovered that by keeping them close he was putting targets on their backs, he let them go. He wanted them to live normal lives before getting sucked into the lifestyle he lived."

"Why now?" Trace whispered. "Why are you telling us this now?"

Andi spoke up. "Because the plan changed."

"What plan?" Trace repeated.

Andi's eyes met mine. What the hell was she talking about? She glanced back at Frank. "The plan was simple… take over the Russian crime family's hold in Chicago, protect me in the process, marry into the Nicolasi family by way of Dante Nicolasi, Luca's son."

Something slammed into my chest — maybe it was my heart, or maybe it was just the feeling of absolute disbelief.

"What?" Trace whispered.

Frank sighed and sat back down in his chair. "Andi was never meant for Sergio. She was meant for Dante. And Dante was meant to take over the Alferos when the time was right."

She wasn't mine.

She wasn't mine.

She wasn't mine.

Why the hell was that the only piece of information I was coming away with during the conversation?

"So why change the plan?" I finally hissed out, my voice sounded a hell of a lot like I'd just swallowed knives.

Frank met my gaze. "Because I made a judgment call. Dante didn't know Andi, doesn't even know this plan exists. And Andi doesn't need a boss as a husband before she dies. She needs a friend."

Dumbstruck, I could only stare and hope my emotions weren't written all over my face. It was part rejection, part shock, part relief.

"I, um…" I stood, my chair scooting against the hardwood floor. "…I need a minute."

I walked toward the back door and didn't glance over my shoulder. Not even when Andi yelled my name.

CHAPTER EIGHTEEN

Andi

SERGIO DIDN'T STOP WALKING. I STARED at the table and let out an exhausted and halfway guilty sigh. He didn't know the whole story.

Or his part in it.

Then again, it wasn't my story to tell. Not by a long shot.

Frank cleared his throat.

"So that's it?" Tex said in a chilling voice. "We just hand over one of the most powerful families to two kids who don't even know what the hell they're doing?"

Frank was silent for a minute, and then he shrugged. "They are nearly the same age as you."

Chase and Nixon shared a look.

The girls at the table were oddly quiet; every one of them eyeing their men like a fight was going to break out at any minute.

Amy gripped Ax's hand.

Trace was still leaning against Nixon, staring at her grandpa hard. Tears pooled in her eyes.

Mil was drumming her fingertips across the table, her gaze weary.

And Mo looked ready to leap across the table at any minute, in case she needed to physically restrain Tex — his hormonal sister looked ready to help.

Phoenix leaned back in his chair; it made a creaking noise, slicing through the tense silence. "It's not like we're going to hand the family over on a platter, Tex. We'll give it months — years. Besides, who's to know Dante will even say yes?"

"Why wouldn't he?" Tex roared, throwing his hands in the air. "The Alferos are worth close to four-hundred-million dollars."

I almost choked on my tongue.

"He'd be stupid to say no."

"Not everyone wants this life," Frank said in a quiet voice. "And I mean to give him something none of you were given."

"Oh yeah, old man?" Tex's frustration was evident in the way his face started turning red. "What's that?"

Frank met his stare head on. "A damn choice."

I quickly looked down at my empty plate. The food on the table was getting cold, and nobody seemed to care that Sergio was still outside, most likely cursing me into the night sky.

"And the girl?" Nixon asked. "What of her?"

Frank shrugged. "I imagine if Dante decides to join us, she'll do the same. It wouldn't be safe for her otherwise."

Ax had been uncharacteristically quiet. He usually didn't speak unless spoken to, and even then I noticed he was a lot like Sergio; he watched, he listened, and then he used information gathered to form a thought. He never spoke out of turn, though I was beginning to notice Sergio was picking up bad habits where I was concerned, talking out of turn, yelling — God forbid — smiling!

"He has a point."

Tex turned his angry stare toward Ax. I was half-tempted to scoot back so I wasn't in the line of sight.

"Oh?" Tex's voice was a hoarse whisper. "How do you figure?"

Ax sighed. "Who else is going to lead the Alferos? You? We need you focusing on our own drama. Phoenix is shit deep in Nicolasi stuff. The De Langes still aren't completely trustworthy — no offense Mil—" She waved him off. "—and my family's been the target of everyone for the past ten years! We need new blood. Plain and simple, and you forget Tex… regardless of where they come from or how they got there. They're blood."

"Damn Abandonatos when they make sense," Tex muttered under his breath.

Mo squeezed his hand reassuringly.

"So that's it." Nixon tucked Trace closer to his body.

"Sort of." Frank's gaze met mine. "Why don't you go find your husband, Andi? We can discuss specifics later."

I didn't need to be told twice. I quickly excused myself and ran outside.

Sergio hadn't made it far.

He was sitting on the lower branch of a giant tree, his legs dangling in the air; it made him look playful, approachable.

"So…" I braced my hands behind my back and strode forward. "…are you pissed?"

"Am I pissed?" he repeated in a bored tone. "Yes and no."

"Ooh, a puzzle." I tried to climb to the first branch but wasn't tall enough or strong enough to pull myself up.

He watched me struggle.

I kicked the stump.

After a few more minutes where he watched me attempt to levitate into the tree, he hoisted me into the air and placed me next to him. "Better?"

"Yes," I gasped, my breathing heavy. "So, you're pissed because I kept something from you?"

"It's stupid."

"What is?"

Sergio chewed his lower lip. "My reason for being pissed."

"Try me."

He turned to face me, his legs straddling the tree. "Alright…" His blue eyes flashed with something, not anger, but something just as intense. "I'm angry because I wasn't the first choice."

"Pride cometh before the fall," I chanted.

He snorted and let out a breath. "Told you it was stupid."

"And it is." I reached for his hand and didn't let go. "Because had I been given a choice, it would have been you."

"Before or after the ass-iness."

"Before." I nodded. "Definitely before. Russians love a good challenge. Hell, you're like my catnip. You rarely smile, you get drunk for no reason, and you like to shoot things. My hero." I batted my eyelashes.

"Too bad I hate vodka."

"I won't tell Dad."

"Oh good. Maybe he won't shoot us next time he sees us then."

I bit back a grin. "I didn't tell you, not because I was trying to hide anything from you…" I licked my lips. "Have you read your folder?"

"Shit, not you too. How the hell do you even—" He paused. "Right, you were in my office."

"Guilty." I winced. "But you should probably read your folder before you go getting all pissed off at everyone."

"What if I don't want to?" He squinted. "What if what's inside of that folder makes me feel worse than I already do?"

"Could you?"

"Could I what?"

"Feel worse?"

"There's always a chance." He squeezed my hand. "Are we having a heart to heart right now?"

"Yup."

"Shit."

"You love it." I tugged his hand hard enough so that he would lean forward. "I'll even let you kiss me."

"Oh, you'll let me, huh?" His grin was wide, unapologetic. I loved the way his eyes almost seemed to darken when he looked at me. He got this lazy, seductive look on his face that had me feeling weak in the knees.

"Uh-huh," I breathed, my voice airy.

"Hmm… I think I like this side of you Andi, falling on your own sword and all that… just to make me feel better."

"Well, you did jump out of a plane with me today, so basically we're stuck with each other."

"Yes, skydiving does mean forever," Sergio said with a serious nod. "Good thing we're already married."

"Right?" I laughed.

He pulled me onto his lap. My legs wrapped around his waist as our mouths touched briefly, for maybe two seconds, before he pulled back. "You're really pretty."

"Wh-what?" All joking left my system. "Since when do you give compliments?"

"Since now." His voice was raspy. He tucked a piece of my blond hair behind my ear and cupped my face. "You're really, really pretty. I'm sorry I didn't say it before."

"You're saying it now."

"And I'll say it every day."

Until I die, I wanted to add, but it seemed too morose and depressing, so instead I added. "Until forever?"

"Until forever," he repeated, his lips meeting mine briefly before he kissed my jaw and then placed a hot open-mouthed kiss to my neck.

"Get a room," a male voice called out.

Sergio grunted, "Bastard," under his breath as he broke our kiss.

Phoenix was standing by the back door. "Sorry to interrupt the special moment, but food's getting cold."

"So eat it!" Sergio yelled back.

"Families eat together." Phoenix smirked. "Come on, Sergio, get out of the tree. Andi won't let you fall."

"You're not funny!"

"He's hilarious," I added.

Sergio shot daggers my way. "People used to cut themselves in his presence. Believe me when I say, this is new."

"I know." It slipped before I knew it.

Sergio paused. "Just how long have you known Phoenix, Andi?"

I swallowed and looked down. "Truth?"

"If you don't mind."

"I've known of him for years. I didn't actually meet him until we were at Eagle Elite, but I had his background memorized."

CHAPTER NINETEEN

Sergio

I THOUGHT ABOUT WHAT ANDI HAD SAID. Just how long had she been watching us? And what more did she know about our family? Hell, what more did she know about me?

Family dinner didn't end in bloodshed, but everyone was pretty quiet throughout the rest of the meal, which wasn't at all normal for any of us.

Hell, normal would have been Tex trying to shoot me with one hand while offering me pasta with the other.

Instead, he was silent.

Nixon looked pissed.

Chase was ready to join him in what I assumed would be a really heated discussion with Frank, once Trace went to bed.

And that left me and Ax.

My brother had been invited to family dinner because he'd been welcomed into the elite fold, not because he actually had any power or say over what happened. It was not like I had any power either.

Then again, sometimes I wondered if they only invited

me so they could keep a watchful eye on my activity — keep your friends close, your enemies closer and all that.

I eyed the bottle of vodka and grimaced. I'd mistakenly admitted to Andi that I'd never tried the good stuff.

The good stuff, according to her, being Stoli.

I wasn't convinced.

I should have kept my mouth shut — because by the time we arrived back at the house she was ready to add getting drunk with me to the top of her honeymoon list.

"Isn't that…" I hated being an ass, but it needed to be said. "…really unhealthy if you're already sick?"

"Riddle me this, Italy." Andi grabbed my hand then lifted it into the air, twirling beneath my arm as we walked into the house. "If you only had one day to live, would you drink water all day, hoping it would prolong those twenty-four hours into twenty-five?"

"You have more than a day to live."

"Answer the question."

I let out a heavy sigh. "No, probably not."

"My point exactly, amigo. It's about quality of life."

"So I'm Mexican now?" I grimaced.

Andi winked and tugged me into the smaller of the two living rooms. Brown leather couches were focused in around a small fireplace, while the back side of the room was lined with bookshelves from floor to ceiling. It resembled more of an office than a living room, but it had a certain coziness about it that the other larger room didn't.

"You..." She poked my chest. "…grab the vodka, and I'm going to go change into something more comfortable."

My mind whirled at that statement, was *comfortable* code word for lingerie? Or was she seriously going to go put on sweats? And why the hell was I still staring at the damn vodka bottle, wondering what she was doing upstairs?

Ten minutes passed.

Then twenty.

I was starting to get worried when, in a flurry of activity, Andi rushed into the room, only stopping long enough to grip my shoulders then hoist herself onto my lap.

I loved how small she was.

Miniature-sized.

My eyes drank in her nearly white, see-through tank top and black spandex shorts.

I cupped the sides of her hips; it made me feel huge — and like I was actually able to protect her. Though the thought was short-lived. I could protect her from environmental things but not internal. That was my horrible reality.

"Okay, my Italian lover," She grabbed the glass bottle and unscrewed the top then tilted her head back and took a long swig. I expected her to wheeze, cough, or at least stutter a bit. Instead, it may as well have been water with the reaction she had.

Damn, her eyes didn't even water.

"Your turn…" She held out the bottle then bit back a grin.

Reluctantly, I grabbed the bottle from her and eyed it warily before taking a long sip — one that matched hers.

The minute the alcohol touched my lips, I regretted ever even agreeing to her plan. It tasted like shit, nothing smooth about vodka as it pours down your throat.

I barely held back a cough as I handed back the bottle and wiped my mouth.

"Good?" She tilted her head.

"Great," I lied, while the vodka cheerfully burnt a hole through my esophagus. "It's like lighter fluid, Andi."

"Now there's a thought. What if I drink, then you light a match, and—"

I covered her mouth with my hand. "No pyrotechnics."

Her tongue reached out and licked my hand.

I jerked it back.

"So that's it? You're just going to give up, huh Italy? You know wine's a chick drink, right?"

I gripped her hips between my hands and squeezed. "You may as well just rip up the Italian flag and burn it! Who says that?"

She took another long swig of vodka and whispered, "Russians."

"I drink whiskey more than wine." Why the hell was I defending myself? "Not that it matters."

"Does that make you feel like more of a man?"

"Does it seem like I need to feel more like a man, Andi?" In frustration, I nipped her lower lip.

Andi leaned backward. "You sure you want to kiss lighter fluid?"

My eyes narrowed as I took the bottle from her outstretched hand. "One more drink."

Famous last words.

Because we finished the bottle.

Because I was completely unable to let the girl drink me under the table. It was a guy thing — not even a pride thing, but a pure masculine need to make sure the pixie didn't destroy me in something I should be able to beat her at.

"Tell me." Damn Russian wasn't even slurring her words, while I was trying to figure out just how many logs I needed to put back on the fire. Everything was double. I blinked a few times at her, hoping to clear my head.

"Tell you what?" There. That sounded good, no slurring, no hesitation. We'd moved from the chair to the floor. She was still semi-straddling me, her left leg behind me, while her right was across my lap. I liked it too much to complain about the fact that I couldn't feel my ass anymore.

"What's the worst thing you've ever done?"

"Andi—"

"Fine, I'll go first." She scooted closer to me, laying her head on my shoulder and wrapping her hands around my arm. "I shot a husband and wife in front of each other."

Horrible that in that moment I wanted to shrug and say,

"Big shit. That all you got?" Instead, I nodded slowly, my brain still buzzing from the alcohol, my tongue heavy. "That's not so bad, Andi."

"Story's not over." She patted my knee. "I shot the husband and wife in front of their kids. Granted their kids were in high school and well on their way to being spies, but hey…" She shuddered. "…I let them live… tried to walk away, then got a text… no loose ends."

"So you went back." I filled in the blank.

"We always go back, don't we, Sergio? People like you and me. We do the job, we get it done, we try to keep our emotions out of it — and the scary part? We're good at it, aren't we? Until one day, you wake up—"

"And suddenly you feel," I finished, "everything."

"Maybe that's our punishment for being so damn good, Sergio. You think? This feeling of invincibility wears off, and humanity kicks in."

"Humanity sucks," I grumbled, trying to keep the emotion from my voice.

"Sometimes…" Andi pressed her cheek to my shoulder. "…sometimes I think I was given cancer as a punishment."

I jerked away from her like she'd just shot me in the stomach. "Andi, no, you can't believe that. Tell me you don't really think that."

She shrugged.

"If that was the case, I should already be dead, and that's the truth." I turned and cupped her face in my hands. Tears were welling in her pretty brown eyes. "I count them."

She blinked in confusion. "What do you mean?"

"I count every single person I kill." I licked my lips. Maybe if I bit down on them, I'd stop talking; instead, everything came out so fast you'd think I was confessing my sins at church. "It started out as a way to keep control over what I did. If I counted, they were just a number, right? They weren't actually a person. So I started with one, then two, then three… after a while it became this weird obsession."

Andi trailed her fingertips across my jaw. "What do you mean?"

I tensed, but the alcohol didn't allow me to stay that way. I pulled back from her enough to pull up my shirt and turn. I'd always kept the tattoo semi-hidden. She hadn't seen it when I was in the shower because my arm did a good job of covering the tally marks.

I had exactly thirty-seven.

For every life I'd taken.

And space to continue — because I wasn't naïve enough to believe that would be my final number, not by a long shot.

"You tattoo them?" She trailed her fingers over the small black marks. "Why?"

"To remember." I shrugged, pulling my shirt back on. "Or to remind myself. I don't know…"

"One of them looked new." Her eyes met mine. "The FBI agent?"

"How do you even know about that?"

She shrugged. "I know a lot of things I shouldn't know. I know she was going to get killed the minute she stepped foot back in the building. I also know you did her a kindness, even though you probably regret having to be the one to do it."

"But that's the thing…" I let out a bitter laugh. "I don't regret it one bit. I gave her control over what happened to her. I could see it in her eyes. She was begging me, Andi. Begging me to end her, so I did."

"She was already dead."

"Does that make taking her life right? Or my right?" I pinched the bridge of my nose. "It's late. We should probably go to bed."

Andi gripped my hands then lifted herself onto my lap, straddling me for the second time that night. "What are you afraid of?"

"You sure get deep when you drink vodka." I tried

ignoring her question; confession time was over.

"Italy..." she warned, kissing both cheeks, "tell me."

I sighed and hung my head. "Then bed?"

"Show me yours, I'll show you mine..."

I blew out air between my cheeks. "I'm afraid that one day I'll stop being afraid. And that's the truth."

"Fear makes it real."

"Fear makes me real." Shrugging, I tried to explain. "It means I'm still human. The minute you stop feeling fear..."

"You turn into a sociopath." She winked. Leave it to Andi to add in some humor to my morose thoughts.

"Right." I chuckled.

"Bed?" She tilted her head.

"Not so fast." I gripped her hips. "What's your fear?"

"You mean other than the dark?" she whispered, the heat of her tongue colliding with my neck, making me want to maul her against the floor.

"Yeah." My breathing slowed in anticipation of what she would say.

"Leaving behind my new best friend — before he has time to realize how much he has to offer the world."

"Best friend?"

"You, silly. Who else do I honor with my presence?"

"We barely know each other."

"Kindred spirits recognize each other. Deny it all you want, but I'm kind of a big deal to you... and I'll continue to be like your lobster, that is, until this love affair ends like a tragic play, and you have to bury me. Oh, and PS, when we do discuss burials, not on a day like today because you're already depressed, can you bury me in white?"

"What the hell, Andi?" I tried to shove her off me, but her damn thighs clenched around my body so tight I could have stood and she'd still be clutching me like a freaking koala. "That's not funny."

"Am I laughing?" She shrugged. "It's only fair that I get a

say in what I get buried in. Don't worry, I'll write things down."

I let out a pitiful groan.

"Okay, bestie." She stood and offered her hand. "Take me to bed and ravish me."

"What?" I croaked.

She rolled her eyes. "Please. We have it written down fifteen times. You better at least take me up on it once."

"And if I don't?"

She leaned down and licked her lips invitingly. "Then I'll doubt your sexuality."

"The hell you will!" I roared, jumping to my feet and pulling her flush against my body, nearly sending us sailing backward into the chair.

My kiss was aggressive, possibly furious, and not just because of her taunting, but because she'd just scared the shit out of me. I'd almost lost the ability to breathe when she started talking about being buried. How could she be so calm?

And how was it possible she was turning my life completely upside down, all within a short week? She was ruining every single wall I had erected, making me want to run in the opposite direction for fear that if I stopped, she'd catch up, she'd catch me, and I'd be left to mourn the most precious thing that's ever been given to me.

"Kiss me," she mouthed against my lips.

So I did.

"Touch me," she urged, rocking her body against mine.

So I did.

"Take me…"

"Andi…"

"Take me…" she pleaded, her hands moving to my head, tugging my hair with ferocity.

I jerked back and looked into her pleading eyes.

And I knew in that moment…

I would.

CHAPTER TWENTY

Andi

HE WAS MARKING ME, HIS FINGERTIPS burning into my wrists as he pressed a hot kiss to my neck then released my arms and took a step back. I'd drunk enough to know it was probably a bad idea to push a guy like Sergio.

The term *healthy fear* rang true in my brain. He was dangerous, and he knew it. I knew it from the dead look in his eyes.

He'd seen too much.

Done even more.

And wasn't so sure he wanted to live to tell about it. I could feel it in the air around him — he wasn't the type of guy you pushed. Sure, I teased him, and, yeah, my body responded to him like he'd been made for me.

I let him have his timeout.

Second thoughts were evident in the way he glanced at me then back down at the ground, like he wasn't sure what to do with me. Like I was a puzzle he couldn't quite figure out. Then again, I don't think my puzzle pieces were ever meant to fit perfectly together.

"Sergio…" I held out my hand. "…let's go upstairs."

He swore and ran his hands through his hair, turning around then facing me again. "Would you believe me if I said I've developed a conscience?"

"After showing me your tattoos?" My eyebrows shot up. "Probably not."

"I'm not that guy."

"What guy?"

"That one…" His eyes turned angry, the blue freezing me on the spot. "I don't make love to girls. I don't do slow. I don't care as long as I get off. I. Don't. Care."

"Ringing endorsement for your sexual prowess." I smirked and leaned against the wall, suddenly exhausted. "Are you warning me away?"

"Maybe that's what you deserve, Andi. Have you thought of that?"

"You sure know a lot about what I need, what I deserve, what I want…" I let out a breath. "Sounds to me like you're trying to come up with reasons not to follow me upstairs."

"You didn't marry the prince."

"Okay…" I said slowly.

"Or the villain."

"Thank God."

"You married the unhappy ending."

I shifted on my feet, uncomfortable that he was right, irritated that he had the ability to take moments, important ones, and screw them up with his depressing logic.

I waited for him to say more. Instead, he took a step back and crossed his arms. "Go to bed, Andi."

I nodded. "You're sure?"

"No," he whispered, "not at all."

"You should be." I took a cautious step toward him, pressing my palm against his chest. "And one day… very soon, you will be."

"What makes you so certain?" His eyes searched mine.

I kissed him softly on the mouth. "You won't be able to resist."

"And if I use you for sex… meaningless sex, sex you know my heart isn't invested in, and then you die… what does that make me?"

"A guy." I shrugged. "Though right now you sound like a chick."

He smiled.

I bit down on my lip while he let out a little groan. His eyes focused in on my bottom lip like he wanted to take another taste.

"See ya in the morning, hubby." I quickly turned on my heel and walked up the stairs, a bit wobbly on my feet. Probably not because of what I had drunk, but because I always got dizzier at night.

Getting ready for bed may as well have been the Boston marathon for as much as I was huffing and puffing.

Damn Sergio. He was probably right about the drinking, but it was my honeymoon! I refused to let the cancer win at everything.

Though right now I felt like I was losing.

I stumbled toward the bed, not doing my usual check for the night where I went to the closet for assassins, my window to make sure it was locked, and under the bed for whatever horror might lurk beneath.

Which is probably why, when someone grabbed me from behind, I wanted to curse myself rather than them.

"Don't." His accent was thick.

Lovely. My biological father had somehow managed to infiltrate the house and send one of his goons after me.

"You scream, I cut your throat before your father gets the pleasure."

I was too far away to reach the knife under my pillow, and my gun was stashed in the nightstand. I could easily outmaneuver him — if I wasn't semi-buzzed and suffering from vertigo.

I'd end up getting killed, and, for some reason it seemed unfair, to die before my time was up. I was banking on enjoying my last few moments with a certain Italian man.

"Soft." He chuckled darkly, his lips tasting my cheek.

I wanted to cut his throat out.

Another laugh invaded the room.

Two men?

"Do you have her?"

Three. Three distinct voices. The man holding me turned around, his grip on me still freakishly tight.

Four men, including the one holding me. There was no way I was getting out of that.

Sergio! He was still downstairs. If I screamed, they'd kill me and go hunt for him; that is, if he was still alive.

A knock sounded at the door.

"Tell him you're sleeping," the man barked in my ear, his grip on my waist tightening. "Now."

"Andi?" Sergio called. "Can I come in?"

"No," I said in a clear voice. "I'm busy painting my nails, Sergio. Go bother someone else."

"What color?" he asked, taking the bait as I'd known he would, because I never called him Sergio, and my nails had been without color ever since he'd known me. Besides, I was Russian. Did I look like a spoiled princess?

"Green," I answered. "Like your eyes." *Please get the hint. Please, please.* He knew I paid attention to detail. I just hoped, in that moment, he'd get it, well, that and that he wasn't as drunk as I first assumed; otherwise, he'd be walking into a trap.

"Okay, goodnight, Andi."

I tensed; footsteps sounded against the wood floor.

Alone.

He hadn't gotten the hint. I wasn't sure if I was relieved

or just sad that my time with him would be so short-lived.

One of the men moved toward the door and slowly opened it, gun raised. He looked both ways down the hall then motioned for all of us to follow. Once we were clear of the hall, we made our way down the stairs and rounded the corner.

I could see the door.

Damn. I needed to do something.

I was just about to make my move when a gunshot rang out. The man holding me jerked my body against his as we moved toward the door.

Two more gunshots.

This was my chance. I used my heel against his foot then brought my other foot back up against his groin.

He stumbled enough for me to break free.

Sergio rounded the corner, gun in hand, dark smile in place. He tilted his head. "Going somewhere, sunshine?"

The man held up his gun. Sergio shot him in the hand. A bored expression crossed his features before he smiled then tossed his gun onto the floor. He held up his fists. "Tell you what, you beat me, you can take her."

The man looked at me then back at Sergio; his laugh had me cringing all over. I stepped back away from them and watched.

Sergio walked right up to him and threw a slow punch. The guy ducked then flew at Sergio's midsection, but Sergio, clearly not as drunk as I'd believed, moved out of the way and kicked the guy in the ass, sending him sailing into the stairs.

He grumbled out a few curses then turned around, blood dripping from his nose.

"Tell me." Sergio cracked his neck. "How'd you get in?"

The man yelled and charged him again.

Sergio sighed and landed two hard punches to the man's nose. He stumbled backward and collided with a large urn. It shattered on contact.

"Hope that wasn't a family heirloom," I said.

"It was." Sergio jerked the guy to his feet by his shirt and slammed him against the wall; a few pictures fell to the ground shattering on contact. "So, you gonna talk, or do I get the pleasure of making you?"

The man grinned and spat in Sergio's face.

I winced.

Knowing what was most likely coming.

Sergio let out a dark laugh and flipped out a knife. There was no warning; he simply made a hard cut across the man's cheek.

The intruder yelled.

Sergio made a cut on the other cheek.

Blood dripped from the man's face, but he kept his lips firmly locked down.

Sergio knocked him back with his head and then tackled him to the floor; knife still in hand, he straddled the man and cleaned off the knife with his shirt. "So here's the thing. I went to medical school for a purpose…" He sighed. "Don't think I ever told you what that was, Andi."

I slowly moved toward them. The man's eyes bugged out; he was terrified, and I knew why.

The air in the room was chilled.

It had shifted into something of Sergio's own creation. He wasn't just a killer because it was necessary.

No, he'd actually come alive in that moment… like he'd been waiting all week for someone to attack him, just so he could come out and play.

"No," I said calmly, "you didn't tell me why."

"I didn't want to save lives," Sergio continued. "I wanted to take them, but here's the thing. Knowledge is power, don't you think?"

The guy squirmed beneath him.

Sergio landed a blow to the man's gut with his free hand and lifted the knife into the air. "Death can be so… creative."

"Oh?" Damn the man was beautiful when he was angry.

His teeth flashed in the moonlight.

"I wanted to learn how to inflict the most pain, without actually killing someone." Sergio held the knife above the man's abdomen. "Cut too low, and you bleed out, and where's the fun in that?"

The man fought like hell.

Sergio held him firm. "But a little higher…" Sergio shrugged. "…and to the right, so I don't puncture a lung, and I can drive this knife at least a few inches in, and twist. The twisting's the best part. Care to know why?"

As he talked, his accent became thicker and thicker. I was frozen in place. Who was this man?

"I don't care," the victim said. "Do your worst."

"I intend to." Sergio stabbed the man in the stomach.

He wailed out in pain.

The knife twisted. I couldn't look away.

"Who sent you?"

"Petrov!" the man yelled.

"Why?" Sergio twisted harder; blood started soaking through the man's shirt.

"He said to bring her!" The man was full on sobbing. "Don't kill me. I have a family. He said he'd pay!"

"A family, you say?" Sergio removed the knife. "Then by all means, I should let you go. It's not like you just tried to take away my family, my reason for living."

I let out a little gasp. Had he really meant that?

"Oh wait." Sergio snapped his fingers. "You did. So you die."

"No!" The man's eyes met mine. "I have children! Please!"

Sergio slapped the man across the face. "You don't look at her, and you don't beg like a little bitch just because you couldn't get the job done."

"But—"

Another punch to the jaw. "You know where I live. You

know where Andi is. No chance in hell you're getting out of here alive." Sergio didn't turn around. "Andi, bring me the largest knife you can find from the kitchen."

I didn't move.

"Now," he said in a calm voice.

I hurried into the kitchen. The largest knife I could find looked more like a machete, which really had me questioning if that was what it was. It wasn't like we lived in the bush and needed to fight our way through it while hunting for antelope.

I came back with the machete and handed it to Sergio.

"I said—" Sergio leaned down. "—don't look at her."

The man continued to sob and wail.

The moonlight reflected sharply from the machete as Sergio brought it over his head and with one fail swoop.

Chopped off the guy's right hand.

I'd never seen anything so gruesome. Even though I'd been around it, I'd never witnessed it firsthand.

I had to fight to keep myself from puking

Blood was everywhere.

The man's body was convulsing.

And then Sergio leaned down and whispered, "You're lucky I didn't cut out your heart, you bastard." He slowly rose to his feet as the man grabbed his hand and tried to scoot away.

Sergio let him make it as far as the door before he bent down and scooped up his discarded gun, firing one shot, directly to the back of the man's head.

The room was silent again.

"Why?" I asked.

"Why what?" Sergio dropped the gun and cleaned off the machete.

"Why give him hope? Why let him think you were letting him go?"

Sergio turned to me, his eyes dark. "Criminals are still human… and it would be inhumane to not give them one last flicker of hope."

"Or maybe," I argued, "it's worse… letting them see freedom, yet taking it from them?"

"Maybe." Sergio calmly placed the knife on the table and walked toward me. "Are you alright?"

I took a step back, holding my hands up.

He frowned. "Andi, I would never hurt you."

The room was tilting, my breathing uneven. I knew — I knew he wouldn't hurt me, but he'd just cut off a man's hand.

"I just need a minute."

Sergio sneered. "So that's it? You see what I'm capable of, and suddenly we're back at square one?"

"No." I shook my head. "I'm just in shock."

"So sit down."

"No." I braced my hands against my legs. "Why did you cut off his hand?"

"To mail it to your father."

"You gonna put a bow on it and wrap it in *Frozen* wrapping paper too?"

"Yeah, and remind me to include a Christmas ham." He pulled out his cell and barked into it. "I need clean up at my house, Nixon."

I could hear yelling in the background.

Sergio sighed. "No. No survivors."

Silence.

He threw the phone onto one of the tables and reached out his hand to me. "Come on. Let's get you cleaned up."

"What?" I looked down at my hands. "I'm not the one draped in blood."

Sergio sighed. "Your clothes… you have blood splatters all over you."

"Well, maybe you shouldn't be so messy next time."

"Did you just make a joke?" Sergio was incredulous. "After I killed four people and tortured one of them?"

"What?" I shrugged. "Did you expect fainting?"

"Yes."

Ignoring him, I crossed my arms. "This wasn't on my honeymoon list."

"No shit." He barked out a laugh. "Really though, are you okay?"

A smile formed across my lips. "I will be."

"Alright."

"If you do one thing for me…"

He frowned.

"Buy me a gun like that… better yet, can I have yours?"

"Hell, no!" He gripped his gun like it was a small child. "Nobody touches my gun."

"Which one?" I winked. "I'm game for both."

"Unbelievable." He swore. "How are you joking right now?"

I reached for his hand then jerked him against my body. The gun clattered to the floor. "Kiss me."

"Andi—"

"You know you want to."

His eyes were burning holes through me.

"And your fighting skills, kinda hot, minus the torture part." I kissed him hard on the mouth.

With a groan, he lifted me into the air and slammed me against the picture less wall, his boots crunching glass beneath them.

I pushed back; he stumbled, his legs colliding with one of the coffee tables. A vase hit the floor.

I smirked as he pushed the rest of the contents off the table and lifted me onto it. My legs wrapped around his waist. His hands were already ripping my shirt off while I started unbuttoning his pants and sliding them off his narrow hips.

The man was ripped.

Chiseled, tightly packed muscles met my fingertips as I pulled his shirt over his head next.

I could really begin to like black boxer briefs.

His mouth was frenzied as he bit along my jaw then took my lips captive. His tongue wickedly teased. I couldn't get enough. I needed him to kiss me harder. With a groan, I tried to pull him onto me, but he wouldn't let me. Instead, he jerked back then reached for something next to me on the table.

The knife.

"Trust me," he whispered, before pressing it against my chest and sliding it down the front, cutting off my bra. It slid lower, down my hip.

I shivered in response as goose bumps broke out across my skin.

The knife dug into my hip and then slid against my underwear. He used the knife to dangle them in front of me. They fell to the floor.

"Cute trick," I breathed.

"I have lots of tricks." Knife still in hand, he gripped me by the arms and slid me backward across the table then crawled on top. He was like a beast stalking his prey. I'd never been so turned on in my life.

He tossed the knife to the ground and pinned me against the table using his body.

"Fifteen." He bit my lip.

What was with him and biting? And why did I like it so much? My body couldn't help but respond, arching toward him, begging for release.

"Aw, you gonna count for me, Dracula?"

"I see what you did there." He licked my lower lip. "I think I like that pet name better than Italy."

"You bite," I said a little breathless as his mouth hovered over mine, his body pressing me against the wood table. I could feel every hard inch of him. "I like it."

He grazed his teeth across my stomach. His hands splayed across my belly as he slid then kicked his briefs off.

Sergio was right in warning me. He wasn't about making love — but he was about making me want him more than anything in my life. Everything about him was hard — rough edges, nothing soft, nothing smooth. There was no taking his time or licking every inch of me. There was possession, plain and simple. No room for adoration in his mind. Just sex.

I shouldn't have been okay with it.

But for some reason, it excited me to know that this man, the one who was so haunted by life — and so controlled and effortless in his killings — couldn't control himself around me.

"I warned you." His mouth met mine in a ferocious kiss, making me forget all the reasons I had in my brain for stopping him.

"More," I whispered.

"Beg."

"More!" I screamed.

He lifted my legs and hooked them over his shoulders. I couldn't help it — my eyes widened.

And then a hard knock sounded at the door.

And another.

Sergio froze.

I blinked, my eyes most likely mirroring the horror in his.

He jumped off me and threw one of the blankets on the couch in my direction, just as the door opened.

He didn't bother to cover himself up.

I, however, wrapped up like it was zero below.

"Holy shit!" Chase burst out laughing. "Really, dude? You do realize there's four dead bodies surrounding your little love nest?"

Sergio started stalking toward him. I grabbed his arm and jerked him back. Did he not realize he was still naked?

Nixon followed, his eyes scanning the mess of blood and bodies before turning to us. "Nice work…"

"Amazing," Chase muttered. "Leave it to Nixon to comment on the dead bodies rather than the naked ones."

Nixon smirked, but other than that, didn't comment.

"Serg…" Chase shook his head and leaned down to

examine the lone bloody hand. "…not your best work. The cut is off a few inches."

"Yeah well," Sergio started pulling on his jeans. "Russia here only managed to find the smaller of the two machetes."

"I knew it!" I shouted.

"Russia…" Chase tsked. "…I'm disappointed. Always grab the bigger machete. Always."

"Life lesson number one," Sergio said under his breath.

"You just make a joke?" Chase tilted his head. "Hmmm, I'm amazed you're in such a good mood, considering what I just walked in on…"

"Thus the good mood," I finished, defending Sergio.

"Ah, the good mood hadn't started yet… or… should I say… finished?" Chase chuckled.

Nixon joined Chase near the floor and sighed. "You gonna mail it out or should I?"

"Allow me." Sergio's jaw clenched. "You know what this means, right?"

"Yeah." Nixon rubbed his face with his hands. "I know. It means you need security."

"Because of me?" I said lamely.

Sergio wrapped his arm around my shoulders. It was completely unexpected but welcome. I curled into him, resting my head on his strong chest.

Nixon glanced up, his eyes piercing through the darkness in the room. "Sorry, Andi. It's what's best for now. Not only would it be horrible if anything happened to you, but if something happened to Sergio too… it would be too big for us as a family to ignore, meaning, a war we don't want to start."

"Hell, we're already in it." Chase nodded in my direction. "The minute we offered her protection."

"They wanted me alive," I offered. "They weren't going to kill me yet."

Nixon stood. "Well, that's interesting."

"Shit..." Sergio gripped me tighter. "…they'd only keep

her alive for one reason, Nixon. You know that."

Nixon's eyes darkened. "Hell."

Chase gave me a sympathetic look before reaching down and searching each of the men's pockets. I assumed for ID.

"What?" I squinted at Nixon. "What's it mean?"

"Intel..." Nixon sighed, then rubbed the back of his head with his hand. "They'd keep you alive only as long as you were valuable. They'd be banking on the fact that Sergio would either come after you, giving them permission to start something — or if he didn't, they'd simply torture you in order to gain as much information as possible before killing you."

"Don't." I jerked away from Sergio. "Don't you ever come after me."

"Wait, what?" Sergio blinked in confusion. "You married into this, Andi. There is no out. I protect you. I keep you safe. That's the deal."

"And I'm saying no." I shook my head. "Protect me as well as you can, but if something happens, if they take me, don't follow."

Sergio rolled his eyes. "Don't be dramatic. I'd have no choice."

I held his gaze. "If I even think you're going to be going all *Robin Hood: Men in Tights* on me, I swear I'll find a way to kill myself."

Chase muttered a curse under his breath while Nixon held up his hands and made quick work moving the bodies.

Sergio stood still as a statue. "That's not your call to make."

"The hell it is!" I hissed, pushing at his naked chest. "You're not putting your family in jeopardy. You're not starting a pissing match with my father over me. It's not worth it. I'm not worth it, remember? Weren't you saying that just a few days ago? What's changed, huh?" It was unfair, baiting him, making him see his own weakness when it came to me. I knew the walls were crumbling, and a few minutes ago I couldn't have been happier, but now I knew there was a reason they needed to stay up.

it wasn't just my life on the line, but his.

Sergio's eyes flashed. "Right." He bit his bottom lip and stomped away from me. The front door opened, a few more men shuffled in and started bagging the bodies.

The hand, however, was left on the floor.

It stared at me.

It represented so many things — all things that could be prevented if Sergio would just get his head out of his ass.

Nixon motioned for one of the men to grab the last body. "Put enough weights in the bags for them to sink fast. I don't want evidence anywhere."

The man nodded, and then Nixon held up his hand and stopped him. He walked over to the last body and snapped a picture of the horror-stricken face.

"Kodak moment." Chase nodded. "Gonna print that out and send it to Pops?"

"With some vodka attached." Nixon smirked. "He'll expect one present... not two." He brought his attention to Sergio, who was leaning against the wall as far away as possible from me. "Think you could bug the hand somehow?"

Sergio shrugged. "It's not a matter of not being able to, but hiding it is a bit difficult. Besides, it's not like they're going to keep the hand hanging out on their kitchen table for a few days so we can gain intel."

"The watch." I pointed. "Put it in the watch."

"Shhh..." Chase winked at me. "The men are talking now."

I rolled my eyes and stomped over to the hand. With a flourish, I picked the bloody mess off the floor and unbuckled the Rolex watch. I flipped it over and held it out. "Put the device inside the watch. I may not know my father, but I know how he operates. The Rolex is always given as good faith that money will be dished out once he completes his assignment. It makes sense, right? Give the guy a Rolex, something more expensive than the car he drives, and suddenly all he sees is money. My father will keep it, believe me. He won't let the hand and the watch go into the trash."

"Because he can't afford more?"

"No." I sighed. "Because he's stingy. He'll use the same watch next time. I guarantee it. It would be a waste not to, and Petrov hates waste."

I tossed the watch to Nixon and smacked Chase on the back. "I'll just let the men have their talk now."

Chase glared while Nixon handed the watch to Sergio. "Make it happen."

"Yup." Sergio was already inspecting the watch like a chocolate addict inspects a Hershey bar. I'd never understand what was so fascinating about listening devices and hacking, but Sergio seemed to be on high just thinking about the technological possibilities.

"Get some sleep." Nixon's voice interrupted my blatant staring.

"Right." I nodded. "I'll get on that."

"Don't you mean under that?" Chase whispered.

I elbowed him in the ribs.

"You forget she stole Tex's gun and landed Sergio on his ass." Nixon chuckled. "Tread carefully, or Mil's going to want to know how you got a black eye."

"Or two," I finished sweetly.

"Fine." Chase yawned. "I'm going to go back to bed now."

The guys left, the door closing softly. I quickly walked over to the lock and turned it hard.

"Nixon will leave men, Andi." Sergio was behind me, his hand placed over my trembling hand. "You're safe tonight."

"Of course I am." I turned to face him. "I have my own Italian assassin in my bed."

His eyes didn't heat.

They were empty again.

Great. I'd successfully pushed him away. At what cost?

"Listen…" He backed me up against the door. "…you tell me what to do in front of the guys again, and I'll follow through on that spanking I promised earlier this week. If I want to jump off a cliff to save your life, you don't talk me out of it. You don't complain or whine. You say thank you and cheer me on." His mouth was hot. I could almost taste him as he leaned in and whispered, "When I said I'd protect you with my life, I meant it. So stop being such a damn martyr and for once in your life let someone save you."

He tilted my chin up, his eyes searching my face for a few seconds before he pulled back and walked away.

CHAPTER TWENTY-ONE

Sergio

I WASHED THE BLOOD FROM MY HANDS, not really sure why I was putting forth such an effort when it wasn't going to come off unless I scrubbed like hell until my skin was raw.

The good news?

I didn't work for the feds anymore, so I had nothing to hide. I could waltz right into Starbucks with a bloodstained shirt and tell people I'd just fallen off my Harley, and people would barely blink.

It irritated me that in the face of something so terrifying — had you not been raised in it, you'd assume it only happened on the movies — Andi had simply watched in fascination.

And then had the nerve to tell me I couldn't protect her.

What the hell?

I slammed my hands against the marble countertop then slammed them again. "Damn it!"

"Easy tiger," Andi said from the doorway.

I looked up at her reflection through the mirror. She

walked hesitantly toward me.

I shook my head and moved away before she could touch me. It was too raw, killing them, nearly losing her, being reminded yet again that this little story wasn't going to end happy. In the end, I would lose her.

It was up to me to decide how.

Shit.

With a scowl, I turned on the shower. "Not now, Andi, I'm not in the mood."

"Not what you said about an hour ago."

I started pulling off my clothes. If she wasn't going to leave, I didn't give a rat's ass; I was still going to shower. I needed to get Russian slime off my body.

Steam billowed out the minute I opened the shower door.

After a few minutes, I assumed Andi had left.

I was just getting ready to turn the handle when a soft delicate hand met mine. With a curse, I closed my eyes and leaned forward, allowing my forehead to press against the glass as water dripped down my face.

Her breasts pressed up against my back; her arms wrapped around my waist. "I'm sorry."

I couldn't trust myself to speak. I'd always been good with words, even better with my intellect, but in that moment I had nothing. I didn't know what to say because I'd never been in a situation so out of my control — so completely out of my element that all I wanted to do was push it to the farthest part of my brain so I wouldn't have to think about it.

So I wouldn't feel.

"I'm sorry I told you not to come after me." Andi sighed, pressing a kiss against my back. "And I'm sorry I did it in front of the guys… but what I'm most sorry about is that you're in this position, somewhere you never wanted to be in the first place."

I let out a heavy sigh, my chest squeezing tight. Slowly, I peeled her hands away from my waist and turned. Her brown eyes were large, focused, sad. It killed me, because Andi wasn't one of those people. Sadness looked completely foreign on her.

I hated it.

I hated it so much I vowed in that moment to do everything in my power to extinguish that emotion forever.

I wasn't a soft person.

A tender lover.

A thinker — when it came to the opposite sex. But everything about her made me think. As water cascaded down her soft face, I thought. I thought so hard I was convinced she could hear my thoughts.

She was beautiful.

Breathtaking.

Brave.

And mine.

My lips found hers. I kissed her softly, tasting the water on her mouth, sucking it between my teeth. "I'm exactly where I want to be. I just never knew it… until now."

Our mouths collided in a heated frenzy as I lifted her into the air then pressed her against the shower wall. My hands slid down her thighs as she clenched around me tightly.

Her blond hair stuck to her cheeks. I moved my lips to her ear, licking the trickle of water down her neck, following its trail all the way to her small breasts.

My mouth sucked along every inch that the water traveled, my lips unable to do anything except taste. I flicked my tongue — and gained a painful jerk as she tugged my hair back and let out a moan.

I wasn't gentleman enough to ask her if she wanted more.

Because I wasn't going to be gentleman enough to stop if she said no.

I was desperate in a way I'd never been before, to feel her, to feel all of her and, most of all, to forget that in a few short months…

I wouldn't be able to feel that heart beat.

I wouldn't be able to lick her skin.

Her taste would be long forgotten.

A frenzied sort of madness over took my senses as I slammed my mouth against hers, willing her to live, willing her to fight, making promises with my lips that I knew I could never speak aloud – because if I did, it would make it real. It would make what we were going to go through real.

And I didn't want real.

Not anymore.

Tension built between us. She jerked my lower lip between her teeth then kissed me deeper, harder, faster.

I didn't ask if she was ready. I didn't need to.

I just… knew.

As if we'd been long lost lovers… as if we'd been made to be together.

One thrust, and I was inside of her, moving with her, living with her. Sharp nails dragged across my back, and then her hands found my hair again. With each movement of my hips, she tugged harder.

Heat surged between our bodies.

Every muscle tensed in her body. I only cared about her – not myself – and that's when I knew I was already gone. Screwed the minute I'd said yes to her.

I softened my kiss as her body slowly tensed and then released. Her big brown eyes blinked at me slowly. I was completely transfixed as my world tilted on its axis and became solely about something other than myself – someone.

Winking, she hooked her ankles tighter around my body. It was uncontrollable, the way I let go, the way she allowed me to.

It was silent except for the sound of the water slamming against the riverrockk and our own labored breathing

"Fourteen." She slid down my body, her teeth tugging my ear as she whispered the number against my skin. "You gonna keep a tally of this on your other side?"

I barked out a laugh. "Epic moments deserve to be remembered."

"Promise me something?"

"Anything." I reached for her hand. Who was this man? This person talking? I didn't recognize myself, wasn't sure I wanted to.

"Remember us."

It took me a while to register what she was referring to. My tattoos, remembering us. I tried to lighten the mood. "I'm not putting Stoli vodka in ink on my body, Andi. I don't care how much you like the stuff."

She burst out laughing then launched herself into my arms, wrapping her legs around my waist for the second time in the past half hour. Our foreheads touched. I brought her underneath the middle of the shower and kissed her mouth.

"Our symbol would be something cooler… like… something from our honeymoon trip."

"Oh, so like the number fifteen?"

"Exactly!" She giggled. "I knew I chose well when I chose you, Italy."

I rolled my eyes and set her on her feet. One minute she was standing; the next she was collapsing into my arms.

"Andi?" I caught her before she hit her head. "Andi, can you hear me?"

"Of course!" She laughed. "You're yelling in a shower."

I rolled my eyes. "Not funny. Are you okay?"

"Yeah." She shrugged. "But shower time probably dehydrated me. Got any Gatorade?"

I sighed, forcing a smile I didn't feel, considering my heart had damn near stopped a few minutes ago. "Yeah, let's Gatorade you up before bed."

"The words… you're so good with them. It's a wonder I swooned."

"Your swoon needs work," I pointed out. "You went in

the wrong direction."

"Drat."

"Drat?" I repeated.

"Read historical romance, Sergio. It will seriously change your outlook on so many words!"

"I like my vocabulary."

"Hmmm…" She patted my chest and yawned. "I'm sorry. I'm just really tired."

"Sure." With a heavy heart I lifted her into my arms and walked out of the shower. I set her on the teak bench, grabbed one of the monogrammed towels, and wrapped her in it before wrapping one around myself.

"Can I lick chocolate off your abs?" she asked in a tired voice.

"I, uh…"

"I promise I'll go slow."

"Is that on the list?"

She crossed her arms.

"Andi…"

"It should be!" She pouted. "I completely underestimated your workout routine!"

"So you thought I'd be a fat Italian?"

"To be fair, you guys eat a lot of pasta."

"When have you ever seen me actually eat pasta?"

She chewed her lower lip. "Good point."

"Look…" I kneeled down in front of her. "…I'll let you lick chocolate off me…"

She clapped her hands.

I held mine up for her to stop. "If you go to sleep. After all, we have honeymoon activities to do, don't we?"

She wrapped her arms around my neck and placed a soft kiss against my cheek. "Yes, Italy. We do."

CHAPTER TWENTY-TWO

Andi

I KNEW SOMETHING WAS WRONG THE MINUTE I tried to open my eyes. My mouth tasted like cotton, and every single bone in my body hurt like I'd been beaten up and left for dead.

With a groan, I tried to turn on my side so I could fall very ungracefully out of bed. My legs felt so weak. I needed more water and to eat, even though I'd been feeling more and more full, just another fun side effect.

I took a few deep breaths holding the air in my cheeks then slowly released a breath as I finally managed to roll onto my side and place my feet on the hardwood floor.

The room was spinning, but I was used to being dizzy. I walked slowly to the door and opened it then shuffled down the hall.

I wasn't paying attention to anything other than getting to the bathroom so I could grab a drink of water and maybe take a shower.

"Andi?" Sergio's voice sounded at the end of the hall.

Crap. I needed to act chipper or he was going to know

something was up. I licked my lips, forced a big smile, and gave him a saucy wave.

I must have looked worse than I thought because his expression went from morning bedroom eyes to horrific, all within the span of a few seconds.

In two strides he was in front of me, gripping my face with both hands. "What the hell happened to you?"

"Huh?"

He turned my face to the side as if he was examining it. Then the weird part happened. He tried to pry my mouth open with his hands.

I jerked away, but he was too strong.

With a curse, he shook his head and lifted me into his arms. He strode into the bathroom and set me on the counter.

"I can walk," I pointed out, though it was nice not having to.

"I know." He swallowed slowly. Face pale, he filled a cup of water and handed it to me. "Swish it around a bit."

"Huh? Why can't I just drink it?"

"Your gums." He reached up and placed his finger in my mouth and pulled it back. Blood mixed with spit slid off his skin.

I covered my mouth in horror then turned to look in the mirror. My gums weren't just bleeding; it looked like I'd suddenly gone vampire during the night and taken out an entire town. Okay, so maybe it wasn't that bad, but my teeth weren't so white, considering the bleeding wouldn't stop.

"Here." Sergio shoved the cup into my hand. "Swish around the water so that you can clean your teeth. Then we'll use some mouthwash. I wouldn't suggest brushing until the bleeding stops, which it should once the day moves on, and you start yakking my ear off again."

He was being sweet.

Which naturally made my eyes well up with tears. "Where'd you learn all this, huh, Italy?"

"Prepare to be awestruck." He smirked, his one eyebrow arching playfully. "I read a book."

"No way!" I punched his shoulder. "You little nerd!"

"I'll probably buy a pocket protector at the end of the week and start ironing my jeans too."

"Don't!" I pointed my finger at him. "Those jeans are designer." I swished the water around and spit it out into the sink. I filled it up again and drank deeply then handed it back to Sergio, only to have him put a bottle of mouthwash in my hand.

"Gargle."

I rolled my eyes but did as he said. When I spit into the porcelain sink, I had to fight the tears welling. Everything was still tinged with blood. Slowly, I turned and smiled weakly in the mirror.

My gums were still bleeding.

I hung my head. "I'm gross."

"Not true," Sergio argued.

I nodded, not trusting my words. Then when I found my voice, I pointed at my mouth and shuddered. "Gross."

Sergio's eyes took on that dark hue that told me he was either really aroused by my vampire mouth or just pissed off. One minute he was staring at me; the next he was kissing me.

I tried to pull back, but he wouldn't let me.

His was invasive, hard; nothing soft about it.

When he pulled back, he still didn't release my head; instead, he looked at me directly in the eyes and said, "I don't want to ever hear you say that about yourself again."

"But—"

His kiss interrupted my words. When he pulled back, I had to admit I was a bit dizzy.

"Never again," he whispered.

I nodded. "Okay."

"Now…" He helped me off the counter. "…let's shower."

"Um…" I raised my hand. "…I can shower on my own."

"I know you can." He lifted his shirt over his head.

Why was I arguing again?

"But do you want to?"

"Have I ever told you how smart you are?"

"No." He smirked. "And don't start now, or it will freak the shit out of me and possibly earn you a trip to the ER. Strip."

I tilted my head. "Can't I just stare? That has to be somewhere on the list — wife watches husband take clothes off and takes mental pictures."

Ignoring me, Sergio gripped my T-shirt and whispered against my mouth, "Strip or I pull out the knife again."

"Ooo, I vote yes on the knife."

His head touched mine. "You're impossible, you know that?"

"Grab the big machete. We can use it as a prop!" I yelled after his retreating form.

I didn't expect him to come back with the knife.

He did.

And the machete, which he placed very far away from me, making it so I'd have to learn how to fly over the counter to actually reach it. "You don't play fair."

"You're dizzy. I'm going to be naked. You don't get sharp objects."

"He has a point." I lifted my arms into the air. "Okay, cut it off me."

"You are so weird." He laughed. It was rich and deep.

I was half-tempted to just stare at his face, but I didn't have time. Soon the knife poked into my shirt. But he put it down.

I pouted.

Then Sergio gripped the shirt and ripped it in half. With. His. Bare. Hands.

My grin was so huge I was officially all vampire, poor guy. Though he didn't seem to mind as he moved his hands to my shorts and did the exact same thing. At that rate, I didn't need to even move.

"Have I told you how hot you are with a knife?" I leaned back, my nakedness fully exposed.

Sergio placed the knife next to me on the counter and kissed my cheek. "Have I told you how hot you are naked?"

"Only naked?"

"If we're taking a vote, I'd say no clothes."

"But you love clothes!"

"So you can see how much I love you being naked…" His eyes flashed with something that appeared to be excitement. "I have an idea."

"Okay."

"Shower, then idea. Well actually, first we have to send the hand."

"Send the hand." I said it in a low voice and raised my hands in the air like I was a ghost. Why? No idea.

"You done now?"

I nodded.

"Great." He picked me up and set me in the shower, then stripped and followed me in.

We washed each other. I would be a liar if I said I wasn't disappointed when he didn't make a move to try anything. I was really hoping for more, especially since my morning had had such a crappy start.

I was just getting ready to turn the water off when he flipped me around and pinned my hands against the shower wall. His teeth nipped my ear as he whispered hoarsely, "Fourteen."

CHAPTER TWENTY-THREE

Sergio

YOU KNOW THINGS ARE ROUGH WHEN you're thankful you have a disembodied hand lying around the house to take your mind off things.

Specifically, to take your mind off the girl who's dying and most likely taking your heart with her to the grave. I still hadn't heard back from Tex, but my appointment was in a week. Either way, at least I could say I'd tried, right?

I put the Rolex back together and made sure to secure it to the hand without making it seem like it had been taken off.

The chip was small enough not to be discovered — that is, unless they took the watch apart. Because it was so small, it would be impossible to hear conversations more than twenty feet away. But it was honestly all we had, so it was worth a shot.

I'd spent the early part of my morning actually tracking down Petrov himself — not an easy task considering he had several houses all over the country, not to mention business in what seemed like every southern state in the US. I didn't want to bank on the fact that he'd be in his home in Chicago, but all trails led to that exact spot.

The man wasn't hiding.

He wasn't even trying to, the cocky son of a bitch.

In a way it was comforting — to know he wasn't underground. The man was known by the feds, but he'd never faced prison time — ever. He had a few judges on his side, not to mention at least two unsavory politicians in Washington state; it was no wonder he kept most of his business in Seattle.

Then again, he had millions tied into a few of the harbors up there.

With a sigh, I started the recording on the computer and was just about to make sure everything worked when Andi walked in.

Sadly, she wasn't naked, but she was wearing skinny jeans and a sweatshirt that hung so loose on her I was afraid it was going to fall off one of her shoulders and hang onto her hips. She was losing more weight. Funny how girls typically love to hear that. But with Andi? I knew it would just take that smile away. Hell, she'd probably leap into the air if I told her she was getting fat.

"Oooo." Andi approached the table. The hand was in the FedEx box, ready to go. "So we flat-rate this stuff, huh?"

I smirked. "Is there any other way?"

"Not sure. Never sent a body part to a person before." She tapped the hand. "Testing one, two, three."

My computer went wild. "Well, it works."

"I can officially mark that off my bucket list. Talked to a hand, hand recorded conversation, and mailed it off to a biological parent."

"Something tells me your bucket list contains a lot more violence than the typical human being."

She shrugged; the sweatshirt fell even farther off her shoulder.

"Will you be cold?" I asked gently. She had half her arm

exposed already.

"No." She smiled. I could tell it was forced. "Besides, most my clothes are getting a bit baggy… probably all that sex."

"All that sex?" I repeated, crossing my arms. "You mean all of two times?"

"In my head, it's been triple that." She nodded emphatically. "Care to make that dream come true?"

"Car." I pointed to the door. "Weren't you just complaining a few days ago about me not participating in our epic honeymoon? You know, the one where I apparently take you on an African safari only to come home and whisk you away to China?"

She chewed her lower lip. "Yes, but doesn't lying in bed sound awesome too?"

I ignored the dark circles under her eyes, just like I ignored the clenching in my stomach that she was starting to bruise more around her hands.

"Of course it does." I grabbed her by the shoulders and pointed her toward the door. "But so does a cinnamon roll and the best mimosa of your life."

Andi let out a slight whimper. "Talk dirty to me, Italy."

"Cinnamon," I said in a deep voice, pulling her back against me.

"Ooo."

"Sugar." I licked the side of her neck.

Andi shivered in my arms. "Don't stop!"

"Hot… buttery…"

"Just a little bit more…" She closed her eyes and clenched my hands within hers.

"Dough," I finished, kissing her head. "You're strange, you know that?"

"Whatever. You're the one making dough a dirty word."

"The woman has a point." I grabbed my keys and swatted her hand when she reached for her purse.

"What?" Her wide eyes blinked up at me.

"You said you wanted one of those fun credit cards. Well, as much as I'm sure you think I can snap my fingers and make them appear, I can't control American Express. Therefore, I put your name on mine."

Her eyes widened even more. "Shut up!"

"No limit." I grabbed her hand and dragged her through the large garage. "Pick a car for your shopping day."

"Shopping day!" She twirled once then winked at me and twirled again, making her way toward the most conspicuous car I owned. "I pick this one."

I cursed. "Of course you'd pick the red Lambo." It wasn't just any red Lambo either. It was a red Lamborghini Veneno Roadster. The thing looked like a happier version of the Batmobile, minus all the toys.

"It's pretty." She ran her hands along the hood then leaned up against it. "Think she'll purr for me?"

I rolled my eyes. I hung up the keys to the Mercedes and quickly grabbed the ones to the Lamborghini. "What can I say? Italians make sexy cars. What's the last thing you did, Russia?"

"You." She blew me a kiss and opened the door. It slowly rose up above her head. With a squeal, she basically flew into the car. So much for trying to keep a low profile. Then again, if Petrov wanted her, he could be my guest; it would be so much easier shooting him in broad daylight.

I got in the car and started the engine.

"Holy…" Andi gripped the seat with her hands. "It sounds like a freaking plane!"

"Yup." I turned up Hozier and pulled out my sunglasses.

"And it vibrates…" She gripped my hand. "…almost like a motorcycle."

"Wow, if I'd known this was all it took to get you all hot and bothered, I would have skipped the shower this morning," I joked.

Andi threw her head back and shouted, "Thirteen!"

I couldn't stop the bark of laughter. "Who was better? Me or the car?"

"Aw..." She lightly punched my shoulder. "...don't ask questions you don't want the answer to." She started petting the seat. I half-expected her to start licking it and whispering sweet nothings to the leather.

"Should I leave you alone?"

"No." She freaking winked at the leather seat. "We'll catch up later." She buckled her seatbelt. "Why? Jealous?"

I shook my head. "Of a car? Never."

"You sure?"

"Positive." I pulled out of the garage. "Besides, you've seen what's under my hood. I don't think I have anything to be worried about."

"That secure, huh?"

I let out a cocky laugh. "Yes."

Her eyes narrowed. "Fine, you win. Wait!" She reached for my arm. "The hand! It's back in the house!"

I peeled out of the driveway. "One of Nixon's men is going to do the honors for us."

"And out of curiosity, what do you guys do? Just drop it off at the FedEx store, or what?"

"Where else would we drop it off?"

"But it's a hand."

"Right."

"From a person."

"Yeah."

"So you can't ship alcohol, but you can ship body parts?"

I let out a little laugh. "It's not like we actually write on the box, *Human Body Part.*"

"Fair enough." She nodded. "Okay, so where to?"

"Downtown." I nodded. "The expensive stores, I think. After all, you're the one with no limit..."

"Are you going to be my personal shopper?"

"I wouldn't trust you with anyone else."

Her smile fell. "You think it's safe for us to be out and about?"

"Of course." I patted my leather jacket. "I have enough guns in the car to take care of us, and I hardly doubt your father's going to be at the mall. If he is, just make sure everyone ducks so I get a good shot in between his eyes."

"Look at you... dirty talk all day long."

The car fell silent for a few minutes. It was comfortable, like we'd known each other for years instead of weeks.

"Italy?"

"Russia."

Andi reached for my hand. "Thanks. I know most girls love clothes, but I really, really love clothes, and mine haven't been fitting and—"

"You're welcome," I interrupted, trying to cut off the conversation so we wouldn't talk about the giant elephant in the room.

It was no longer cancer.

But the clock.

CHAPTER TWENTY-FOUR

Andi

I'D MADE HIM UNCOMFORTABLE.

I could tell from the way he clenched his jaw and drummed his fingertips against the steering wheel — like the car wasn't moving fast enough, and he wanted to hurry up and get to where we were going so he could flee the small space and actually breathe.

I knew the feeling well.

Sometimes it hurt to breathe, not because I was sick, but because the knowledge of being sick had a way of choking you physically, even if it was just a mental thing.

We made small talk until we reached downtown. There was a huge shopping center in the distance. He kept driving.

I opened my mouth to ask why, but he just shrugged and drove a few more blocks and stopped directly in front of Neimen Marcus.

"Hmm..." I tapped my chin. "...I like the way you think."

"Knew you would." He flashed me a sexy smile that had

my heart skipping. We parked and suddenly, as I was getting out of the car, I felt very, very underdressed.

I was wearing combat boots, an ill-fitting Lacrosse sweatshirt, and baggy jeans. Self-consciously, I tugged the sweatshirt up over my shoulder and braced myself for the looks I knew I would get from the salesclerks.

Sergio walked around the ridiculously loud car and reached for my hand. When we touched, he briefly looked down and frowned.

Bruises were making themselves known around my thumb and on the back of my wrist. I tried to jerk my hand free so he wouldn't have to see them; instead, he simply held my hand a bit tighter. Then, in a move I wouldn't have expected, lifted my fingers to his lips and kissed every single one.

I shivered, unaccustomed to affection, especially from a sexy guy who was just as dangerous as he was addicting.

"Shall we?" Sergio asked. He was still frowning.

I wasn't sure if it was at me or because of me; regardless, I figured I had a lot to do with it and immediately felt guilty.

To be fair — I hadn't planned it.

Falling for him.

I mean, any girl would, but he'd always been such an ass I honestly assumed he'd get tired of my constant chatter and just lock me in a room or a really large box.

Instead, it broke him down.

And turned him into a completely different person — one I knew I would be devastated to say goodbye to.

"Smile." Sergio shoved me lightly "You're at Neiman Marcus."

"Oh, I'm happy," I gushed. "Just thinking about… dresses."

"Dresses?" His eyebrows shot up as he held open the door and ushered me through it. "What kind of dresses."

"The short kind."

"We should get lots of those for you to wear around the house..."

"The house is chilly."

He was thoughtful for a minute then said, "I'll break the air conditioner."

"Or you could just turn it off."

"Right, but breaking sounds a lot more aggressive, and I guarantee if you start wearing short dresses around the house, I'll be aggressive, possibly violent."

I let out a little laugh and followed him closely as he led me through the hundreds of perfumes and cosmetics on the ground floor. Once we hit the escalator, he wrapped his arm around me and pulled me close.

It seemed natural for him.

It wasn't for me.

I'd never had an actual boyfriend or someone steady in my life — so having someone hold me in public, felt... foreign, but extremely nice.

A group of teenage girls were riding down; as we passed, I could have sworn I heard each of their hearts stop. As it was, all talking ceased, mouths dropped open, one girl let out a little whimper, and — yup — a camera phone quickly snapped a profile shot of Sergio.

"Happen often?" I joked.

Sergio narrowed his eyes. "What?"

"Teen girls." I jerked my head in their direction; most of them were still staring, so when Sergio turned around, they all froze in place and nearly fell off the bottom of the escalator.

He shook his head in disbelief then flashed me an amused smile. "They're probably just confused as to why a giant would be with such a small little pixie."

I growled. "I'm short, but I can still dropkick your ass."

"Oh, I know." He nodded escorting me off. "I still have a bruise on my ass to prove it."

"Aw, it's like a love mark."

"Yeah, that's what I think every time it hurts to sit. A love mark."

I smacked his ass hard.

He let out a little groan.

A saleslady stopped walking and eyed us suspiciously.

"Sorry." I licked my lips and elbowed Sergio. "He's just really sexually frustrated."

Her eyes bugged out of her head as she scurried past us and nearly collided with a mannequin.

"That went well." I nodded and turned to Sergio. His eyes were dark and hungry as he gazed down at me.

I gulped.

"If you wouldn't have chosen my car over me, I wouldn't be so..." He leaned forward and tilted my chin up. "...frustrated."

"They have changing rooms for a reason."

"With cameras."

"So put on a good show."

He sighed and released my chin. "Let's shop first..." He quickly looked around then grabbed my arm and basically pulled me toward designers I'd never worn before. In fact, I was pretty sure they didn't let just anyone walk up to those little sections of the store that have glass surrounding them.

Dolce & Gabbana was first.

Followed by Versace.

We ended up in Prada, and then when Sergio still wasn't happy, we moved into another section that I couldn't really pronounce.

A tank top was six-hundred-and-ninety dollars.

Sergio was like a man possessed. I imagined seeing him shop was like watching an animal finally return to its natural habitat. Yes, Sergio was the great white shark finally getting released back into the ocean.

You know, if people saved sharks.

Then healed them.

Then returned them to their natural habitat where they'd most likely kill all the other endangered animals.

Bad example, but I couldn't exactly say he was like a turtle finally finding its way into the ocean.

He was all aggression.

His eyes took in each thread count; he was the Clark Kent of shopping, using super-human eyesight to read through any sort of cheaply made fabric.

"This." He tossed me a dress. Didn't ask if I liked it, simply ordered me to hold it. And so it went. He said "this" and tossed; I caught and tried not to trip.

In three hours, he'd picked out complete outfits.

Not just shirts that I could wear around the house…

But silky things that hung on my body like I wasn't sick. Pants that hugged my legs like they weren't losing muscle.

Every outfit fit.

Sergio was officially magic.

He didn't complain when I took a long time getting in and out of the clothes; then again, he was actually in the changing room with me, considering a few of the outfits made no sense whatsoever.

You know you officially have no style when a guy has to tell you which way the front is on the shirt.

Sergio got that irritated look on his face then told me to open up the door or "so help me, I'm going to break it down."

Another saleslady scurried by after that…

Leaving us all alone in our own dressing area.

"So what do you think?" I'd just tried on a beautiful, short, black lace dress with three-quarter sleeves. It hugged every curve. I already imagined wearing bright blue shoes with it or something equally loud. Maybe I'd go red and match his car.

"Hmm." Sergio leaned back against the wall and folded his arms. "Twirl for me?"

I twirled once.

He frowned harder.

My face fell. "It's ugly?"

"Twirl again," he instructed. "Stop if you get dizzy."

I twirled again, slower this time, so I didn't fall over.

Still no emotion. The guy said he was Italian, but in moments like these I wondered if he didn't have some Russian blood running through those ice veins of his.

"One more time."

Rolling my eyes, I twirled one more time; halfway around, I felt his hands on my hips, helping me finish the twirl. When I faced him again, his eyes were hooded. "It was a three-twirl dress."

"Aw, that good?" I wrapped my arms around his neck.

"Not just good…" His knuckles grazed my ribs, his fingertips spread across my hips and landed on my ass. "Gorgeous."

"It's over twenty-seven-hundred dollars."

He shrugged.

"That's more than most people's house payment," I added.

"How do you feel in it, Andi?"

I thought about it for a minute. "It's not necessarily how I feel. I mean, I feel great, but when I see the way you look at me… I feel invincible."

"Exactly." Sergio brought his mouth to mine, kissing me softly then stepping away. "I know not everyone can afford to shop like this. I can. So don't think about the price tag. What I want you to think about is how you feel. You spend all day and all night in clothes. Well, all night we're working on. But you get my point. They should better your day. They should complement your skin, from the color to the lush feel. Clothes make you… you. It's important to me." He put his hands on his hips and hung his head. "It's important that you feel like the best you that you can possibly be."

"Careful, Italy. Your romance is showing."

I could have sworn I saw a blush tinge his cheeks before he coughed and looked away. "Yeah, well." He burst out laughing. "I have nothing. Shit." He rubbed his face with his hands. "Sorry, forgive my psychotic break, I just… in any other situation I'd try to defend myself, or maybe just ignore that you called me romantic."

"So what gives?"

His eyes met mine. "You make me want to be."

I swallowed the dryness in my throat. "What else do I make you want to do?"

"You want a list?"

I opened my mouth to scream *yes* when a knock sounded at the door.

"Uh, sir, I have those items you asked for."

I crooked an eyebrow in Sergio's direction.

In two strides, he was at the door; he opened it, pulled the items from the lady, and said, "Thanks. That will be all."

Dismissed.

Any other guy would have sounded like a complete ass, but coming from Sergio, it almost seemed like he'd really meant it as a compliment: *Thanks for helping, but your services aren't needed because I can probably do your job better than you do your job.*

His confidence was one of the sexiest things about him.

"Andi…" Sergio held up two very small pieces of lingerie. "…these are for you."

My mouth dropped open. "Isn't underwear supposed to cover?"

His smile was heated. "It covers… enough."

"Enough," I repeated. "Fine, but you can't be in here while I'm trying it on."

"I'm sorry. Are we negotiating now?"

"Out." I shooed him toward the door. "I'll give you a play by play."

It took every ounce of strength I had to push him out the

door, and even then, he complained the entire way. But hey, technically, we were still on our honeymoon, and I wanted some things to still be a surprise.

"Ready yet?" Sergio called.

"Three seconds, Italy. It's been three seconds."

A few more seconds went by. "And now it's been ten. You ready yet?"

I rolled my eyes and made quick work about getting out of my dress so my slave driver wouldn't start pounding down the door.

On second thought…

I smiled as an evil plan took root…

CHAPTER TWENTY-FIVE

Sergio

I WAITED IMPATIENTLY OUTSIDE THE DRESSING ROOM. My phone hadn't stopped going off since we'd started shopping, and for once I didn't give a rat's ass what any of the guys needed.

I didn't want to be interrupted. I could hear Andi undressing; it was painfully arousing, so much so that I finally pulled out my phone, desperate for a distraction that wouldn't have me breaking down the door and crossing number twelve off that damn list, landing us both in prison for indecent exposure.

Five messages were from Phoenix with strict instructions to yet again check the black folder. Somehow he'd gone from a psychopath with suicidal tendencies to a nagging father figure who wouldn't leave me the hell alone.

I sent him an emoji of a gun back.

He sent me a picture of his middle finger in return.

With a sigh, I clicked through the rest of the messages and paused when I saw one that needed attention.

Nixon: *Hand sent out, but two of my men were injured while someone tried to infiltrate the house again.*
Me: *Did they take anything?*
Nixon: *No. And this time they just left once they knew nobody was home.*
Me: *Well that's reassuring.*
Nixon: *Why the hell are you at Neiman Marcus?*
Me: *Why the hell do you care? And turn off the damn Find a Friend. It's annoying as hell.*
Nixon: *Phoenix told me to tell you to read the black folder.*

"Ouch!" Andi yelped.

Me: *Phoenix can kiss my ass.*

I quickly shoved my phone back in my pocket and whistled out a breath of air. "Doing okay in there?"

"Yeah." She was seriously out of breath. Was trying on lingerie an Olympic sport or something? Maybe she wasn't feeling well. My gut clenched.

"It's just that — oh, wow."

"Wow?"

"Italy…" She let out a dark chuckle. "My boobs look amazing in this."

I sighed and gripped the handle to the door. "I bet."

"And my ass?" she added, "looks… firm. Do you think it's firm?"

I banged my head against the door and let out a curse. Whose stupid idea was this? Oh, right. Mine. "Your ass is… firm."

"Ooo!" Clapping came from the other side of the door. "I think I like this lacy bodice thing better. Holy crap, do you think they have a whip that comes with? I could dig that."

I let out a strangled cough as a salesclerk re-entered the dressing area, stopped, then turned around.

At this rate, they were all going to quit by the end of the day.

"Damn." Andi let out a whistle. "You should see this."

I gripped the handle harder. "Can't. It seems my wife's locked me out."

"So pick the lock."

"You can't pick a lock that slides, Andi."

"Hmm, if you were Russian, you could find a way to get in here."

"Are you serious right now?"

"Russians know all the tricks."

I pulled against the lock then slammed my hand against the door while Andi continued talking about her mother country. I half expected her to break out in song.

Desperate, I looked up. I could probably climb over the top. What the hell was I thinking?

With a growl, I glanced down at the floor. At least two feet separated the door and the ground.

Crawling.

I was going to crawl.

On my hands and knees.

Wow, if the guys could see me now.

Shaking my head at myself, I got down on my stomach and slid under the dressing room. My eyes were met with combat boots. Slowly, my eyes inched up Andi's already-dressed form.

"Looking for something?"

"Low…" I shook my head. "…even for you."

She knelt down and blew me a kiss. "I did you a favor. Now for the rest of the day, you can imagine what I looked like — and how you'll get to take off the lingerie tonight."

"I vote now."

"Hmm… maybe later. You said I could shop."

"I regret those words. Really. I do."

She smirked. "I can tell. Now grab the clothes and swipe,

swipe, swipe."

With a groan, I moved to my feet and grabbed the hangers off the hooks. My phone buzzed again in my pocket. With a curse, I put the clothes on one arm and answered. "Kinda busy, Nixon."

"Shopping, I know."

I rolled my eyes. "What did you need?"

"The men said the alarm was de-activated."

"The house alarm?" I blinked. "But that's impossible. Only a few people know the code — me, Jules, and Andi." I hadn't exactly told Andi the alarm code but figured she knew it because she'd watched me plug it in.

"And Jules was one of the guys that was knocked out," Nixon grumbled. "So how did they get in the house without tripping the alarm?"

I narrowed my eyes at Andi; she was busy petting the clothes on my arm. No way would she do that, and I hated myself that I'd even thought it.

"I'll figure it out," I huffed. "That all?"

"Yeah. And Sergio?"

"What?" I barked.

"It's good to see you showing interest…"

"In Andi?"

"In clothes."

"Bite me."

I hung up while he laughed his ass off.

"You weren't kidding about those mimosas." Andi yawned behind her hand as we walked through Lincoln Park. I'd originally thought to take her to the zoo since she had that odd fascination with animals, but after seeing how tired she was, I decided to save it for another day.

"Well…" I held in my chuckle. "…when you have five of

them…"

"I had three." She held up four fingers.

"Good to know you're just fine." I laughed. "Should I carry you?"

"Probably." She gave me a dopey grin. "But I think I can at least make it to the car."

"It's about a mile away."

"Oh." Her face fell.

"How about a piggyback ride?" I offered lamely, hating that a simple walk to the car was making her sad because she was so exhausted.

She stopped walking and crossed her arms. "Riding a cowboy was on the list."

"I'm not following."

"Talk to me in a southern accent, and I'll imagine a cowboy hat on that gorgeous head of hair and boom… I'm riding a cowboy."

I pinched the bridge of my nose. "Andi, I have so many different scenarios that would fit perfectly with that statement. None of them, however, include me carrying you through the park while singing 'Achy Breaky Heart.'"

"Oh good. You know it then?"

"I need to learn the art of silence."

"Probably true." She nodded.

"And teach it to you," I added.

"Aw, come on cowboy…"

I rolled my eyes and turned around so she could jump onto my back. "Should I find a park bench, or can you actually jump this high?"

"Never ask a ninja if she can jump — it's degrading."

"My mistake. I thought you were a short Russian masquerading as a baker. Go ahead, ninja. Jump."

She did, probably using the rest of the energy she had left. Her arms wrapped around my neck tightly. "Mush."

"I thought I was a horse."

"I changed my mind. Girls can do that on occasion."

Damn, the girl made me smile. The afternoon sun was starting to set as we walked along the path. Andi was encouraging me to use a southern accent in her most Russian accent.

And I was trying to pay attention to our surroundings, just in case we'd somehow been followed.

I thought we were in the clear until we reached the edge of the park. I could see the street, and immediately regretted that simple fact the minute two black sedans pulled up to the curb.

Five men got out.

Two from the first car.

Three from the second.

Andi tensed behind me.

"Andi." I kept my smile in place like there wasn't anything wrong. "Got any energy left?"

"Enough." She shuddered behind me.

"My gun," I whispered. "It's in the back of my pants. Reach between your legs and slide it up so nobody sees."

"You know in any other situation…" she muttered as I felt the gun slide up my back.

"Good," I encouraged. "The minute I put you down I want you to aim for the guy to the left. Don't shoot for the head. Hit his kneecap so he goes down. If he reaches for his gun—"

"This isn't my first rodeo, cowboy."

"You're right. I forget."

"I'm good. Don't worry about me."

The tension left my body. "I won't. Just don't get shot. I hate having to sew up bullet wounds."

"Please." I could feel the energy riding off her body. "You owe me a massage if my body count's higher."

"So now it's a competition?"

"Russians rarely lose."

"Well, you should get used to it. Because this Italian's going to hand you your ass."

"I'd like to see you try."

The men were trying to look nonchalant, outside their cars, smoking cigars like they weren't waiting for the perfect opportunity to attack.

"One," I whispered.

Andi slid farther down my back. "Two."

"Three." The word fell from my lips just as I ducked to the right. Andi went to my left and popped off two rounds directly into the guy's kneecaps — not just one, but both of them. A crunching sound broke out across the park as he fell on bones, cracking them further. He wailed in pain and surprisingly didn't reach for his gun.

Three of the men started charging me. Gun less, I could only rely on the fact that my fists were just as deadly as any gun could be, and I punched the first man in the throat then turned and elbowed the next. They stumbled back. Another gunshot went off. Andi was seriously picking them off like she was shooting fish in a bucket.

The three men turned their heads to glare at her. Then, rather than attacking, came at me again.

Surprised, I was knocked in the face by the first guy but sidestepped the next hit then landed a hard blow to his stomach followed by a knee to the groin. With a growl, I head-butted the next guy then punched him in the jaw; the sound of teeth breaking was my only indication that he'd be down for the count.

The final man circled me.

"Let me get him," Andi pleaded behind me.

"He's mine," I barked.

The man shrugged and held up his hands. "You should let girl do your work."

I rolled my eyes. "I'll never hear the end of it."

"Andi," the man called, "why not come with us, huh?

You've done job. Time to come home."

"Job?" I repeated.

Andi came up beside me and aimed the gun for his forehead. "I've never worked for you."

"Oh?" The man chuckled and glanced at me. "He knows as well as I know… you are never out."

"Please let me pull the trigger."

The man ran at us.

I ducked then heaved my body into his, sending him backward against the park bench. Punch after punch I landed to his face, his blood mixing with the slices breaking out on my knuckles.

The sound of sirens interrupted my blatant mutilation of his body.

"Serg…" Andi kicked me. "…gotta disappear."

I backed up, chest heaving. "Right."

With one last kick to his body, I grabbed her hand and ran like hell toward our car, our very easy-to-spot car.

"Shit!" I tossed her the keys. "Start the car." I opened the trunk and hit the red button. A new license plate slid over the old one; it said *New Mexico*. Good enough.

I jumped into the car and waited for the cops to pass the street then sped off in the other direction.

"You think they know we're in this car?" Andi asked breathlessly.

"Andi, NASA probably knows we're in this car," I muttered and glanced in the rearview mirror. "But I changed plates so even if they grab a picture of the plates, they'll think we're a retired couple living on a farm raising ducks."

"People do that?"

"Retire?"

"Raise ducks."

"Mr. and Mrs. Thomas do."

"Good for them." Andi nodded. "Any money in that, you think?"

The car hugged the corner tightly as I quickly got us on the freeway. "Are we seriously having a conversation about ducks after killing some people?"

"Correction." Andi placed the gun on the console. "I killed. You maimed."

"You killed?"

"Well, technically they're dead anyway. Either the cops get them, they die in jail, or my father finds them and shoots them. All dead."

"True."

"So when's your birthday?"

I jerked the wheel to the right in shock. "What?"

"Sorry." She bit her lip. "I just get chatty after a good fight."

I burst out laughing and hit the accelerator. "Wouldn't want you any other way."

CHAPTER TWENTY-SIX

Sergio

WE WALKED INTO THE SILENT HOUSE. I frowned when I glanced at the keypad for the alarm. It bothered me.

The whole situation bothered me.

Like I was missing something important.

Did I question Andi? More doubt crept in at the man's words in the park. Was she still working for her father?

No. It would be impossible.

What would she possibly have to gain? When she was already dead. Harsh but true.

Andi disappeared the minute we walked into the house, and for once, I was grateful. I needed to think, and it was hard to do that when she was constantly smiling and pulling out her damn list.

I reached into the fridge and pulled out a chilled bottle of pinot grigio.

"That's chick wine," Andi said from behind me.

"I've never understood that reference." I turned around and placed the wine on the table, while Andi went to the sideboard and pulled out two glasses.

"What reference?"

"Chicks. It sounds so... I don't know... surfer, a bit uneducated, maybe I'm just old."

Andi placed the glasses in front of me, her steps faltering a bit before she pulled up a barstool and leaned her elbows against the table. "Just how old are you?"

I smirked and began pouring the wine into her glass first. "I'm old enough to know that using the word *chick* makes me look like an ass."

"Wow. So over thirty, huh?"

I stopped pouring and glanced up at her. "Do I look that old?"

"Some say thirty is the new twenty." She yawned. "I'm not judging, just making conversation."

"Twenty-nine," I said smoothly.

"So thirty."

"What?"

"Twenty-nine is basically thirty, Sergio."

I handed her a glass. "How do you figure?"

"It's all downhill from twenty-nine, my friend. Achy bones, Viagra, and gray hair are your future." She took a sip of the wine; her face scrunched up then relaxed as if the little bit she had wasn't as bad as she'd expected. "It's probably a good thing I'm not going to be here to see it. Nobody wants to see a Viagra-popping Sergio."

"I don't want to see a Viagra-popping Sergio," I snapped. "And that won't ever happen."

"Don't say never."

"I said ever."

"Drink your wine so you stop arguing," I instructed, wagging my finger at her.

She shrugged and kept drinking. I tried not to focus on her bruised hands or the fact that there was some slight bruising on the side of her face, possibly from the fight we'd just finished.

"Andi…" I licked my lips and pulled out a barstool next to her. "…did you ever work for your father?"

"Which one?"

"The one who likes vodka."

She shrugged. "Not really. I mean, I always worked for the FBI as a double agent, so did I technically work for my real father? Yes, in a way, but only because I was pushed into it by the feds."

I nodded.

"Why?" She'd already finished her glass of wine and was slinking her hand toward mine.

I slid it backward and shook my head.

"No reason."

She reached farther behind me, her fingers securing the stem. "Sergio?"

"Andi?" I breathed; her face was inches from mine.

"I'm really tired…"

"I know."

"But…" She hopped off her barstool and stood between my legs, releasing my hostage wine glass and wrapping her arms around my neck. "I wouldn't mind working on twelve."

"Wouldn't it be thirteen?"

"Um, your car gave me thirteen."

"Damn machinery didn't give you what I can."

She leaned forward and tugged my ear with her teeth. "Care to wager on that?"

With a growl, I lifted her by the ass and carried her out of the kitchen.

We spent two days in bed.

And knocked off numbers, from thirteen down to four.

Andi started making tally marks with a black felt tip pen

on the inside of her ribcage so she could match me. Her marks were for love; mine were for death. She thought it was hilarious; it just made me feel like a bit of a monster.

"We need to get up." Andi's naked body was sprawled against mine. "The guys keep texting you, and if we don't answer soon, they're going to send a search party."

I weaved my fingers through her tangled mess of blond hair. "Let them."

She let out a heavy sigh. "Sergio?"

"Yeah?"

The air all but got sucked out of the room. It felt like she was about to say something big, something that would alter or maybe steal the bit of happiness I'd been experiencing with her over the past few weeks.

"I'm sick."

My body tensed. "I know."

She ran her hands along my stomach; her cheek pressed against my chest. I was sure she could hear my erratic heartbeat. Shit, I really didn't want to talk about it.

"I missed another doctor's appointment."

I froze. "What? Why?"

"We were in bed, and I just… I wanted to pretend."

I kissed the top of her head. "Pretend what, Russia?"

"That it was real." She leaned up, her chin on my chest, her eyes filling with tears as they gazed into mine. "Just for a few hours I wanted to pretend that outside didn't exist. That it was just you and me. I'll never forget you… I want you to know that. You give me moments, moments where I don't remember I'm sick, moments where only we exist. They're like tiny presents sprinkled throughout my life."

"I wish it worked that way, Andi..." God above, I wished it worked that way. Where if we willed something enough to happen, it inevitably would. "…but you can't miss any more appointments, alright? I'll never forgive myself if something happened to you all because I wanted to keep you in bed a little bit longer, kiss you a little bit harder, make love to you deeper."

She leaned up and kissed my mouth softly. "Then we should probably go in sometime today."

I nodded.

She frowned.

"What is it?"

She shook her head as tears filled her eyes. "I'll miss you."

"Andi, you aren't going anywhere."

At least not for now.

Because we both knew that the odds were she was going somewhere. And I was staying.

Damn. I would do anything in my power — to follow.

CHAPTER TWENTY-SEVEN

Sergio

MY NERVES WERE SHOT. THEY WERE able to fit us into the doctor the following day. It was the same hospital doing my lab work, so I inevitably asked if I could get the test done at the same time.

The plan was to have Andi go to her appointment with the girls so she could be cheered up, while I went and pretended to do something for Nixon.

Unfortunately, Nixon actually did need me for something; the listening device had picked up bits and pieces, but the words were fuzzy, which was really strange, considering I'd done a hell of a job actually making sure it worked in the first place. We argued over when I was going to stop by his house, but I ended up going to my appointment first, just in case I needed some extra hours to hide out and crash so Andi wouldn't be suspicious.

With a sigh, I walked briskly down the hall.

I hated hospitals.

I'd only gone to med school to do exactly what I'd told

Andi — learn how to take life, efficiently, effectively. Did that make me a monster? Maybe, but at least I embraced that part of me — the dark side that knew without a doubt I could reign hell on my enemies and be the only one to come out on the other side.

In the beginning, it had meant I could protect myself, protect my brother, Ax.

Now? It just meant I could protect those I loved. Andi. Did I love her? My chest ached whenever I even thought her name, let alone spent time with her. I couldn't focus when she was gone, and I couldn't focus when she was right in front of me. Every time I tried to breathe, it felt like I was suffocating.

If this was love?

I wanted out.

Because it officially wrecked me.

I glanced at my watch. Right on time.

"You sure about this?" Tex said from the end of the hall, arms crossed, his expression unreadable.

"Yeah." I licked my dry lips. "Besides, if I go the other route, Andi will get suspicious."

He nodded. "I already talked with Nixon. We're going to double the security at your house, but I don't see you being out for longer than a few hours."

We walked into outpatient surgery together.

I needed him to have my back, just in case. We didn't want to take any chances that someone would knife me while I was under the knife, pun intended.

"Sergio Smith?" the nurse called.

"Aw, you took her fake last name," Tex whispered under his breath. "How cute."

I rolled my eyes and held out my hand as the nurse approached. "That's me."

"Alright." She shook my hand and took one long glance at Tex, her face paling by the second. The guy sweated intimidation. While I at least tried to appear normal, Tex didn't. Mainly because he didn't give a shit. I had to respect that about him, even if half the time I wanted to strangle him.

"So..." She looked away from him, swallowing hard. "...it looks like you've got a bone-marrow harvest today."

"Yes."

"Great." She nodded toward the door. "If you and your partner will just follow me..."

Tex choked while I barked out a laugh.

"No." Tex held up his hands and managed a smile. "We're..." He shared a look with me. "...we're family..." His eyes were serious. "...basically brothers."

"Oh." She shrugged. "Sorry. I just assumed."

"No problem," I said quickly then under my breath to Tex murmured, "I think that makes me the bitch in this scenario."

He laughed loudly. "How do you figure?"

"You're taller." I nodded. "I dress better."

"You do have a nice shoe collection."

"Was that a compliment?" I didn't hide the surprise from my voice.

He shrugged. "Maybe. Look, I know this isn't easy for you... I may hate you most the time, I have trouble forgiving and forgetting, but what you're doing for Andi..." We stopped at one of the surgery prep rooms. "...it's commendable."

"It's not like you didn't do the same." I shrugged.

"Ha," Tex shook his head. "We all did it the normal way – five days' worth of injections, basically no side effects. You're getting bone marrow pulled from your freaking hipbone. Yeah, good luck with that. I may love inflicting pain, but needles in my bone? No thanks."

"Wow, great pep talk, Tex." I pulled off my shirt.

He smirked. "Alright, this is where I leave you. Try not to die."

"And again with the encouraging words."

"Hey, I'm Italian." He nodded. "I'll bring you wine later,

we cool?"

I burst out laughing. "Yeah, if you bring wine."

"Chase can cook some pasta."

"Tell him to bake some bread while he's at it."

"Anything else you want me to tell my bitch?" he joked.

"Hey, I thought I was your bitch!"

A nurse walked by. Her steps faltered before she raced past our door.

Tex kept laughing. "You can both be my bitches."

"Now you're talking."

Tex sobered. "Be careful, alright?"

"I'll do my best to lie very still."

"Wouldn't want that knife to slip."

I rolled my eyes. "Leave already before you talk me out of it, and make sure the girls distract Andi long enough for me to wake up and at least be able to carry on a decent conversation."

"When have your conversations ever been decent?"

"Maybe not with you…"

"Valid point." He knocked his hand against the door and waved. "See ya on the other side."

"Yeah." I swallowed as he closed the door, leaving me in silence. The last time I'd been in this hospital had been when my mom had died and then again when Andi was in here. I'd vowed to never come back again.

I'd vowed never to even have surgery.

I'd even told both Ax and Nixon that if I got a bullet wound to take me anywhere but there.

Because in my mind, this hospital was where people went to die.

And yet, there I was, facing a fear, doing something I swore I would never do. Hell, I would have rather died.

So yeah. It was love.

Because it couldn't be anything else.

Nothing else would have brought me back to this place.

Nothing else would be able to keep me here.

But Andi.

I loved her.

I just hoped it would be enough — because it hadn't been with my mother and something in the back of my head told me, it wouldn't be for Andi either.

CHAPTER TWENTY-EIGHT

Andi

THE NEWS WAS BAD. I KNEW before the doctor even walked in, report in hand. I wasn't stupid. It wasn't like I didn't know my body backward and forward.

Bruises weren't healing.

The dizzy spells were getting worse — another reason I wanted to stay in bed with Sergio. At least, having sex distracted me from the fact that when I wasn't horizontal I wanted to fall down onto my hands and knees just to keep the room from spinning.

But more so than the physical symptoms, I just… knew. I felt it in the way each breath of air left my lips — those breaths were counted. They were numbered. My soul knew it even before my doctor did, and that was the sucky part. Modern medicine could perform miracles — but I was beyond saving.

I put on my brave face, which basically meant I forced a toothy grin and tried extremely hard not to let my eyes fill with tears. Basically, there was a lot of fanning my hand in front of my face. I probably looked like a southern debutante after winning another pageant, but whatever; if it worked, it worked.

"Miss Smith…" Doctor McHotpants held out his hand.

I shook it, firm — always firm. He wasn't one of those doctors with sad eyes. I appreciated that about him. He was too good-looking to be sad, something I would never tell Sergio, lest the good doctor find himself strapped to C-4 for blinking too long in my direction.

Sergio wasn't the type of guy to half-ass a threat, and I was pretty sure that he'd see the good doctor as a threat, especially considering McHotpants rarely kept his hands to himself.

He was one of those doctors.

He felt things.

A lot.

He cried with me once.

I was still trying to figure out if I liked the fact that he empathized, or if it just made me want to punch him in the face and give him some Midol.

"So…" My smile felt so forced I almost just gave up and cried. "…what's the diagnosis?"

His smile looked how mine felt. His normally radiant green eyes were dull, his sandy brown hair messy. Black-framed glasses fell low on his nose, and I could see dark circles under his eyes.

"Andi…" he began, his voice low.

I sighed. "Just tell me."

"…at this point…" He licked his lips and stared directly through me.

Ah, I knew that stare; it was the one that said the doctor was trying to emotionally detach from the patient. Look at the patient like an object, not a person, because it would hurt too bad otherwise.

Hell, I knew it already did. He was a good man, and I was young. Too young.

Cancer didn't care if you were six months old or sixty; it had no prejudices; it just was.

"...I've taken it upon myself to come up with a two-month plan." He nodded encouragingly. "I think if you take a look at the—"

I held up my hand.

"Andi—"

I shook my head. "How long?"

His face took on a greenish-white color. Oh good, always a promising sign when your own doctor starts getting sick. "I can't give you an adequate timeline, Andi."

I let out a frustrated sigh.

"It's spread."

"From my blood?"

"Andi..." He leaned forward, pressing his arms against his thighs. "...I don't know how else to say this, but the cancer is in your lymph nodes, and we found a few spots on your lungs as well."

I smiled. "Hey, I still have my kidneys and boobs, right?"

He didn't laugh.

It was probably a bad joke anyway.

I played with a loose thread on my jeans. I'd known this would happen, knew it was happening now; I didn't really feel sad — numb was more like it. Like I was hearing it or watching it play out, but that it wasn't happening to me, but an entirely different person, because I honestly didn't feel all that horrible.

It's weird.

Something was eating me alive from the inside out. My own blood was basically poison. And I didn't really feel it.

"You'll need to come in three times a week for blood transfusions. That should help at least give you some more time. There's also the chance that we can try chemo again, some radiation. There are options, Andi."

"Give me numbers." Wow, if Sergio could hear me now.

"What are the odds that chemo or radiation will work a second time?"

"Five percent." He sighed. "Maybe less."

"So get violently ill and spend my remaining days in the hospital or… just go to sleep?"

"Andi, it will get more painful… your joints will start swelling, you're going to bruise a lot more, your skin will even hurt. I'll prescribe some medicine, but maybe you should just take some time, talk to your family, and get back to me."

My family.

I had no family.

No one but Sergio.

He was my only family now.

And if I told him the truth, it would either scare him to death or make him resent me. After all, he'd never wanted this.

Would it be selfish for me to leave him? Or selfless? What would be easier? Running away so he didn't have to see me die? Or selfishly staying so he could hold my hand while I did it?

"Knock, knock." Bee's voice sounded at the door. She let herself in and walked around the bed. Her eyes took in the doctor's solemn expression. Immediately, her hand touched my shoulder and squeezed.

"I'll go get your meds, Andi." The doctor stood and walked out the door; it shut softly behind him.

"So…" Bee grabbed a stool and nodded. "…your doctor should totally be on *Grey's Anatomy.*"

I burst out laughing. "I'm so glad you agree. I told him he should get an agent. I think he thinks I'm kidding."

"With that face—" She nodded. "—he could do quite well at Seattle Grace."

"From your mouth to Dr. Hotty's ears."

Bee grinned. She was gorgeous in a totally irritating and baffling way. It wasn't just one thing that made her pretty, but every single part of her face working together to form perfection. I'd told her that on numerous occasions, but she'd just waved me off. I loved that she didn't have a prideful bone in her body.

Pregnancy looked amazing on her; she wasn't even showing yet, but I could tell that once she did, she'd still look like a rock star with her dark hair and light features.

"Question," I leaned back in the chair and crossed my arms. "Would you be willing to come with me to a few appointments? I'd ask Sergio, but I'm not sure I want him to know it's come to this point."

"This point being?"

"Death."

Bee didn't gasp or cry. She simply nodded and said, "Whatever you need."

"Well, right now I need you to cheer me up."

"I have wine for that."

"You little slut, please tell me you stole from your brother's ridiculously expensive wine cellar."

Bee laughed. "I did it for you."

"You're a great friend."

"No…" Bee reached over and gripped my hand. "…I'm family… we're sisters… all of us. It's what we do."

"We?"

"We," a few voices said in unison.

I turned and gaped at the door as Trace, Mil, and Mo barged into my room, bags in hand.

"Did you guys rob a Nordstrom on the way in?" I pointed to the bags.

"Who needs to rob when you have Nixon's card?" Trace shrugged and winked in my direction. "I think it's time for lunch."

The doctor made his way back into my crowded room, took one look at all the gorgeous girls, and wrote down the wrong prescription three times before he finally was able to give me a legible one — and that was by doctor's standards.

"See ya later." Bee winked at the doctor and blew him a kiss.

I loved that girl.

Mo pulled me in for a side hug while Trace looped arms with me.

"To lunch and wine!" Mil shouted, and the rest of us followed.

We earned some odd looks from bystanders, but I didn't care. They were, as Bee said, really the only family I had.

And suddenly I felt so much better that a few years ago I'd tried to kill a man. Because had I not met him — I wouldn't be here, living my last few weeks with some of the most caring and amazing people in the world.

Had I not met Luca.

I wouldn't have met Sergio.

I owed Luca Nicolasi my life, my everything, and a small part of me had to wonder, if he somehow had known it would come to this.

And I would need someone to hold my hand in the end.

CHAPTER TWENTY-NINE

Sergio

I THINK I PREFERRED GETTING SHOT. That was my first thought when the needle went into my body. They'd given me drugs, but I didn't want drugs. Drugs meant I would recover slower. So I told them to give me the bare minimum and tried to think of anything but strangling the nurse when the procedure started.

The nurse with the needle and kind eyes told me it would take a few hours to get the results back from the lab. Luckily, everything would be done on site so I wouldn't have to wait very long.

In the meantime, my only job was to not fall on my ass and make sure I powered through the pain so Andi didn't find out. The last thing I needed was her getting suspicious.

It would mean pestering.

And questions.

And it would be exhausting.

"Hey!" Tex said from the door. "You're alive!"

I gave him a thumbs up.

"Did they stick a catheter up your—"

"Mr. Smith?" The nurse gave Tex a wary eye and sidestepped him. "Your discharge papers."

"Ma'am." Tex nodded his head and gave her what I'm sure he thought was a reassuring smile, but he bared way too many teeth.

She took a step away from him and handed me my papers. "Now remember, you may be sore for a day or so. If you have any excessive bleeding, please come back to the hospital."

"Great." I winced and rose from the hospital bed. "You'll call with the results?"

"As soon as we have them." She flashed a smile and left the room, careful to give Tex a wide berth.

"Huh." Tex scratched his face. "Is it because I'm tall?"

"Your gun's showing." I pointed.

He looked down.

"Kidding." I laughed; it kind of hurt, but the look on his face was worth it.

"Jackass." Tex punched me in the shoulder. "Seriously, you feeling okay? They didn't switch your man parts out for girl parts or do anything freaky, right? That nurse looked a bit handsy..."

"No bad touching." I rolled my eyes. "Not that I would have cared. I was on drugs, you know."

"Clearly not enough if you can still hold a conversation with me."

I winced as I took a step toward him. "Don't suppose you'd give me a piggyback ride?"

"Burn in hell."

"That's what I thought." I bit back a curse and finally met him at the door. "You know, Nixon would at least have given me a high five or something."

Tex nodded. "You're right." He slammed his fist into my shoulder. "Good job. You lived."

"Now who's the ass?"

"Don't forget it, bitch."

The nurses had horrible timing in that hospital, plain and simple; we scared at least two more on the way out when Tex started clapping behind me and yelling, "Mush!"

He needed a kid to torture. I almost felt sorry for Mo; no wonder she was packing half the time.

"How did Andi's appointment go?" I asked once we were out in the parking lot.

Tex's face didn't give away anything, but his body tensed. Every single muscle seemed to stand at attention.

"Shit."

"What?" He shrugged. "I didn't say anything."

"Didn't have to," I muttered, trying to will my body to get into the car without my hip actually breaking off my body. Damn, walking hurt more than it should have. Hell even breathing hurt more than it should have.

Tex, probably irritated with my turtle-like speed, came over and helped shove me very lovingly into the passenger side of the car and nearly slammed the door on my foot.

Once we were both in and driving out of the hospital, he spoke again. "Look, all I know is that Mo sent me an *I love you* text. It's not that I don't get those type of texts, but lately she only sends them when she's really upset about something, like she doesn't want me to forget we're a team and— Why the hell am I sharing this with you?"

"No idea," I muttered, "but for what it's worth… thanks."

"Serg…" Tex tapped his fingers against the steering wheel then gripped it tightly with both hands. "I have a bad feeling."

I swallowed the hollow feeling in my chest and glanced out the window so he wouldn't see the fear in my eyes. "Yeah, Tex. Me too."

"Sergio…" A soft voice said my name, whispered it in my ear. "…wake up."

I shook my head and hugged the pillow tighter.

"Wake up, and I'll show you my boobs."

"Huh?" I mumbled, blinking my eyes open.

Andi was hovering over me, her smile wide. "You've been sleeping for a really long time."

"What?" I covered my yawn with my hand. "What time is it?"

"Well…" She grabbed my hand and read my watch aloud. "…six at night."

"Shit!" I tried to jolt up then remembered that I'd already met with Nixon, and because Andi had been out with the girls, he'd agreed to drop me off at my house so I could sleep in my own bed. "I'm so sorry."

She frowned. "For sleeping? Right… you should be."

Six. Six meant the hospital had to have called. I frantically searched my pockets for my phone.

"Whoa. You okay?" Andi sat on the bed and tucked her feet under her body.

"Yeah." I finally located my phone on my nightstand. One missed call. "I just… was expecting someone."

"Oh, your other lover." She winked.

"She's a redhead." I nodded solemnly. "Hates Russians. Loves cats though."

"Ah, so she has that going for her."

I smiled and held up my phone to my ear. *"Mr. Smith, this is Nurse Holingway. While I'd much rather have this conversation in person, I understand you need the test results as soon as possible. It appears we won't have the final results for another twenty-four hours. If you are somehow a match, we will need to start the process sooner rather than later, as your wife's condition has, as you know, worsened. Expect to hear from us soon."*

I dropped the phone onto the bed.

The room was silent.

Andi cleared her throat and reached for my hand. "Everything okay?"

I jerked my hand away. "What happened at your appointment?"

"Well…" She bit down on her lower lip. "…I tried to convince my doctor to try the entertainment industry again."

"Andi…"

"And…" She sighed. "…the girls came and rescued me."

"Andi…"

Her face fell. I reached for her hand, this time squeezing it tight.

"It's not good, Sergio. I kind of have the black lung and all that."

"This isn't *Zoolander*."

"Wow!" She tilted her head in appreciation. "Points for the movie reference. See? You're not that old!"

"Andi!" I yelled her name, not because I was angry, but because I knew her, backward and forward. She was trying to let me down lightly, trying to make light of a very serious situation. "What did he say?"

Her brown eyes filled with tears. "It's in my lymph nodes… and they found a few spots in my lungs. I can't do chemo. The chances are pretty rare that it would help in the first place. Once you've done it, your body doesn't respond as well the second or third time."

"And a donor?"

She shrugged.

"Andi, I have something to tell you."

"Can we not?" She wiped away a few stray tears. "At least for the next hour, can we just lie here? Can you just hold me? I don't want to talk about it, not yet… please?"

I sighed heavily. "Yeah." No use in upsetting her more. But we would have that conversation. And it would be soon. If there was a chance at saving her, I was going to take it, even if I died trying.

"Kiss me." She pressed her hands against my shoulders and pushed me against the bed, straddling my body with her legs.

I was finding it extremely hard to stick to my promise, to not shed any tears. I had to be strong for her, for us. "Kiss you, huh?"

"Yes." I would never get tired of her smile, of the way it lit up her entire face. Shit, the way it lit up my entire world.

I brought her head down and met her mouth with mine in a tender, desperate kiss. Every touch inflicted a slow-burning fever of need — not to just kiss her, to make her mine again and again — but to mark her, to possibly mark her so hard that she stayed with me.

Logic, numbers… hell, even reality told me that it was an impossibility. That no matter how hard I kissed her she wouldn't stay, but I had to try, right? I would be foolish not to.

So I kissed her harder.

I dove deeper into the madness of our feelings — the desperation of the love I felt for her.

When the kissing wasn't enough, I pulled her shirt over her head, my fingers making a slow trail down her stomach, memorizing that feeling right there and holding onto it, just in case.

She didn't fight me. She didn't even flinch when I started slowly pulling down her yoga pants.

"Andi," I whispered against her lips, "I have to tell you something."

"What?" Her hands cupped my face.

I was lost in that look, the very look that said she loved me, would die for me, knew she was but wanted to take that risk anyway — the risk that before death her heart would be broken, and she wouldn't get a second chance to fix it or to allow me to put the pieces back together again.

Had there ever been a love like ours before?

I doubted it.

And if there had been, I pitied those people, because every touch felt like the last… when it should have been the first of many.

Every kiss that should have been hello was goodbye.

Once her pants were dangling by her ankle, I reached for her bra and removed it. "You're too beautiful for me."

"For an Italian like you?" she countered, then slid off her underwear and crawled on top of me, her breasts pressing against my chest. Andi kissed up my neck, her hands drawing my T-shirt over my head and tossing it aside.

I closed my eyes and ran my hands slowly down her hips, my fingers pressing into her soft skin. With a sigh, I took her mouth in a slow, agonizing kiss, a kiss that I had a hard time stopping — because stopping meant ending, and ending just reminded me of the time that kept slipping through our fingers.

"Sergio?"

I opened my eyes and paused while my heart cracked against my chest.

"It's okay to be scared, right?"

I nodded, not trusting my voice. "Yes." I tucked her hair behind her ears. "But we're together. When you have a partner, things are less scary because suddenly you aren't facing giants all by yourself."

"I like the idea of facing them with you." She sniffed and looked down. A single tear slid down her cheek and landed on my chest.

It may as well have been acid; I felt the burn of that tear in the depths of my soul, crushing in its weight, devastating in its truth.

I kissed her harder, deeper. Our bodies slammed against one another. With a grunt, I flipped her onto her back and kissed between her breasts, sliding my hands down her legs. I refused to stop until I gave her every ounce of pleasure she deserved.

She cried out when my hand slid between her legs.

"I thought you just screwed," she said, breathless.

I retreated then pressed forward again, this time replacing my hand with my mouth.

Every arch of her body, every whimper was music to my ears. When she was finally ready for me, our bodies slid together in a perfect match.

I moved, deeper, harder.

Andi's eyes closed.

I could have sworn in that moment I felt the air; I could taste its bittersweet reminder that time was against us.

It wasn't just about sex.

Not anymore.

Not ever, if I was being completely honest with myself.

It was about sharing every single part of my soul — my body — with her, and hoping she did the same with me.

Because she was it.

We were quiet, passionate; both of us realizing we were experiencing one of those rare moments in life where words were useless and actions meant everything.

Her hands clenched my arms as I continued my slow, languid movements, taking time to relish each sensation of our bodies connecting, communicating. It was bliss — it was everything.

"Feels so…" She exhaled. "…good."

"Italians are always good."

"Had to joke," she hissed, her nails digging into my flesh. "Sergio, I'm—"

I felt her body clench around mine as a shudder wracked her body. I watched, absolutely dumbstruck by the beauty before me and utterly wrecked that it wouldn't last.

"Andi…" Sweat trickled down my cheek and landed on her bare stomach. My body soon followed hers as I collapsed onto the bed, trying not to crush her. "…I love you."

Her hand drew slow circles along my back. "I know."

I lifted my head. "That's it? You know?" I smiled tightly. "Harsh, Russia."

"Let me finish." She pressed a fingertip to my lips. "I love you too. And I'm sorry."

"Sorry?"

She shrugged. "My love is short."

"No." I shook my head and gripped her hands between mine. "Just because our love feels short doesn't mean it is. Our love is forever."

CHAPTER THIRTY

Andi

I WATCHED HIM SLEEP. I WASN'T sure I believed in heaven. I'd seen too many horrible things in my short life — but if heaven was real, Sergio had to be a gift from above, because he was everything I didn't know I even wanted.

And at the same time needed, more than oxygen.

His breathing was heavy. He'd woken me twice in the middle of the night, both times kissing me, making love to me, not caring that I was fragile, but acting like he was desperate for every inch of my body.

I was exhausted.

In the best way possible.

He mumbled in his sleep and turned on his back. That silly scar stared back at me — I stuck out my tongue — his one imperfection if you could even call it that.

The longer I stared, the sadder I became. Tears soon filled my eyes as a thought occurred. I wouldn't get to stare at the scar much longer, and soon, well hopefully, he'd be able to move on — to live his life — and someone else would be sleeping in my place, staring at that scar, wondering about its story.

It was an eerie feeling.

Knowing that the sheets would be, and should be, warmed by another body, by another soul.

I wished in that moment I had control over what would happen when I was gone, or that I could at least help him.

An idea popped into my head.

A slow smile met the tears streaming down my face. "Oh, Sergio, you're either going to love me more or hate me. But at least you'll be forced to live, and that's the greatest gift I could ever leave you."

I kissed his forehead and went off to find a piece of paper. Ha, the man made fun of my lists; he was going to want to strangle me over this little piece of paper.

It was two hours before I finally made it back into bed. It was quiet around the house, which wasn't all that normal, considering a lot of the men Nixon had left took shifts, meaning the TV was almost always on downstairs.

Frowning, I glanced into the living room.

Empty.

I called down the hall, careful to keep my voice low.

Again nothing.

And then a hand slammed across my mouth. Someone pulled my body back. I was too weak to fight.

The man dragged me up the stairs; once we were back in Sergio's bedroom, he placed a gun against my back and whispered, "Talk and I shoot."

I didn't recognize the voice.

Soon footsteps sounded up the stairs.

Another man burst into our bedroom as Sergio was starting to wake up.

"Ah, Andi."

My eyes widened in horror. It was my father, my real father.

"Did you have to screw him so hard he blacked out?"

Sergio jumped to his feet just in time to get shot through the shoulder by my father. He crumpled to the floor.

I yelled. The gun pressed harder against my back.

My father moved over Sergio and whispered, "Well done, Andi. I knew you could do it."

What? What the hell was he talking about? I opened my mouth to yell when I was hit in the back of the head.

Everything went black.

CHAPTER THIRTY-ONE

Sergio

BLOOD FILLED MY MOUTH. THE METALLIC taste made me want to puke; instead, I spit out as much as I could and tried to take in my surroundings.

Well, at least I wasn't in a warehouse — or worse, dead.

I was in a living room, my sad ass tied to a chair right in front of a baby grand piano.

Heavy black curtains decorated each of the large bay windows.

An expensive leather sectional was in the middle of the room; a bookcase covered one end, while a large desk sat in the other.

One door.

One exit. One entry.

Well, there went my escape plan unless I wanted to jump out the window, but I wasn't sure if I was up high or if I was on the bottom floor of whoever's house I was in.

I assumed it was Petrov's.

Memories of what had taken place came flooding back. I

flinched in pain as I remembered being shot in the shoulder. I glanced to my right. It was bandaged. Ah, so they wanted to keep me alive before they killed me. Fantastic.

Andi! I tried to jump to my feet, but they were tied too.

It was fuzzy, but Petrov had said something about her… doing a good job? Or was it something else? I blinked, straining to remember what he'd said.

She would never double-cross me.

Or would she?

No. I had to trust my instincts, and my instincts said she was good; besides, she was being held at gunpoint. If she was bad, they would have pulled the gun away.

Or was there a gun?

Again, I couldn't tell; the memory was too fuzzy.

She'd been standing in front of another man…

Her face broken.

But I couldn't recall a gun.

"Shit," I mumbled.

"Ah, he's awake." Petrov walked in, wiping his hands on a towel and tossing it onto the couch. It was covered in blood, which made me wonder what else he had in his house of horrors.

"Petrov." I grinned. "Care to explain why you have me tied to a chair?"

He shrugged. "Think about such things hard enough, and you'll come up with a solution."

I glared.

He was a large man, who one could surmise quite enjoyed his food and vodka, if his gut was any indication. He was at least six four with a girth that made me cringe. His black suit fit him to perfection.

With a sigh, he pulled out a cigar, clipped the end, and lit it. Puffs of smoke filled the air, making me want to gag.

"She betrayed you."

I rolled my eyes. "I highly doubt that."

He shrugged. "Believe what you want, but know this. She's been working for me the entire time, and now I have a greater prize than my own daughter."

I burst out laughing. Even though my entire world felt like it was crumbling, I had to save face. "I'm not a boss. I mean nothing to the families. I mean nothing to the FBI."

"See?" He nodded. "That is where you are wrong." He puffed again on his cigar and set it on a dish then pulled a small syringe from his pocket. "You are blood, and blood always fights for blood. You will draw out one, if not all, of the leaders. I shall finish what my idiot son and Director Smith started. I will destroy the heads of the families. I will take over what should have been mine in the first place, Italian scum," he spat.

"Save the dramatics," I hissed.

"You have control of seven of our docks in Seattle. Seven." He ground his teeth. "You've infiltrated every single major harbor in the United States. How can I run drugs if the Italians are constantly trouncing all over my territory?"

"Well, here's a thought." I leaned forward as much as I could. "Go back to Russia. This is our home, our right. We've been here a hell of a lot longer than you and have a shitload more money. Just try to take out the families — cut off one head… two more will appear. Besides, killing me would be doing them a favor. Believe me."

"Oh yes." He nodded. "Double agent. You've been a bad man, haven't you?"

I was really tired of this conversation.

"It matters not." He flicked the syringe with his forefinger. "I won't have to kill them. You'll do that for me."

"Oh, I will?"

His grin was malicious. "Truth serum is often misused."

I squirmed in my seat, my eyes frantic for a weapon I could use to kill him. I stalled instead. "I imagine you're going to tell me why."

"Of course." He chuckled, taking two steps closer to me. "It rarely works when asked direct questions, but the power of suggestion? Oh now, that is a different beast entirely. I inject this..." He held up the needle. "...and I tell you so many falsehoods you forget your own damn name. I imagine if you're weak enough, I could even convince you that your cousin Nixon was Satan himself."

"Doubt it." I jerked at my hand restraints.

He sighed and with a nod set down the needle. "You know, you're right. What am I thinking? Truth serum!" He laughed loudly. "Sleep, dehydration — those are even better — but why don't I inject you first, cloud your vision, cloud your logic a bit before we begin, yes? Oh, and I do hope you enjoy the heat."

"What?"

He clapped his hands.

The fireplace turned on.

And a loud noise sounded.

"Hear that?" He cupped his ear. "The heat has just been turned on in this glorious state-of-the-art prison. The walls are triple insulated, the door lets no air in or out, by this time tomorrow morning, you'll be begging for release. You'll be so dehydrated you can't see straight, and the best part? Just when you're ready to take a nap, to escape the hell I've put you in..." He pulled a black collar from his pocket and fastened it around my neck.

I tried to bite him, but he was too fast.

"...I'll simply shock you awake. Let the games begin. I imagine it will take them at least twenty-four hours to locate you. Another twenty-four to form a plan, and by then, well, let's just say by then I'll have you eating out of my hand. Just think!" He started waltzing toward the door. "In the end, you will betray them all, just like you should have a month ago."

"I won't," I vowed.

He didn't turn around. He simply answered, "We'll see."

I was trying to figure out why I was strapped next to the piano, facing the door, when the heat started searing my back.

I was backed against the fireplace.

My kidneys.

"Shit," I hissed. He really was trying to dehydrate me. I closed my eyes and tried to meditate on keeping my breathing even.

The guys would come; I prayed they wouldn't.

I prayed they'd stay and just let me die. Funny, this morning I'd dreamed about following Andi into the afterlife, and now, I would be preceding her.

"Don't," I whispered. "Don't come for me."

CHAPTER THIRTY-TWO

Sergio

MY HEAD WAS SO HEAVY IT didn't even feel like it was part of my body anymore; it hung forward. A beeping sounded, and then I was zapped twice around the neck, stunned so hard that I had to clench my teeth.

The fire continued to lick at my back. Sweat drenched the borrowed shirt and jeans they'd put me in.

I was thankful they were larger than I needed, at least providing some vent for the air to come up my back.

I was tired, so incredibly tired that my eyes were having trouble focusing. It didn't help that the bastard had injected me again with whatever the hell was in that syringe.

Voices sounded down the hall.

Either that, or I was truly going insane.

The door opened.

"Twenty-four hours have passed…" Petrov had two heads.

I blinked, trying to clear the image. Nope, still two heads.

"…and your friends have not come."

"Told you." Sweat dripped into my mouth.

"The room is over a hundred degrees, the fire still roaring. I bet water sounds like a slice of heaven."

I ignored the thirst burning my throat. My mouth was sandpaper; the desire to drink so strong I couldn't recall a time I'd ever been so thirsty.

"She betrayed you." Petrov stood in front of me and crossed his arms.

"She wouldn't." My voice was weak, unconvincing.

Petrov laughed. "Oh, to be in love. Tell me, did she give you the sob story about her sickness? Did you feel sorry for her? That was part of the plan you know. The easiest way to infiltrate is through the heart — through pity."

I shook my head.

"You're an idiot if you think she loves you. She feels nothing — she's my flesh and blood, after all. She hates Italians. I imagine you saw that hate quite often."

I ignored the voice in my head that said he was right.

"Haven't you wondered how we were able to get into your house all those times?"

"Luck." I clenched my jaw as the fire seemed to roar against my back. I arched and let out a little cry. So. Damn. Hot.

"Ha." Petrov wagged a finger at me. "She gave us the alarm code."

My head started to hang.

"You're a smart man, Sergio. I bet you even suspected her, but, because of your love, you ignored that voice in your head, that voice of logic — reason. She's good. I'll give you that. Many a man would fall for her blonde hair and innocent act. Didn't she tell you? She was trained in the art of manipulation."

"Stop!" I roared, lunging against the rope that was chaffing my wrists. "Stop!"

"She played you…" Petrov leaned down and slapped my

cheek. "…like a fiddle."

He grabbed me by the hair and slammed his head against mine. Pain sliced through my forehead. I fell forward, and another zap hit my neck.

"Admit it," he whispered, his eyes black with hatred. "She bested you, and now… you are nothing."

"You won't win." Why was I still fighting when I knew he was right? When I knew— What did I know? The images were blurring more; I saw her snapping a picture of the code with her phone. Was that real? Did that happen? Memories replayed; they all seemed right, but they didn't fit.

Her kiss had been real.

Our love was real.

"Ah, the doubt." Petrov stepped back and nodded. "That's the first to happen, and then the images… the images your brain stored up suddenly float to the surface. Take your time, Sergio. I imagine a man like you will come to the same conclusion."

"Why?" My voice was ragged from lack of spit. "Why would you go after her then? The first night?"

"A truly good predator is always able to throw off its own scent." Petrov twisted a large ring around his middle finger. "We wanted to get the layout of the house, and what better way for us to grab you? We get you to focus on Andi, keeping her safe without any regard to yourself." He let out a low chuckle. "I bet you started sleeping with your gun and knife in the nightstand instead of under your pillow. After all, the bed is for making love, not war."

Damn it, he was right.

Foolishness washed over me.

"And there it is." He clapped his large hands slowly. "Admission. She betrayed you."

She betrayed me.

The love of my life had betrayed me.

I blinked back tears as the fire roared to life behind me.

"She betrayed me."

"Good." Petrov nodded. "And what are you going to do about it?"

I was silent.

He sniffed, walked away from me, and pulled open the door. "One more syringe, another twenty-four hours, and we'll get our answer."

She was so beautiful, like a black widow spinning her web of deceit, just waiting for me, someone so weak, so desperate for love to fall into her clutches.

She waited.

The heat was too intense between us.

I wanted to escape.

Still she waited while I dangled in her web.

And then, she struck.

The poison spread from my back to my legs — heavy, so heavy. The pain seared through my hip and up my shoulder.

So much pain.

I strained against her bite, bucking my body away from her.

She simply smiled and bit harder.

My head fell back. A buzzing hit me in the neck—

I jolted awake.

The room was spinning; my back was on fire; my face fell forward again, this time slamming against the keys of the piano.

The zap jerked my head up.

Eyelids heavy, I fought for the sleep I needed, prayed that water would pour from the ceiling as I tried to lick my dry lips.

Andi's fault.

She'd done this.

She was the reason I was here.

Rage burst inside of me. I let out a hoarse yell.

The door to the room opened. Petrov walked in, his boots slamming against the hardwood. I saw four of him, maybe six — I lost count of how many blurs were in front of me. All I knew was that he was the key to everything. The key to water.

Sleep.

God, I'd do anything for sleep — for hydration.

Petrov pulled out a chair and snapped his fingers. The door opened again.

Water.

I moaned.

"Ah, see?" Petrov took the pitcher of water and poured it into the glass that accompanied it. "See how I take care of what is mine?"

He lifted the water to his lips and sipped, droplets fell down his large chin onto his chest. "It's very fresh. Cold."

My breathing was erratic; I couldn't focus on anything but the water. The drops he was wasting… the drops I would lick off him if I could just reach… That was all I needed in life — two drops of water.

"She betrayed you," he said as he slowly dumped water from the pitcher onto the floor.

"No!" I screamed.

"Yes," he whispered.

"Y-yes." I hung my head. The zap didn't come, but neither did sleep; instead, a frenzied madness took its place. "Yes!" I lifted my head. "The bitch betrayed me."

Petrov rose, his knees cracked as he held the water to my lips. "And what are you going to do about it?"

I met his glare. "I'm going to kill them all."

CHAPTER THIRTY-THREE

Andi

"NIXON!" I YELLED INTO MY CELL PHONE as it went to voicemail yet again. "Answer your damn phone!"

I hit the accelerator harder, ready to ram the gate that led into his house. Dying before my time wouldn't help Sergio. I rubbed my head where I'd been hit; the bruise looked horrific. It had probably caused brain damage, but I couldn't think of that right now.

Sergio had been taken…

By my father.

And I was going to get him back even if it killed me — or if I needed to kill my own flesh and blood to do so.

The stupid-ass idiot who'd knocked me out had tied my hands and feet together and stuffed me in a closet then dropped what felt like a hundred pounds of clothes on top of me…

I wasn't sure what he was trying to accomplish, other than suffocating me, but once I had fought through the clothes I had a new problem.

How was I going to get to a phone?

By the time I managed to kick down the closet door, I was exhausted. My sickness wasn't allowing any sort of Xena-warrior-princess tendencies. Instead, I turned on my side and puked.

When I was done tossing my guts I inched and hopped down the hall. He'd put me in the farthest room in the house — a million miles away from a phone.

When I passed the upstairs' study, I noticed that it was already starting to get dark again.

How long had I been out?

The pain in my ass was intense; bruises would cover my body by the time I made it to the phone.

I had no concept of time — only that I had to call Nixon… or find a knife.

When I reached Sergio's room, I nearly burst into tears. No phone. They'd taken all communication from his room. No cells, nothing.

Knife. I needed a knife.

Or a machete.

Another few hours, and I was at the stairway.

It was going to hurt. But time wasn't on my side. Gritting my teeth, I rolled to my hip and tucked my head toward my chest, causing myself to roll down the stairs. Each stair bit into me. I held my scream in — I wouldn't scream, I wouldn't focus on me. Only him, the man I loved.

I was going to save Sergio…

And put a bullet between my father's eyes.

He was trying to start a war, and I was going to be the one to end it, after I cut off his head and put it on a freaking spike.

I hit the bottom floor hard. Something cracked in my wrist as I tried to catch myself. Ignoring the jarring pain radiating down my arm, I inched into the kitchen and located the knife drawer.

With a wince, I leaned back and kicked my legs up. The drawer slowly opened. I kicked out harder. One final kick, and the drawer fell to the ground.

I'd never been so happy to see a machete…

"Nixon!" I honked my horn for the fifth time. I was driving one of Sergio's cars and doing a crap job of it, if the scratches on the sides were any indication.

I pressed the buzzer to the gate again.

"What the hell, Sergio?" the voice barked on the other end.

"He's been taken!" I yelled frantically. "Nixon, let me in, or so help me God, I'm going to use Sergio's machete to cut out your heart and feed it to you!"

The gate opened.

I hit the floor with the accelerator and barely put it into park when Nixon and Trace came running out of the house.

Nixon helped me out of the car. His eyes took in my appearance. "Shit, Trace, call the guys now."

He threw a phone at her; she caught it mid-air and started dialing, not missing a beat.

Nixon didn't say anything else; he simply lifted me into his arms and carried me inside the house. I knew if I relaxed, the pain would be worse. If I stopped freaking out, the stress would stop protecting me, the adrenaline would stop, and I'd feel all the broken parts of me. Rigid, I waited until we were in the house, until he set me down.

And then I started screaming.

Trace's eyes widened briefly before she ran out of the room, returning minutes later with a syringe.

"No!" I held up my hands. "No drugs. Let me feel the pain."

Nixon cursed and kicked the couch. "Have you seen yourself?"

"No." I shook my head violently. "Don't want to. We need to go get Sergio, now."

Nixon checked his watch. "Shit, they need to drive faster."

"Nixon..." I pleaded, tears in my eyes, "...my father has him."

Nixon's eyes narrowed. He leaned over my body, his face menacing, so frightening it was like staring into the depths of hell. "If you double-crossed him, I'll be the one cutting your heart out, princess — while you're breathing."

"No!" I slammed my hands against his chest. "I would never. I LOVE HIM!"

Trace joined me on the couch and grabbed my hand. "Nixon, she wouldn't."

"How the hell are we supposed to know that?" Nixon kicked the couch again then reached for his gun and pointed it at me. "You've left me no choice."

I closed my eyes and hung my head.

The gun never went off.

I opened one eye then two.

"A liar would fight for her life." Nixon lowered the gun.

"Or maybe I just don't value my life anymore — but I do value *his* — and I promise you I'll kill my father before you get the chance."

"If I suspect anything—" Nixon pointed the gun back at my face. "—I end you."

"Deal." I exhaled.

The door opened. Tex stormed in followed by Frank, Mil, Chase, and Phoenix.

"What the hell happened to you?" Tex glanced between me and Nixon.

"Sergio," I choked. "Petrov took him."

"Not you?" Tex's eyes narrowed. "Swear on my unborn child I will chop off that pretty blond head of yours if you double-crossed him."

I sighed. "Look this is getting old. Nixon's already threatened me. I get it. You guys actually like him, which is a giant shock to me, considering you haven't even visited."

Tex gritted his teeth hard. "You don't know shit."

"Oh yeah?" I was picking a fight with a giant. I knew it, but I didn't care. I was too upset; all my feelings were boiling to the surface. I was helpless to stop them.

"Girls..." Chase stood between us. "...stop. This is about Sergio. Time's wasting."

"Any idea where they took him?" Mil asked, voice calm, demeanor rigid.

I shook my head; that small movement hurt every bone in my body. "No idea."

"His phone on?" This from Frank.

I rolled my eyes. "No offense, but I'm not stupid. I've already tried to use the GPS locater."

Phoenix cleared his throat. "The listening device in the hand."

"What about it?" I shrugged.

Phoenix's eyes met mine. "Sergio put the listening device in. He also put a locator in it, remember? My money's on Petrov taking Sergio to his compound on the lake."

I nodded. "Well, how do we turn the thing on? Our resident nerd has been captured!"

Nixon rushed out of the room and returned with an iPad Mini. His fingers worked smoothly across the surface, his eyes frantically searching the screen until they stopped. "Got him."

"That easy?" I was dumbfounded. What the hell kind of technology did they have?

Nixon flipped the screen around and pointed to a green dot. "The hand is still at the same location. There's no way of knowing if Sergio is actually in the same location. The transmission from the watch wasn't functioning properly, and we were unable to gain any useful information."

I blew out an exhale between my cheeks. "Okay, so what are you saying?"

The room fell silent.

"No." I shook my head violently. "No. I'll go myself if I have to."

Tex cursed under his breath. "Sergio wouldn't want you to."

"The hell he wouldn't!" I yelled, though in my heart I knew there was truth to what Tex was saying. "I'm going after him."

"Think about it." Tex held up his hands. "We all go. We storm the compound, and he's there… How many men do you think are holed up inside? At least twenty — maybe more. Say he's not there, and it's a trap. Petrov gets all our heads on a platter."

My legs felt weak; I crumpled onto the couch and put my head in my hands. "We can't just leave him."

Mil walked over to me and leaned down. "Think logically about this, Andi. If you were in his position, what would you do?"

I lifted my head, my eyes blurring with tears. "Or you can think of it this way. If it was Tex in that house, what would you do?"

Mil's nostrils flared. "Storm the freaking castle and get my man."

"Right." I stood. "Thanks, boys, but I think I'm going to go with my own plan. Firearms?"

Nobody moved.

"I said…" I yelled. "…firearms? At least arm me before I go marching off into enemy territory."

Tex nodded at Nixon, but Nixon didn't budge. He stared at me, hard, like he was trying to figure me out, like he couldn't figure me out.

Tears filled my eyes. If there was a way to open up my chest and show him my heart, show him how desperately I needed Sergio, if only for a few short weeks before I left this earth, I would.

He nodded slowly then tilted his head. I followed him down a large hallway. We stopped at what I thought was the door to the garage; instead, he opened the door and then another immediately to his left. We went down a flight of stairs.

Lights flickered on.

Holy super-hero sanctuary, Batman.

Rifles lined one wall.

Nice rifles.

The kind you pay a lot of money for.

Knives, daggers, machetes — all hanging from the opposite wall.

Nixon pressed another button; another door opened. Right. Another door.

Inside that room were semi-automatic guns, tear gas, bullet proof vests, C-4, scuba equipment, and a few terrifying looking contraptions that reminded me of every single historical romance I'd read that had talked about medieval torture.

"I'd start with the tear gas." He threw a few cans at me then pulled out a duffel bag. "…then the smoke." He tossed something else into the bag. "Once the smoke clears and the fire alarms go off, the sprinkler system will be activated." He sighed and grabbed two semi-automatics. "You'll have five minutes, maybe six, before men start running to your location. You'll either need to fight or create another diversion so you can search the house."

"Or…" I reached for one of the guns. "…I kill all but one, torture him, then find out where Sergio is."

"Too much time, Andi. You won't make it."

"Watch me."

"Andi…" Nixon's hand closed over the gun. "…this is a suicide mission. You get that, right? Chances of him coming out of there alive are next to zero. We don't know how Petrov works. We've never been to his compound. Hell, we don't even know if he's there. This could all be for nothing."

I jerked the gun away. "I have to try. Besides, I'm Russian. We live for zero odds. Makes the victory that much sweeter."

Nixon smirked, dropping his head. "Shit, Trace is going to kill me."

"Why?"

He grabbed a vest and put it over his head. "I'm his boss. I'm also his cousin. I go in with you, or you don't go in at all."

"The hell you will!"

He pushed me back, actually pushed me. "That's right." He nodded. "I have no issue with pushing you, punching you, shooting you. You're my equal, and he's my family. I go in, or we don't go at all. Those are your options."

"I could just dropkick your ass."

"Sweetheart…" Nixon licked his lips, another smirk forming. "…I'd really like to see you try."

I backed away then turned around, trying to trip him with the back of my leg. I was out of practice and already severely wounded, so it wasn't surprising at all that he'd seen it coming a mile away. He gripped me by the ankle and flipped my entire body onto the ground then hovered over me; a gun pressed to my chin. "Keep wasting my time. See what I do. See how far I'll go."

I nodded; the tip of the gun was cold against my skin. "Fine, but we do it my way."

"Not surprised, you're shit at taking directions anyway." He got off the ground and held out his hand. "Oh, and don't tell the others. They'll just follow. We go out the back, we take—"

"Dibs on the Chiappa shotgun. That bad boy hasn't been used yet, and I plan to get dirty." Chase burst into the room and reached for a vest.

"What are you doing?" Nixon asked in a calm voice.

"We had a family meeting while you were in here being all self-sacrificial." Chase shrugged. "I know you, Nixon. You wouldn't let her go on her own. Where you go I follow. It's kind of the deal since we're brothers from another father. Ha!

Get it?"

Nixon clenched his jaw. "Chase—"

"Make sure they all have silencers. We don't want nosey neighbors calling the cops on us." Tex entered the room followed by Frank and Mil.

Mil was already grabbing knives and strapping them to her leg.

Mo followed and then Trace.

"Wait." I held up my hands. "What's going on?"

Phoenix entered last and offered an unapologetic smile. "It's an Italian thing."

"Blood." Frank moved to the middle of the small armory. "But we do this the old way, not the new way where you children run in guns blazing."

"Love it when he calls us children," Chase sang in a bored voice.

Frank smacked him on the back of the head. "Listen closely and listen well."

CHAPTER THIRTY-FOUR

Sergio

SOMETHING JAMMED INTO MY WRIST. I tried to pull away, but I was too weak, too hot, too tired. I lazily glanced down. An IV had been started. What the hell? Where was I?

A hand slapped my cheek. I blinked hard, trying to focus.

The man chuckled. "Wouldn't give you the satisfaction of tasting the water. This way you don't die of dehydration, but you don't get to feel the coolness against your lips."

I was going to murder him.

I lunged, but I was so weak it felt like I had barely moved, barely blinked.

"Ah-ah..." Petrov held up a finger. "Remember who the real enemy is."

The real enemy.

Andi?

No. Yes. My mind and my heart were at war with one another. I felt like I was missing something — but I had no idea what.

"She betrayed you... and it's been two days. Your family

has yet to come for you. I bet they're in on it too. In fact, they are. Aren't they, Sergio?"

"No." I shook my head. "They would never."

"But they did, Sergio. None of them truly care about you. They hate you. They left you for dead. Andi despises you. Even if they do come for you, it will be pointless because they are the enemy, aren't they?"

I nodded. Why was I nodding?

"Very good." He clapped. "I think you've earned a respite from the fire."

A knock sounded at the door, and then a loud blast followed from a fire alarm.

"Boss..." Someone else entered the room. "...they're here."

"Well..." Petrov rubbed his hands together. "...I do hate to miss this, but in case things go badly, I'll just be off the premises. Have fun, Sergio, and it really has been a pleasure. Be sure to say goodbye to my daughter before you shoot her in the heart."

I was angry — so angry — but I didn't know who I was angry with, myself? Andi? Nixon? Tex?

My eyes couldn't focus. I rubbed them then realized my hands were no longer restrained.

I glanced down. My feet were free. When had that happened?

With a grimace, I ripped the IV from my arm and tried to stand. My legs were wobbly, but at least I was able to move a foot before needing to take a break. I was defenseless. Frantic, I held my head in my hands and looked down. Two guns were near my feet.

Why would they leave guns?

I'm going to kill them all.

Had I said that?

Had I meant it?

Kill who? And why?

Andi… she was why I was here. She'd done this to me, hadn't she? I just wanted to lie down, to rest.

Gunshots sounded, and then more followed. I heard screaming, and then an honest-to-God explosion erupted.

I could feel the heat from the bomb as if it was right in front of me. What the hell was going on!

I fell to my knees and covered my head as pieces of debris flew past the door and into the room.

Everything fell silent except for the water that was now pouring from the sprinkler system in the house.

The cold felt so good I didn't even think. I tilted my head back and opened my mouth. My entire body shuddered as water coated me from head to toe.

"Got him," a faint voice called.

I looked up. Andi was walking toward me. Without thinking, I reached for the gun at my feet and pointed it at her.

She dropped her gun to the ground. "Sergio, it's me… It's fine… See? I put my gun down."

Nixon stepped into the room; his gun was drawn too. I was supposed to pull the trigger, right? She was the enemy.

"You," I said hoarsely, "betrayed me."

"No." Tears filled her eyes.

Why was she crying?

"I didn't. I swear, Sergio. I love you."

"No." I shook the gun. "No."

"Andi." Nixon reached slowly for her; blood trickled down his arm. Had he been shot? "He's not in his right mind."

"Stop!" I yelled at both of them, pointing the gun at Nixon then back at her.

Another figure stepped into the room. Phoenix. He eyed the gun then stepped around Nixon, shielding him with his body.

"Oh, that's rich," I spat. "Protect him? He was in on it. You all were!"

The words coming out of my mouth confused me; I

believed them, but a part of my consciousness told me I was wrong — they were wrong.

"Sergio…" Andi stepped closer. "…you've been brainwashed."

I slowly lowered the gun, but when she got closer, I panicked; rage flew out of me. I pointed it at her head and pressed my finger against the trigger. "You. Betrayed. Me."

"No." Bruises covered the side of her face.

Who did that? Who hurt her? Was I going to hurt her?

"Screw this." Nixon pushed Phoenix out of the way and pointed his gun in my direction; my reflexes were too slow. Two gunshots.

One went directly into my shoulder; the gun dropped out of my hand.

The next shot hit me in the thigh.

I crumpled to the ground and closed my eyes.

CHAPTER THIRTY-FIVE

Andi

"NIXON!" I YELLED HIS NAME, BUT he still shot Sergio. I was terrified he would kill him, but he didn't. Both were good shots, but the bleeding…

It wasn't stopping.

"He's severely dehydrated," Phoenix said at my side, dropping to his knees. "We need to get him to the hospital now."

"No hospitals!" Nixon roared.

"Then your cousin's going to die!" Phoenix yelled back. "Look!" The bandage on Sergio's other shoulder was turning a weird yellow-orange-green color. Phoenix pulled it back. It looked septic. No doubt about it. I could only imagine what they'd done to him.

Our infiltration had been quick — thanks to Frank. He didn't want anyone injured, so he took a chance, a big chance that Sergio would either be on a second-level floor or in a basement.

We bombed the entry to the house.

Then used tear gas to fight our way in. There were around thirty men altogether, but most of them weren't prepared for the gas; we had masks on, so picking them off was easy.

Finding Sergio was hard.

Until I saw Petrov rush out of one of the upstairs rooms just as I was clearing the hall.

Coward was probably halfway to Seattle by now.

"Help me get him up." Nixon gripped Sergio by the shoulders.

My husband let out a pitiful moan.

Tears rushed down my face as Tex hurried into the room.

It didn't take us long to clear the house and put Sergio in one of the waiting cars down the street. I held his head in my lap and cried.

He didn't look so perfect anymore.

His lips were cracked and dry, his face had bruises covering it, and he was bleeding — everywhere.

"Call ahead." Nixon tossed the phone at Mil. "Make sure Stephen's working the shift today. If not, get him in the hospital now!"

"Stephen?" I repeated.

"Surgeon. Doctor. De Lange." That was the only explanation Chase gave as we drove the rest of the way to the hospital.

A man was waiting outside with a gurney and a team.

When the door opened, he cursed then started firing off orders to everyone around him.

Sergio was basically tossed onto the gurney. With a moan, he fluttered open his eyes. "I'm a matsh!" he slurred. "Tell Andi. Tell her if I'm a matsh, they have to do the surgery before I die."

I froze. "Is he delirious?"

They were still strapping him in when Tex came to my side. "He had us tested. All of us, the entire family. Would have tested dogs and goldfish if that's what it took."

"What?" I gripped Sergio's bloody hand. "What do you mean?"

Tex turned his blue eyes on me. "To see if you were a match. He wanted to donate his bone marrow, but to do that type of surgery now, or hell, even a week from now?"

I nodded in understanding.

Sergio was willing to give his life for mine.

But it wasn't his call to make, not when my time was so short, not when I knew he had so much more to give.

"No." I gripped his hand tighter as Nixon and Phoenix stood over the gurney telling Stephen what happened.

"Drive-by shooting." Nixon ran his hands through his hair. "He was hit in the shoulder a few days ago at the shooting range then was out going for a walk to clear his head and was shot twice."

Stephen nodded, while the rest of the nurses didn't blink an eye.

Gunshot wounds were always investigated in hospitals. I'd always been the type of person that frowned at law enforcement or government officials being in the pocket of organized crime.

But now? With Sergio's life at stake?

I prayed to God that Nixon had sent the police chief a Christmas goose.

"Hold him!" Stephen pushed Sergio down on the gurney as Sergio's body started convulsing; blood soaked the inside of his leg. "Damn it!"

The doctor didn't need to tell me what I was seeing. An artery had been hit, and the seizure was making it worse. I closed my eyes. I couldn't watch, didn't trust myself not to fall to my knees and cry.

"It was supposed to be me," I whispered. "Not him."

CHAPTER THIRTY-SIX

Sergio

THE FLUORESCENT LIGHTS BURNED MY EYES. I blinked them rapidly — thinking it would make the stinging go away, but it only made everything worse. The pain was indescribable, like someone had broken my body in half, repaired it, then repeated the process.

"He's not going to make it."

I recognized the voice. It was Nixon's. Why the hell was Nixon there? Wasn't he dead? No wait. That was me. I'd taken that bullet.

Memories of the past few days flashed across my line of vision, causing a searing headache to build at my temples.

The fight.

The gunshots.

The agreement.

My wife.

Tears burned the back of my eyes.

Wife…

"I'll do it. I'm a match." I gripped her hand firmly in

mine.

"You'll die," Tex whispered. "Your body… it's too weak from everything else."

"We're running out of time!" I screamed, my voice hoarse, eyes wide frantic. "Do it now!"

"No." She wrapped her frail arms around my neck. "No."

"Yes." I pushed her away. "If I don't — you could die. The doctor says it needs to be now, so operate."

Her eyes were sad.

Both Tex and Phoenix looked down at the blue and white tile floor, faces pale. I knew what they were thinking. I'd already lost too much blood, my kidneys were barely working, and I wanted to give her part of my life.

I knew going in I would most likely die.

But I'd do everything within my power to save her.

It's odd, when you face death every day, when you elude it, when you finally come to terms with the fact that you won't be on earth forever — that's when you think you're at peace.

I'd thought I was okay with dying.

Until I met her.

And then I was faced with someone else's death every damn day. It's harder. People don't tell you that. It's one thing to come to terms with your own mortality; it's quite another to stare down death of the one you love, knowing there is nothing in this world that will stop it.

My vision blurred again.

"He's flat lining," a voice said in the distance.

I tried to keep my eyes open. I saw white blond hair, big brown eyes, and that tender smile. I reached for it and held onto it, held onto the memory of her. The girl who'd changed my world from darkness to light.

The girl I never wanted.

But desperately needed.

"Tell her I'll love her…" I didn't recognize my own gravelly voice. "…forever."

With a gasp, I felt my heart stutter to a stop.

Blackness overtook me just as a searing pain hit me square in the chest.

CHAPTER THIRTY-SEVEN

Andi

HE'D FLAT-LINED TWICE.

Both times, I felt my own heart stop as I waited for his to start pumping again. Those seconds, those moments, were the worst I'd ever experienced in my life. Nothing would make me feel better — nothing but hearing his voice again.

"Andi…" Nixon nudged me with his arm. "…you should get some sleep. I'll watch over him."

I shook my head and stayed glued to his bedside. He'd been in surgery for eight hours. His body had gone into such shock from dehydration that he'd seized; the bullet that Nixon had put in his leg was just close enough to his main artery that when he seized, it had caused a small tear.

He'd nearly bled out.

He would have had we brought him back to the house instead of the hospital. I gripped his rough hand harder, willing him to open his eyes.

Nixon sighed and pulled out a chair. "Fine. Stay, but I'm staying too."

I shrugged. I didn't care either way.

A knock sounded at the door. Tex pushed it open halfway, peeking his head around the side before he entered. "So I have some news."

I covered a yawn with my hand and laid my head against Sergio's chest. "Good news or bad news?"

"Bad." Tex's eyes fell. "He's not a match."

Sergio groaned.

"Sergio?" I cupped his face. "Can you hear me? Open your eyes."

"Water." His voice sounded rough, like he'd swallowed sandpaper. "I need water."

I quickly lifted the cup to his lips. He drank greedily then blinked his eyes harder as if trying to focus on me. "Why aren't you in surgery?"

"Uh…" I set the water down. "…because I wasn't the one shot?"

"No." His eyebrows knit together in frustration. "I'm a match, right? Why aren't you in surgery getting my blood? Why am I alive?"

Tex cursed softly behind me. I held onto Sergio's hand tighter. "I don't know how to tell you this, Sergio, but… you're not a match."

"Yes, I am!" His voice rose an octave. "Tex, you were there, and Nixon, I told you guys to operate while they were taking me in the hospital. I said—" His eyes darted between the three of us. "I said to do it… to tell Andi I loved her. I said…" His voice died.

Nixon was instantly at Sergio's other side. "You were severely dehydrated, drugged — you technically died. Whatever you imagined happening… didn't… happen, Sergio. Tex and I were there. So were Andi, Phoenix, Frank — all of us — and you did talk about being a match, but you aren't. Tex just came in to tell us."

"But—" Sergio's face fell. "—it was real. It felt so real."

I wiped the stray tears rolling down my face. This man, his love was so incredible. I didn't deserve it. "I'm so sorry, Sergio."

"Why are *you* sorry?" He jerked his hand back. "It's my fault!" The heart monitor started going crazy. "I didn't save you!" Tears welled in his eyes. "I can't save you, damn it!"

A nurse rushed into the room. "What's going on?"

"He's upset," I said dumbly as more tears collected on my cheeks.

The nurse frowned. "Well, try to keep him calm." She inserted something into his IV and checked his vitals. "Quite a close call, Mr. Abandonato. I imagine you'll be more careful what neighborhoods you walk around in next time."

Sergio didn't miss a beat. "Right, it was foolish of me to think I was safe in that area of Chicago."

She nodded and handed him his call button. "Be sure to let me know if you need anything. The police have already been by, so for now, just rest."

When the door closed, he glanced at Nixon. "Police."

"Gunshot wounds." He shrugged. "But me and the chief go way back. His sons always wanted to attend Elite."

"Amazing," I whispered under my breath.

Tex grinned in my direction. "What's amazing is the amount of cops we have on the ledger."

Sergio's breathing had evened out.

I glanced back at him. "I'm glad you're okay."

"But you're not." His eyes focused in on my hand; he gripped my fingers tight. "And I think I pointed a gun at you."

"Thus, why Nixon shot your sorry ass," Tex said.

"Caught that." Sergio pointed at his clipboard. I handed it to him while he quickly read it. His face paled as he set it back down. "Maybe next time my cousin should aim for the less important arteries?"

"You seized." Nixon crossed his arms and sat down in his chair. "I couldn't have predicted that."

"Yeah, well..." Sergio licked his lips. "...thank you... for coming for me. I should kick your asses but then I wouldn't be here, with Andi, so... thank you."

Nixon grinned. "You think this one..." He pointed an accusing finger at me. "...would have it any other way? She was ready to bomb the house just to find you."

"I briefly recall a bomb actually going off." He squinted in my direction while Tex and Nixon muttered, "Frank," under their breaths.

Tex nodded at Nixon. "We should let them talk."

Nixon rose from his chair and followed Tex out. "Let us know if you need anything."

Sergio waited until the door closed before he turned his attention to me. His eyes were sad. I'd always heard that expression — even read about it — but never had actually experienced it.

His blue eyes were glassy like he was trying to hold tears back, his expression grim, his face pale. When he gazed at me, it was with utter hopelessness, and I hated that he'd been brought to that point.

"Chin up." I winked. "At least Nixon didn't kill you."

"Remember how you said I sucked at pep talks?" He frowned, gripping my other hand in his.

"Vaguely," I said innocently.

He cracked a smile. "Yeah, well... you're not so good yourself."

"Russians don't have feelings."

"We Italians feel all over the place. It's in our blood. We feel, we worry, we eat pasta, we drink copious amounts of wine, and we shoot things to defend our family honor."

I sighed and moved to the bed so I could lie by his side. "And what is this Italian feeling right this moment?"

Sergio let out a long sigh. "A bit helpless."

"Well, you do have a few holes in your body."

"I couldn't care less about the gunshots or the pain or

almost dying."

I knew what was coming. I even closed my eyes, thinking it would help the impact of the words.

"I'm really not a match?" he whispered, releasing my hand and rubbing his fingertips up and down my arm.

I shook my head, not trusting myself.

His hand paused. "I believed it. I seriously believed it, Andi. I thought maybe if I believed it hard enough, it would make it true."

I glanced up at him through hooded lashes. "Sergio, you can't save the world."

"I don't want to save the world — I just want to save you."

I pressed my palm against his chest. I could feel the heat of his body through the hospital gown, his heartbeat steady.

"Do you think you can miss people? Even when you die?" I blurted. "Because I can't imagine not missing you."

"Andi—" Sergio pressed a kiss to my forehead. "—it's only over when it's over, right? Until then, you fight, and I'll fight right alongside you."

"A lot of good that will do me. You're basically handicapped. "I winked.

He chuckled low in his throat and ran his fingers through my hair.

"Italy?"

"Hmm?"

"I'm glad we didn't blow you up."

"You really know how to romance a man," he teased.

I rolled my eyes. "Please, your idea of romance is using family members as target practice then washing down the blood with a large glass of wine."

"Look who's talking, bloodthirsty little Russian."

I smiled against his chest. My cheek pressed against him, just wishing the moment would last forever. "You should sleep."

He wrapped his arms around my body. "Only if you stay with me."

"Where else would I go?"

He tensed.

I tensed right along with him.

Because we both knew… eventually, I would go – and neither of us could stop it.

CHAPTER THIRTY-EIGHT

Sergio

I WOKE UP IN A COLD SWEAT. Probably one of the worst ways to wake up, in a pool of water that came from your body. I shuddered then tried to nudge Andi awake so she could at least shower.

"Andi," I whispered, "wake up."

She didn't move.

"Andi?"

Still no movement. I felt for a pulse, like a complete psycho. Her heart was beating, but it wasn't strong.

I hit my call button twice, three times. A nurse came walking in like she had all the time in the world.

"My wife!" I yelled. "She's — something's wrong! She has leukemia, and she's not waking up."

The nurse took Andi's pulse.

I gritted my teeth, wanting to yell that I'd already done that.

She nodded then felt Andi's forehead. "She's burning up. Has she been sick recently?"

What was I supposed to say? *"No, but she did survive an explosion and a fun day of being held at gunpoint, so it wouldn't surprise me if her immunity is a bit low."*

"No," I lied. "She's been just fine, other than the dizzy spells."

The nurse pressed a button on the side of my bed; two more nurses walked in followed by another nurse with a gurney. "Wait, where are you taking her?"

"Mr. Abandonato, you've been through a lot in the past day. Try to stay calm. We're putting her in her own room, and I'll be contacting the doctor on call. She's fine, she's breathing, she's okay, but for now, I need you to concentrate on getting well."

"But—"

"—for your wife," the nurse said.

I lay back down and frowned when I realized, it wasn't me sweating. It was Andi.

We were in a pool of her sweat. Not mine.

"Just try to stay calm." The nurse patted my hand. If one more person gave me that pitiful look, I was going to lose my shit.

Thankfully, Nixon had chosen that perfect moment to walk in. "What the hell's going on?"

"It's Andi." My voice cracked. "I think something's wrong."

I lifted my hands in the air to brace my head, but they were shaking so bad I realized it wouldn't do me any good.

"Serg…" Nixon was immediately at my bedside. "…I'll go with her, alright? Just try not to think of the worst. I'll send someone to sit with you."

"I'm not an invalid."

"No..." Nixon let out a choke of laughter. "…but I know you. The minute she's out of here you're going to try to get out of bed and follow. Stay. She needs you to heal, alright?"

I said nothing.

"Serg… promise me."

I gave him a curt nod.

Two hours later, and I still hadn't heard from Nixon or from the nurse. I was ready to lose my mind.

Things got progressively worse when Phoenix, Chase, and Tex all showed up as reinforcements.

"Housekeeping…" Chase said in a high-pitched voice. "You want me fluff pillow?"

I chucked my pillow at the door just as he waltzed in with the coffee and food he'd promised everyone. I wasn't allowed coffee on account my ass had been so dehydrated, but I did want food — anything to take my mind off Andi being in another room. Andi waking up without me. Andi thinking I wasn't there.

"Shit." I pounded the bed with my fist; my eyes filled with tears again. I'd never been an overly emotional guy — in fact, I'm pretty sure every single member of my family assumed I'd up and shot myself in the heart to keep from feeling any sort of emotion.

But with Andi? I found myself constantly on the verge of tears, always wondering if that last kiss would be the last, and trying to selfishly hold onto it as long as humanly possible.

"You look like hell..." Chase placed a small bag on my tray. "…which is why I brought you two muffins, muffin."

"Call me muffin again."

Tex made his way over to the bed and pulled out a chair. "Do it, Chase. I wanna see how fast he can move with three bullet wounds."

I flipped them both off.

Phoenix was on the phone talking quietly in the corner. I nodded in his direction. "What's with him?"

"Phoenix is having a hell of a time telling his wife that it's not okay for her to participate in sparring with Trace while pregnant." Chase took a giant bite out of his own muffin and shrugged. "I say good luck with that."

Phoenix ended the phone call and gripped the cell in his hand, glaring at all three of us like it was our fault he couldn't control his wife.

"Trace will go easy on her," I said helpfully. "She's not going to kick her or anything. The girls aren't stupid, and you know Bee, she has too much energy. You tell her no, she'll just keep asking until you say yes."

Phoenix pinched the bridge of his nose. "Sometimes I forget how young she is… and immature."

Tex snorted. "I don't. That's my sister you're screwing."

"Get over it," Phoenix snapped then sighed. "Sorry, Tex, not your fault. I'm just worried about her."

"That makes you a good husband," Chase piped up. "Worry."

"I hate worry," I grumbled, the muffin suddenly going dry in my throat.

The guys gave me that look — the same look I was sure doctors gave their patients just before they were about to tell them there was nothing they could do. It sucked balls.

The door to my room opened. I straightened a bit, hoping it was the nurse. I was pleasantly surprised when it was Andi who walked in, though she was connected to an IV.

"Hey." She gave me a small smile and cleared her throat, arching her eyebrows at each of the guys.

"Uh…" Tex scratched his head and stood. "…I'll just go… to the bathroom."

"Me too." Phoenix followed him.

Chase remained.

Andi cleared her throat again.

Chase leveled her with a glare. "What you gonna do? Drop kick my ass?"

I sighed. "Chase, just go. She'll beat you up later."

He stood, albeit slowly, and patted me on the leg then walked out of the room.

"How are you?" I blurted.

Andi shrugged. Her face was pale; her smile a bit weak. Her bruising looked like shit around her face, but she was still beautiful to me. Always beautiful.

I patted the bed.

She took a seat, rolling the IV with her. "I need blood transfusions three times a week."

"Okay," I said slowly. "I'm assuming that's good, right?"

She looked down at the ground. "No… I mean it sounds good, right? Fresh blood!" Her shoulders sagged. "But typically, in a case like mine it just means the end is—" She swallowed. "—close."

I reached for her hand. She pulled away. "You don't have to go through this with me, Sergio. If you want me to leave, if it's too hard, I would understand." Her eyes filled with tears. "I swear to you, I'd get it if you want me to just stay at the hospital until the end."

"Hell no!" I yelled, gripping her hand, pulling her as close as I could without hurting her. "I'm with you until the end, whatever that means for us. I'm here."

She nodded. A tear fell down her cheek. "They said I can stay here, or we can do hospice, and when I heard the word hospice I just freaked. I mean, I thought I had come to this place where my heart and my head were one. But now? Now it just sucks, Sergio. And I want to stay positive. I want to be happy. For you I want to be those things, but I need at least an hour where you let me cry."

My heart shattered.

"Please," she pleaded. "I can be strong the rest of the time. I can be optimistic. I can be happy — because honestly, that's how I've always been, but I think… I think I need to grieve first. I need to grieve over us. I need to grieve over what should have been — what could have been."

My eyes were so blurred with tears I couldn't make out her small form. "Come here," I whispered.

She burst into tears and crawled into me, her tiny body

sitting halfway across my body as I held her tightly.

"I love you, you know." She sobbed into my chest. "You're the best friend I've ever had."

"You're my best friend too." My voice cracked. I needed to be strong for her; this was not the time for me to cry. I'd do plenty of that, I imagined, in my future. But for now... I was going to be her rock. "I've never had one of those before. Does this mean we get to exchange bracelets or something?"

Her sob turned into a laugh. "Yeah, I'll be sure to get one made."

"You do that." I squeezed her tight and kissed her head. "Cry as hard and as long as you want, and when you're done, if you have to cry some more, that's okay."

She took my words to heart, sobbing her little heart out, while I hugged her, kissed her face, squeezed her hands, and told myself not to break.

When she quieted down about a half-hour later, I set her back and looked at her tear-stained face.

"I was your punishment." She sniffled.

"Wrong." I tilted her chin up. "You were my gift."

CHAPTER THIRTY-NINE

Sergio

COMING HOME FROM THE HOSPITAL WAS bittersweet. Damn, I was using that word a lot lately. After spending a week there, I was more than ready to be home — and so was Andi.

She was getting weaker by the day.

Watching someone you love deteriorate before your very eyes was indescribable. I was getting healthier; she was getting sicker. And there was nothing I could do to stop the clock; it seemed each minute I took in a hearty breath I noticed hers was more labored. She'd done three transfusions over the last week, and though she said they'd helped, I knew they'd only done so much.

"Home!" Andi spread out her hands then clung to me to keep from falling. Her balance had been seriously suffering, and I knew it would only get worse.

I had to blink back tears. Soon my house would be silent again — no more baseball bats and pans, no more arguing, yelling, fighting.

I pushed the morose thoughts away just as the doorbell

rang.

Frowning, I set Andi down on the stairway and walked over to answer the door.

"Do you have Cheetos?" Bee asked, hands on hips, then pushed past me. "Phoenix promised you'd have Cheetos." She walked briskly by and gave Andi a high five on the way to the kitchen.

"Sorry." Phoenix moved into the doorway. "She's on a Cheetos kick. God help me if this pregnancy has her eating every color of the rainbow. You know how I feel about color," he joked. Once upon a time he refused to eat anything that wasn't a leafy green — long story.

He pushed past me, carrying two duffel bags. "My old room, okay?"

"Okay?" I repeated. "For what?"

"Aw," Tex's low voice crooned, "did you really think you would get rid of us so easy? Dibs on the bigger room. Mo wants the attached marble bathroom!"

Tex shoved past me. Mo kissed me on the cheek and followed.

Nixon and Trace were next. Bags in hand. Trace winked and skipped after the rest of the group while Nixon shrugged. "We're family. Family sticks together."

Chase and Mil drove up and parked directly in front of the door. Mil was yelling at Chase for driving too fast, and Frank was climbing out of the back seat, looking like he was going to puke.

"Frank too?" I frowned.

"Frank gets lonely!" Chase yelled up at me. "Imagine that? He actually likes having us around."

Frank rolled his eyes and grabbed his bag from the car. "I do love getting talked about as if I don't exist."

I couldn't hold in my smile. While the rest of the gang had just one duffel bag, Frank had a duffel bag, a garment bag, a hat, and a cane. A man after my own heart; even worse, he wore scarves. He probably had a closet that made mine look small and cheap.

Frank pointed up toward the house. "I'll just take the room farthest away from my granddaughter."

"Good idea," I choked.

Once everyone was in the house, I went back to grab Andi, only to find her missing.

Laughter echoed out of the kitchen. I followed it.

Wine was open. Lots and lots of wine.

And Andi was talking animatedly about our honeymoon list. Oh shit. She actually had it pulled out.

"We went from thirteen to—"

"Andi." I coughed and shook my head.

"Damn," Chase grabbed the Cheetos from Bee. "The story was just getting good."

The doorbell rang again. "What the hell?"

Nixon moved past me. "It's probably Ax and Ames, the last of the crew. I'll get it."

Sure enough, Ax and Amy walked into the kitchen.

I looked around and fought to keep my emotions from getting the best of me.

It was suddenly so loud in that house that I couldn't even hear myself think. Mil and Chase were arguing. Typical. Mo was punching Tex in the shoulder repeatedly. Andi was singing the Russian national anthem. Frank was finding more wine — smart man. Nixon and Trace were kissing, moving on, and Ax and Amy were opening the fridge. Phoenix was trying to pry the chips away from Bee, and Chase was reaching past Mil to grab them.

"So," Andi said loudly, "you guys are all staying the night or what?"

The room fell silent.

"What?" She looked around. "Did you not like my rendition of Mother Russia?"

Chase bit down on a Cheeto. "Doesn't matter how loud

you sing it, honey. You're Italian now."

"Oh really?" Andi's face lit up. "How do you figure?"

"You fight like hell." Tex nodded in appreciation. "Married one of our men… risked your life to save his. I'd say you're more Italian than Russian."

Andi beamed. "Does that mean I have to drink wine now?"

"You and your vodka," I muttered.

"Admit it." Chase chuckled. "You scrunch up your nose at wine to piss Sergio off."

Andi grinned. "Guilty."

"Real mature, Andi." I wrapped my arms around her from behind and set my chin on her head.

"So…" Andi shrugged. "…you guys are here for a while then?"

Thank God, she didn't say *the end*.

"Yup." Nixon nodded. "Now what's for dinner?"

All eyes fell to Chase.

"Damn it." Chase slammed his hand onto the counter. "I'm not your bitch. You can't make me cook every night!"

Mil whispered something in his ear.

Chase's grin grew to epic proportions. "Homemade lasagna okay?"

Phoenix groaned. "I don't even want to know what my sister just uttered."

"Nope." Chase bit down on his lip and started swiveling his hips. "But just so you know. We're trying to get pregnant… and we're trying really, really, really hard."

"Say hard again," Tex joked.

"Hard," Chase whispered, this time in Phoenix's ear.

Phoenix raised his hand to smack Chase away, but Nixon intervened. "So lasagna."

"Buzzkill," Chase accused.

Frank moved to the middle of the room. "There is not enough wine."

"What?" I frowned. "I have an entire cellar."

Fighting erupted again. I could have sworn I saw Chase pull out a gun on Phoenix. I turned to Frank and nodded. "I'll make some calls."

"Good man." He patted my shoulder. "Good man."

CHAPTER FORTY

Andi

CHASE WAS AN EXCELLENT COOK. IF I hadn't already been dying, his homemade lasagna would have seriously done me in. The room was buzzing with conversation and laughter – it felt like a real family. One I was a part of.

Frank had already gone upstairs for the evening. Apparently, his being old meant he was not only allowed his own bottle of wine during dinner – but also an eight o'clock bed time.

Bee yawned and put her head on Phoenix. "Bed?"

"It's eight," Chase pointed out.

Mil whispered something else in his ear.

He gripped her by the butt and heaved her over his shoulder. "Which I've always said is the perfect time to hit the sack." He slapped her ass and moved out of the large dining room.

Everyone else made similar excuses. I knew what they were doing, giving me and Sergio some time together.

Sergio walked over to me and slid our honeymoon list

across the table. "Pick one."

"Only one?" I jutted out my lower lip. "How about two?"

His blue eyes narrowed as a few pieces of long hair fell across his face. I loved that he was growing it out; it made him look even more like the duke from my romance novels. "Fine, two."

"So I say we work on number four out of our thirteen? And…" I tapped my chin. "…this one."

His eyebrows shot up. "You've really never done that?"

"Have you?" I countered.

"If I say yes, will you judge me?"

"Absolutely."

"In my defense, I wanted to see what all the fuss was about." He crossed his arms.

"Oh really?"

He swore. "Fine, up you go."

He walked over to my chair and lifted me into his arms, carrying me effortlessly into his giant media room. It wasn't just a theatre room. It was like an actual theatre, with games lining the walls, movie posters, a full bar, and a hot tub.

Semi-ridiculous. Then again, I imagined he had enough money that it had just seemed practical. Why party outside the house when you can have the party inside?

"Pick your poison." He sat me on the leather couch and walked over to the bar.

"Hmm… in my fantasies, all the bartenders are shirtless."

Without arguing he peeled the shirt off his body and braced his hands against the counter. "Better?"

"Hmm…" I rubbed my lips together. "…flex."

He glared.

"Flex!" I shouted. "It's part of the list."

"The hell it is," he grumbled then flexed.

"I really like your abs." I tilted my head. "They're tight. How do they get so tight? And your ass…" I fanned my face. "C'mon, turn around and bend over."

"I'm a person, Andi." He slammed his fist onto the counter, his lips curving into a gorgeous; *I may need to take a cold shower* smile. "Drink?"

"Sprite," I decided. "You really won't bend over?"

He ignored my plea and made my drink then walked over to the couch and set it in my cup holder. His naked chest brushed my fingers as he leaned over and then kissed me on the head. "So, ready to bang out that list?"

"Bang." I laughed. "Good one."

"I thought so." He lifted me into the air, sat down, then placed me on top of him. "*Frozen* singalong — and then we work on number four."

"Is it wrong to have sex after *Frozen?*" I grimaced.

Sergio shrugged. "Just don't start singing that you want to want to build a snowman while we're in the middle of it, and we'll be good."

"I don't know that song." I frowned.

"Oh…" Sergio clicked on the giant TV. "…believe me, you will."

I cried.

It was pathetic. But the whole *sister saving her sister* thing really did me in. Probably because I knew I'd never actually meet my real sister. I'd heard about her, known she existed, but would never know that type of affection. Feeling sorry for myself was stupid, but I was still a bit bummed about it.

"So…" Sergio turned off the TV. "…thoughts?"

"I suddenly want to build a snowman."

"Told you so."

The room was quiet. I felt relaxed and surprisingly not dizzy, probably because I was sitting down.

Sergio shifted me on his lap so that I was facing him. "What are you thinking?"

"I'm thinking…" I ran my hand up and down his abs. "…that I'd really like you to kiss me."

"I can do that."

"And after you kiss me at least four times, I think you should take my clothes off."

Sergio's mouth met mine. He whispered against my lips, "Consider it done."

"And…" I pressed my finger to his mouth. "…I want you to go really, really, really slow."

"Uh-huh."

"And then fast."

He laughed. "Okay."

"And then slow again."

His lips lingered over mine. "How about you just let me do what I do best?"

"And what's that?"

"Love you, of course."

CHAPTER FORTY-ONE

Sergio

I CARRIED ANDI UP TO OUR BEDROOM and silently hoped that the surprise I'd planned for her wouldn't be ruined. I'd never taken her on a honeymoon, and she was right. She deserved one.

So I brought the honeymoon to her.

I carefully opened the door and set her on her feet.

Andi covered her mouth with her hands then spoke between her fingers. "What did you do?"

"Well, someone..." I grabbed her hand and led her through the room. "...said I would have taken her to Africa." A few stuffed lions and zebras lined one side of the room. "And then she said I would take her to China." Chinese food was on the table with perfect little origami creations; chopsticks were placed across both plates.

She nodded, tears welling in her eyes.

"But she was wrong."

"What?" Andi wiped at a few spraystray tears and turned. "She was?"

"Yup." I turned her around to face the other side of the room. Her back was to me. I wrapped my arms around her and whispered, "I wouldn't have stopped at Africa or China. I would have taken her to London." A small Ferris wheel was outside, facing the window. "It's not the London Eye but… it will have to do."

Andi didn't say anything. So I walked her closer to the window and pulled the curtains. "But who stops at London?" I whispered, my ears grazing her ear, my tongue trailing the soft skin. "Especially when France is so close." A miniature version of a lit-up Eiffel tower stood next to the Ferris wheel.

"And then…" I turned her back around to face me as I pulled a small postcard out of my pocket. "…when all was said and done, I would have taken you home."

I handed her the postcard of the Kremlin.

Andi's hands shook as she took it, her eyes sad. "I've never been."

"Well, it was a bit hard to find a miniature version of the Kremlin. Believe me, I tried, so I figured a postcard would work just as well."

She frowned. "How do you figure?"

I grabbed the pen from my back pocket. "Because you can write it as if you were there and send it to whomever you want."

"But if I've never been—"

"The colors…" I twirled her around to face the window. "…I've heard are like fireworks…" I checked my watch and sighed in relief as the first blue firework went off. "…constantly changing before your very eyes." Another firework, this one green. "The building itself looks magical, almost unreal, but it's the color of the building that creates an atmosphere of pure beauty." More fireworks filled the sky above the house.

Andi covered her mouth with her hands.

"And just when you think you've stared long enough,

just when you think you understand the beauty it represents…" The fireworks went crazy; it looked like hundreds of them were going off. "…it surprises you again."

"It's beautiful," she whispered in reverence.

Slowly, I let her go.

When she turned to face me, I was already on my knees.

Andi covered her mouth with her hands.

"I never asked." My voice trembled. "I never had the honor of asking you to be my wife." I reached into my pocket and pulled out a three-karat princess-cut diamond ring. "And I wondered, if you felt as cheated as I did, that we never had this moment."

Tears poured down her face.

"So Andi…" I held up the ring higher. "…will you do me the greatest honor of my life – and be my wife?"

"Yes!" She didn't even grab the ring but grabbed me instead, kissing me so hard on the mouth that I stumbled backward. "I love you."

Laughing, I swung her around. "I love you too."

I swung her around again, knowing she liked more than one twirl, and placed the ring on her finger. "So, did you really want to work on number four now, or did you want to ride the Ferris wheel?"

"The Ferris wheel can wait." She pulled her shirt over her head and tossed it at my face. "I can't."

CHAPTER FORTY-TWO

Sergio

I THINK, LOOKING BACK AT THIS MOMENT, I would always struggle with fully describing the way my heart hammered against my chest, the electric feeling of my hands as they roamed freely across her body.

How do you describe something that's indescribable? You don't. You can't. It's impossible. And I knew, five years from now – or ten, maybe twenty – I'd still be walking around with a smile on my face when I recalled the moment she was mine – the moments I owned her, and she owned me, the moments our hearts were one, our souls united.

"Sergio..."

Her shirt went flying, her bra followed, her jeans. I'd never seen someone undress so fast and was slightly humiliated that I couldn't keep up, that I wanted her to go slow so I could savor every second my eyes were allowed the pleasure to gaze upon her beauty.

"...make love to me. Make it good."

"I can make it good," I whispered. "But you'll have to

forgive me."

She frowned.

"Forgive me..." I smiled. "...if I stand here a moment longer than I should — because I feel like you deserve to be stared at. Hell, you deserve to be worshipped, but I'm not that patient of a man, so at least give me this — one minute, sixty seconds — give me that, and I'll make love to you. I'll make it so good you never forget."

"Even in my death."

"In life or death." I shook my head and licked my lips as I took a cautious step toward her. "You'll never forget this — or forget us. I swear it."

She nodded, her eyes pooling with tears again.

I reached out and touched her arm, my hand slowly caressing up toward her shoulder. I could never understand how her skin could be so soft. "Every touch feels like the first."

Her eyes closed. "It does... it really does."

"I think... I'll remember this moment..." I sighed. "...forever."

Andi pulled back, then twirled once, twice, and winked. "Since it's forever, I figured I better make it good."

"It's a two-twirl moment," I agreed.

She giggled. "I thought so."

"Come here." I held out my hands.

Tentatively, she walked toward me, naked, her perky breasts like a siren call, her curvy body my ultimate demise.

"This," I said once she reached me and I was able to press a kiss against her hot lips, "this is what people wait for."

"It's fair." Her forehead touched mine.

"What?"

She shrugged and then wrapped her tiny arms around my neck. "I've been saying it over and over again. How is it fair that I only get you for a few short weeks, a month, maybe two?" She sighed against my mouth. "But in this moment, right now, I can honestly say it's fair."

"Yeah?" I croaked. "Why's that?"

"Because we get to live... we get to love... together. We get this." She pressed her palm against my chest. "Regardless of the journey, of how hard it was, of how hard it is or how short we— The time — we still had it — and that, my friend, is a beautiful ending."

"I've always loved the end." I fought to keep my tears back. For her, I smiled when I wanted to cry.

"They're my favorite too," Andi agreed, her lips teasing mine. "Because you know, after everything, they'll be okay."

I nodded. "They'll be okay."

"You will be." Andi cupped my face. "You know that, right?"

"No," I blurted. "But for you... I'll try."

She crushed her mouth against mine, and I savored it. I lived for that feeling right there where everything was right in the world, where sex was making love, and making love to my wife, Andi, was my destiny, my purpose — the reason I'd been spared.

The reason I hadn't been killed up until this point...

Was in order to love her.

Amazing, I'd always wanted a higher purpose. I'd had no idea it would be my wife.

Yet it was.

"I love you..." I choked. "...so damn much."

She wrapped her legs around me as I walked us back toward the bed. The back of my knees touched the mattress. She jumped down and crawled on top of me as I scooted up on my elbows.

"Show me..." She winked. "...just how much."

"Pretty sure I just did." I pointed around the room.

She burst out laughing. "Aw, Italy, you can do so much better."

"I can." I gripped her hips and tossed her next to me. "Wanna see?"

Andi laughed as I made quick work of stripping my body of the rest of my clothes.

I started at her foot.

It made sense.

To start at the bottom, work my way up.

She tried to kick me. I pulled her leg tighter. "Hey now, let me do my job."

"But it tickles."

"Good." I kissed the inside of her ankle. "Shh… you're going to wake up the animals."

"What?" Andi squealed. "They're stuffed!"

"Shh, they'll hear you!" My lips met the inside of her knee.

The covers bunched up in her hands as her head thrust back. "You're the devil. That really, really tickles."

"Andi, Andi, Andi…" I licked the inside of her thigh. "…you taste so soft."

"Mmm…" Her body arched.

My mouth inched higher.

Every muscle tensed.

"Shh..." I blew across her skin. "Enjoy this. I know I am."

"Sergio," she panted, "hurry up before I kill you."

"Please, I hid all the knives." My mouth licked at her core.

A yelp and then, "You're evil."

"I'm your husband." I sucked until she squirmed. "Your fault."

No more words, just panting and cursing.

Andi fisted my hair into her hands and tugged my head up then slammed her mouth against mine.

I rolled onto my back as she straddled me. "You were going too slow."

"Oh?" I choked out a laugh then stopped when she slowly lowered herself onto my body, inch by aggravating inch.

"Who's laughing now?"

I lifted her up, then slowly down. "Not me."

She gasped. "Me either."

"Faster."

I tsked. "Slower."

"Damn you, Sergio!"

"Let me enjoy this." I rolled my hips.

She cursed again, her nails making permanent marks on my chest as she pushed against me, her way of trying to go faster.

"You feel amazing." Her eyes closed.

I moved faster. She kept my same tempo and then threw her head back, her hair flying across her shoulders, whipping my hands where they were placed against her skin, causing such an erotic sensation and vision I had to grit my teeth to keep from finishing.

"Let go," I said through clenched teeth.

"If I let go…" She blinked open her eyes.

And I knew the truth; it was just another moment passed, another second closer to the end, which is why she wanted fast. Because she wouldn't have to think. With a growl, I pulled out and tossed her onto her stomach and covered her with my body, with my warmth, my strength. I gripped her hands and slowly inched into her then moved.

Seconds went by.

Minutes.

Hours?

Who knew?

It was a moment that didn't need definition, that just was — perfection as I felt her body tense then ease under mine, as I followed and experienced such completion at our joining that I knew I could follow her into heaven and know—

—I'd done good.

I'd done good by her.

By me.

And I'd accomplished what I'd been set on Earth to do. Love Andi.

CHAPTER FORTY-THREE

Andi

"DUDE!" TEX STOOD FROM THE TABLE and stretched. "You look like you got some last night. Well done, Andi. Always get yours, that's what I say."

"Oh is it?" Mo countered from her end of the table. "Is that what you always say, baby?"

"I sense a fight." I held up my hands. "Don't put me in the middle of your drama. I'm too small."

"Please." Sergio snorted and met us with a bowl of popcorn. "You pack a punch and stole Tex's gun right out of his hands."

"Oh?" Mo's eyebrows shot up. "Baby, you didn't tell me that. Had something in your eye, did ya?"

Tex shot me a glare. "Whatever happened to you being my bitch, and I'm your bro, and you don't go blabbing to my wife?"

"Oh, I'm sorry." Sergio grinned and tossed a piece of popcorn into his mouth. "I was unaware of the rules."

"Rules." Mo flashed a smile. "Who likes those?"

"Nixon." Trace waltzed into the room. "Dibs on popcorn — oh, you know what would be great?"

All eyes fell to her. For the past week, since my return from the hospital Trace had been eating peanut butter like it was going out of style and chomping down on every piece of fruit in the house; she was constantly eating, and I do mean constantly. It was weird, though a bit hilarious, considering Sergio had finally sent his housekeeper out to get groceries on account that Trace and Bee had eaten everyone out of—

"Holy crap!" I jumped out of my chair and covered my mouth with my hands. "Trace!"

She frowned, reaching a fist into the popcorn and stuffing it into her mouth.

I shook my head. "You're pregnant."

She paled.

Tex burst out laughing. "Nixon, you dirty dog…"

"Huh?" Nixon walked into the kitchen, a gun in hand

Seriously, did the guy ever turn it off? Or put it away? Probably why Trace was preggers. I smirked at my own joke.

"Why am I dirty?"

"Trace!" Mo pointed an accusing finger in Trace's direction. "You got your wife pregnant. Well done, evil twin. Well done."

Nixon's face broke out into a smile. "Oh…" He winked at Tex. "…that."

Popcorn fell out of Trace's hand as she started counting on her fingers.

"Six weeks," Nixon said, looking bored.

Trace's eyes widened.

Nixon shrugged. "What? I know your cycle better than you do. You're about six weeks along. I was waiting for you to say something, thought maybe you didn't know." His grin was shameless. "Apparently, someone's been distracted."

Trace launched herself at Nixon, wrapping her arms around his neck. "Why didn't you tell me?"

Nixon kissed her across the mouth. "I honestly thought you were just waiting to tell me until you were further along — until you knew. Don't girls do that?"

"No…" Phoenix stumbled into the room, his eyes tired. "…they tell you right away and then cause you to freak out at the exact same time they find out, making you lose sleep and wonder if your child is going to inherit the same awful tendencies to stay up ALL THE NIGHT LONG!"

"Just me?" Tex frowned. "Or did Phoenix just say 'all *the* night long'? Like he was born in the eighteen hundreds."

"Coffee," Phoenix croaked.

"Bee not sleeping well?" I guessed.

Phoenix shot me a glare. "Insomnia. Which means I don't sleep either. Which means nobody's happy."

Bee entered the kitchen humming.

"Ha, someone's happy." I pointed.

Phoenix sighed and glanced at Sergio. "Tell me you have coffee, man, or else I'm heading to Starbucks, and nobody wants to see me drive into a tree because I can't keep my eyes open."

"Same cupboard." Sergio pointed.

Phoenix mumbled a "Thank God" into the air and started making coffee.

Nixon was still kissing Trace.

"Get a room," I called.

Trace blushed and pulled away from her husband. "Sorry, I just… this is crazy, right? Me and Bee at the same time."

"Same time what?" Bee said mid-mouthful of popcorn.

"I think I'm pregnant." Trace bit down on her lower lip. "I mean I—"

"YES!" Bee jumped into the air. "I was wondering if you'd be next, though I honestly thought my brother's sperm would have found their way to Mo. Weird… must be slow swimmers."

"Now see here," Tex said in a booming voice as he stood. "My swimmers are just fine, and please, don't think about them, or talk about them, or—"

Bee waved him off. "I'll believe it when I see it."

Tex turned bright red. "You aren't seeing jack shit."

"Chill." Bee rolled her eyes. "I meant the pregnancy, bro. I don't actually want to see *it*." She scrunched up her nose. "This conversation just took a turn for the worse."

Sergio snorted. "Good thing Chase isn't here."

"Ladies, I have arrived," Chase announced from the bottom of the stairs. "Who's the siren that made the call, because I could have sworn I heard my name."

"Tex." I nodded. "He needs reassurance his swimmers aren't crap."

"Tex swims just fine." Chase nodded his head then tilted it. "Wait, are we talking swimming or…" He swallowed then grinned. "*swimming*."

"Oh, good Lord." Tex hung his head. "Trace is pregnant!"

"What?!" Chase's eyes widened. "No way! Who's the father?"

Nixon growled.

Chase inched past him and pulled Trace in for a giant hug, lifting her off the ground. "Just kidding." He kissed her cheek. "Congrats, Trace… I can't wait to be the godfather."

Nixon let out a groan.

Chase shrugged and wrapped his arm around Trace. "It only makes sense," he whispered in Trace's ear. "Go ahead. Tell him."

"Er..." Trace giggled. "…it really does, Nixon."

"Family's fun." Tex chuckled. "Don't you think, Serg?"

Sergio had been pretty quiet. I expected him to be scowling; instead, he was laughing, his face bright, happy. My stomach clenched. I wanted him to be like that forever — and I had no way of securing his happiness, except for the plan I'd put into motion, the plan I wasn't even sure he would go along with.

It was a long shot.

But it was all I had.

"Nixon…" Sergio tossed some popcorn into his mouth. "…just think how much fun it will be to have Chase as the godfather…"

"Hey…" Trace looked around the room. "…where's Mil?"

"Movie." Chase released Trace and opened his arms. "She felt like we should have a movie night to celebrate a week since Andi and Serg have been home — oh, and the fact that nobody's been shot at."

"Throw a damn parade." Frank entered the kitchen, wine glass in hand. "Sergio, a word?"

Sergio's smile fell.

Damn.

"Sure." He cleared his throat. "No problem."

"Phoenix..." Frank nodded. "…you too."

Why did it feel like the parent had just come into the room only to end all the fun?

"Let's go." Tex helped me up from my chair. "Time for the movie."

Sergio walked over to me and kissed my head. "I'll be right in. Save me a seat."

"'Kay." I gripped his hand then released it and followed Tex out, but I didn't miss Phoenix's morose expression or the look of confusion on Sergio's. I had a sneaking suspicion my plan was already getting set into motion.

Not by way of me.

But by way of Luca.

Someone who wasn't even living anymore — carrying out his wishes.

Funny, we'd soon have that in common.

CHAPTER FORTY-FOUR

Sergio

FRANK POURED EACH OF US A GLASS of wine.

We drank wine all the time—it was like water; if you weren't drinking it, you were either dead or dead. Seriously. Every other occasion called for it.

So I shouldn't have been suspicious, and I wouldn't have been — had Frank not asked Phoenix to stay as well.

Two bosses and me.

It wasn't good news.

But would it be bad? What could be worse than what I'd already experienced or what I was currently experiencing?

Frank cleared his throat and slid the wine toward me slowly. His frosted black and gray hair looked more dominant in the light, casting a glow across his sharp features. I imagined around thirty years ago he probably could have given all of us guys a run for our money in the looks and all around muscle department. But now he just had the look of the patriarch of a very old and very organized business.

He swirled the wine in his glass then took a long sip.

"Have you read your black folder?

I suppressed a groan. "No. And I don't think I will."

Phoenix tensed next to me.

I wasn't sure why.

What the hell was so important about that damn folder?

"You should," he encouraged. "Luca kept great tabs on not only you but some other key players in our… family."

"I see what you're doing." I toyed with the stem of my wine glass. "But it won't work. I'm curious but not so curious that I feel like reading about all the horrible things I've done — the horrible things I'm capable of."

"Like you should talk," Phoenix said under his breath.

I shot him a guilty look.

Phoenix scratched his head and leaned back. He looked less tired than he had a few minutes ago. "Look, it would be in your best interest to read it."

I glanced between the two of them. They'd never been on the same team. Hell, the more I thought about it, they were basically natural enemies. Phoenix had tried to rape Trace; granted, that seemed like a million lifetimes ago, but Phoenix was basically the big bad wolf, the monster, the loose cannon. Out of all of us, he's the one I'd say who was around two seconds away from losing his shit and just bombing the house because he felt like it. It made no sense.

"What's going on here?" I leaned forward. How had I missed this? The way Frank looked at Phoenix, the way Phoenix almost… cowered in Frank's presence — not that he was intimidated, but that he was uncomfortable with the weight of his own knowledge.

"Luca knew everything about everyone," Phoenix said slowly. "Everything. And Sergio… it's hard to explain, but it's almost like he took every possible scenario that could have happened in our family and planned for it."

I snorted. "What? So now he's a ghost? Freaking psychic? Controlling the family from the grave?"

Frank gulped and looked down at the table. "You know nothing, and you'll continue to be in the dark until you read the folder, the one Luca specifically left for you, about you, with instructions only you can carry out."

I met Frank's gaze, my gaze unwavering, giving nothing away. "And what if I burn it? What happens then?"

Frank licked his lips and cracked a smile. "I imagine my brother even planned for that outcome as well. His mind worked in very mysterious ways."

Phoenix tapped his fingers against the wood table. "Sergio, we still need you. That's what this is about. We need you in this family. Don't check out. Not yet."

"Yet," I repeated.

Frank's eyes were kind when he said, "She will die."

I averted my gaze. "I know."

"And when she does…" His voice was soft, reassuring. "…we will still need you, Sergio. Do you understand what I'm saying?"

I snorted. "Don't go off and shooting myself in the face? Is that what you're saying?" I shook my head. "Well, let me put your mind at ease. I would never do that. Ever. Andi would be ashamed of me if I did, and I live for that woman." My voice shook. "I'm a man because of her, and I'll be damned if I take the coward's way out because I can't live without her."

Frank stared long and hard at me, his blue eyes piercing, his body taut. "Fine," he finally said. "Good." Standing, he gave me another once-over and said again, "Read the folder, Sergio, I think you'll be pleasantly surprised… or burn it. Either way, life… it is meant to be lived, it is meant to be felt, regardless of how painful or sorrowful the journey."

I nodded and whispered, "It's not how you start."

Frank smiled softly. "Son, it's how you finish."

"A beautiful ending." I repeated what Andi and I had said.

"Yes," he agreed, "it is."

Frank walked slowly out of the room; his footsteps echoed for a good while before they disappeared, leaving just me and Phoenix at the table.

"I have to say something." Phoenix's eyes were glassy with tears. "And I'm sorry if I'm being that guy right now, but I have to say it."

"What?" I'd never in my life seen Phoenix show emotion, not really, not in the way he was showing now, like any second he was going to break down and sob all over the table. "What's wrong?"

"I've never…" He shook his head as tears filled his eyes. "…respected a man as much as I respect you, right now, in this moment."

I swallowed the knot in my throat. "Oh yeah? Why?"

"Because I see it, Sergio. I feel it. I know it. What it's like to be saved, to have someone see you for you, not just what you want people to see. But who grasps the innermost parts of your darkness and calls bullshit on your own insecurities, who takes you for who you are and says its okay. I know." He licked his lips and looked down at the table. "I know it, probably better than most, and now, so do you. She's dying, man, and I can't… my brain can't comprehend the gravity or the depth of the sorrow you feel, and I can't help you — none of us can — and it's choking to watch, to live through, so I can't imagine being you, I can't imagine being her, and because of that, I respect you so much that now, right here, right now, I vow to do my damnedest to help you when this is done. I'll get your ass out of bed when it seems too hard. I'll shoot you in the ass if you don't eat. I'll do what I can because I owe you at least that much for showing me what it's really like to be selfless — to love."

I had no words.

So, for the first time since my promise to Andi, I let it go. I collapsed against my enemy — the one guy I probably hated just as much as Tex.

And I cried.

Big heaving sobs wracked my body.

And Phoenix De Lange of all people…

Held me.

And told me it was going to be okay.

I just wish I believed him.

CHAPTER FORTY-FIVE

Andi

THIS WAS FAMILY. IT WAS DISORGANIZED, messy, chaotic, hilarious, heartbreaking—it was perfect.

Trace had quickly decided that we didn't need a movie but a karaoke night.

Nixon was not amused.

And watching Trace try to get Nixon to sing *Frozen's* "Let it Go" was officially going down in my all-time favorite moments. He looked livid, yet he was up there, clutching the microphone with a death grip while Trace danced around him.

Awesome.

I clapped.

Tex kept booing.

And Chase kept asking Nixon to take off his shirt.

Somehow the song took a turn for the worse when Trace tried to spank Nixon. He tossed her over his shoulder and carried her out of the room.

The song was finished anyway.

I imagine she was going to get punished — in the best

way imaginable. Homeboy seemed to have a lot of anger — but the good kind — like the kind that you knew if timed right could be… exciting.

I giggled when Chase and Mil took the stage.

I'd never seen a better pair in my entire life. She was feisty; he was hilarious but had this underlying intensity that I think he tried to hide in order not to terrify small children. It worked.

They sang "A Whole New World."

Chase was the magic carpet.

You can imagine how that went.

Mil got on top of him and… well, it was Chase; he immediately flipped her around and started kissing her.

The song never even finished before Mil stopped singing and flushed a bright red.

"Get a room!" Tex yelled.

"We have one!" Mil gripped Chase's hand and led him to the door just as Phoenix and Sergio made their way in.

"What's going on in here?" Phoenix shoved his hands into his pockets and grinned.

"Singing!" I announced.

Sergio tried to leave.

Chase barricaded the door with help from Mil.

"Yay!" I yelled. "Our turn!"

I jumped to my feet and quickly fell back to my chair.

Sergio was at my side immediately. "Are you okay? Do you need to go to bed?"

"No," I lied. The room was spinning, but I was having so much fun, and I just wanted to pretend the night could last a little bit longer. "Let's sing!"

"Huzzah!" Tex yelled.

"Historical romance nod." Chase held up his fist to Tex. "That's my man."

Sergio rolled his eyes and gripped my hands. "Alright, Russia, what do you want to sing? I swear to all that is holy if you say the Russian national anthem, I'm going to Taser your ass and hide your gun."

I pouted. "But my gun is special."

He smirked. "So's mine."

"Fine. You win."

"Ha." He kissed the corner of my mouth. "Okay, so what will it be?"

The only song I could think of wasn't fun. But it had meaning, so I pressed my finger to his lips and went over to the little machine and picked my song then grabbed the microphone.

"'If I die young, bury me in satin, lay me down on a bed of roses…'" I kept singing and twirled around on the stage, but I got dizzy super-fast and had to stop.

Sergio was there instantly. He sat on the makeshift stage and put me on his lap as I kept singing.

I was on his lap…

Singing about getting buried.

And he was rocking back and forth like it was okay.

Tex and Mo sobered.

Phoenix turned off the lights, and soon cell phones lit up the small dark room.

"The sharp knife of a short life… oh well, I've had just enough time," I crooned. "'And I'll be wearing white…'"

Sergio grabbed the microphone when I couldn't finish and started singing with me. I was breathless, maybe from my cancer, maybe from the fact that it was so true, so close to home — being buried in white, leaving the boy from town.

"'So put on your best, boys, and I'll wear my pearls,'" I sang

"'A penny for my thoughts…'" Sergio countered in a low voice that was smooth, effortlessly beautiful.

Nixon and Trace came back and immediately held up their cell phones.

It was like a tribute concert.

The end of something great.

A ballad of beauty.

I closed my eyes and cherished the moment — where I had family, where I had love, where I had in that night everything I could have ever hoped or dreamed for.

It was short.

But it was beautiful.

And it was enough.

CHAPTER FORTY-SIX

Sergio

"ANDI?" I'D NEVER TIRE OF KISSING her mouth, of pressing my lips against hers, of tasting her, of exploring. My tongue met hers. She was tired. I wouldn't pressure her or anything. I just wanted — needed — to be close.

"Hmm?" It was early morning; the sun had just started to rise over the horizon. "Everything okay?"

"Yup." My hands found her hips as I pulled her against me. "It is now."

Her eyes were still closed as she nestled her head under my chin. "You smell sexy."

"Oh yeah?"

"Yup." She sighed happily. "I've always thought so, like expensive cologne."

I laughed.

Andi was quiet. I'd assumed she'd fallen back asleep when suddenly she let out a tiny whimper.

"Hey..." I tilted her chin toward me. "...you okay?"

Her eyes blinked and then rolled up in the back of her

head.

"Andi!" I gripped her by the arms and set her on her back. "Come on, sweetheart. Talk to me. Stay awake."

She jolted and then blinked. "Sorry, sorry… I just… sorry."

My eyes narrowed. "What's going on?"

She licked her lips. "My face just felt… funny and…" Her eyes kept blinking wildly at me.

"Andi?" I hated to ask. "Double vision?"

"Yeah…" She frowned. "…and a bit of a headache."

Shit. I'd read every brochure, researched until I felt like I was going to go blind from the glare of the computer.

I knew it was possible.

I just hadn't thought it would happen.

She'd had a stroke. I looked closer as part of the right side of her face sagged just a bit; only noticeable to someone who was obsessed with every angle of her.

"Maybe…" I swallowed the lump in my throat. "…we should call the hospice nurse, just in case."

Typically, our nurse only checked in once a day.

I dreaded the time I'd have to call her to stay more than an hour.

The time was upon us.

Andi shook her head and reached for my hand. She gripped it tight, which wasn't tight; it was weak, again making me feel sick to my stomach.

"Please, wait, just… just until the sunrise."

I licked my lips, not sure if I should wait. I mean, what if?

"Please," she begged. "Things always look better in the morning, right? And it's not morning yet. Technically, it's still night. So wait until morning, wait until the sun shines on a new day, and we'll call."

I nodded. "Okay."

She sighed and pressed a kiss to my lips. "Good, now let's put a chair in front of the window and watch. Let's watch life together."

It was the last good day we had.

That was cancer for you. It had no schedule, no timetable — it just was. One day she was laughing and joking with me.

The next…

She was a shell of her former self.

A week had gone by since her stroke.

A week where I watched my wife, the love of my life, fade before my very eyes. The weight continued to fall off; her appetite was nonexistent; muscle deteriorated. It was almost like I was watching the cancer actually eat her.

I tried to cheer her up.

We watched movies in bed. I sang to her even — though I sang like shit.

And when she was too tired to read…

I read to her.

Her stupid historical romance books.

About dukes and London and far away kingdoms that no longer existed in society.

She loved it.

So I loved it.

"Shergio…" Andi slurred, her speech had started to go, especially at night. "Promise me another sunset."

"I promise." I kissed her forehead. "Sleep."

She fell asleep within seconds.

I set the book down and left the room, not because I wanted to be away from her, but because I hadn't eaten anything all day. I'd been too consumed by her.

Too sad.

It was around eight at night when I made it down to the kitchen.

Chase was pulling something out of the oven. Frank was pouring wine, and the rest of the group paused.

It wasn't awkward, just… depressing.

"My other bitch made food," Tex finally blurted.

And suddenly everything was right again.

I cracked a smile. "He better have buttered my bread.

"You slut, butter your own bread!" Chase snapped.

I laughed.

Probably for the first time in a week.

Fighting commenced over dinner.

Four bottles of wine all but disappeared, and I knew, one day, maybe not soon, I'd be okay. Because I had family — I really had family.

CHAPTER FORTY-SEVEN

Andi

I FELT IT.

Maybe that was normal — maybe not. But it was like an alarm clock had suddenly gone off in my heart, beckoning me, calling to me. And a peace like I'd never experienced in my entire life fell over me. It was warm, like a blanket on a cold winter's night.

I woke up from my sleep and smiled a real smile — like the ones I saved for Sergio and only Sergio.

I looked around the room. Things had been set into motion, the plans for his life set, even though he had no idea.

I'd done what I could.

And I'd done well; I knew that in my soul. The peace I felt in that moment was enough to help me get out of bed.

I wrapped an afghan around me and kissed Sergio on the top of his head. He stirred, then woke up just as I walked out of the room.

He would follow.

He would always follow.

But this was the last time he'd do such a thing. It was the last time he'd follow me, and that was how it should be, how it was supposed to be.

I ran my fingers along the wood banister as I made my way down the stairs, my naked feet sinking into the warm plush carpet. The house smelled like pasta; I imagined they'd had a really good meal the night before — with wine and laughter.

Good. He would need that.

A lot of it.

Night blanketed the house, its shadows casting a comforting glow as I finally found myself in the main entryway.

I heard Sergio's soft steps behind me.

I opened the front door and walked outside. The moon was starting to set, the sun just beginning to peek from the east.

The smell of winter was long gone, and spring was starting to seep its way into the atmosphere with its growth, its life.

It was poetic really, if I thought about it. The timing… more perfect than I'd originally thought.

One step.

Two.

Three… and I was walking out into the field, the same field I'd run into in my wedding dress when my husband had pissed me off.

Again, so poetic, so romantic that this was where life had brought us.

Together.

In that same field.

I blinked back the tears as I watched the sky swirl with life.

I would miss him.

Desperately.

Our time had been short.

But it had been good.

And that's how life is measured — not by the length, but by the strength of those moments spent together.

I turned around as Sergio slowly approached, his hair disheveled, his face calm, his body strong. I'd remember him always — his sharp jaw, his defined lips, his gorgeous icy-blue eyes, long shaggy pirate hair… or as I'd remember… historical-romance duke hair that would make any girl with a pulse swoon.

He was my hero.

My white knight.

Granted, he was missing a horse.

But his heart — damn, it was strong.

He didn't have armor… then again, men like Sergio? Rarely needed it.

His steps were purposeful, his full mouth curving into a sad smile.

Beautiful… and mine — a gift I'd never deserve but forever cherish. I winked and then sat down, the grass tickling my legs. I pulled the afghan tighter against my body as I waited for his approach.

For the final moment.

CHAPTER FORTY-EIGHT

Sergio

I'D KNOWN IT BEFORE SHE'D EVEN woke me up.

Something in my soul had stirred… maybe it was because we were connected at such a deep level that her thoughts were my own; her feelings, the same.

I followed her into the field, grinning when she gave me that coy look I'd been so used to seeing — the same one that had been missing from her face for the past week.

"Wanted to go for a midnight run, huh?" I teased.

Andi laughed. "Yeah, well, you know me. I like to keep you on your toes and all that. Italians aren't known for their spontaneity."

"Who uses big words this early in the morning?"

Her eyebrows arched. "Russians."

I held out my hand.

She stood and gripped it.

"Twirl."

"Huh?"

I kissed her softly. "This…" I stood back and glanced at

her pajama pants and T-shirt. "…is a two-twirl outfit — maybe three."

"Oh yeah?" Tears welled in her eyes.

"Yeah." I nodded then slowly twirled her, one, two, three times, bringing her into my arms and kissing her again, slowly dancing side to side. "You're beautiful."

"Nope." She pulled back. "Not doing this. You know we never would have worked, right?"

I sat on the ground and pulled her into my lap. "Oh yeah?" My hands danced across her arms, rubbing them back and forth, trying to bring warmth into her cold body. "Why's that?"

"You hate vodka and never even finished the honeymoon list!"

I laughed. "We finished the important parts."

"True." She laid her head against my chest and let out a huge sigh. "You know you don't really love me, right?"

"Yes, I do. Don't tell me how to feel." I pulled her against me and kissed her nose, feeling semi-aggravated she would doubt me.

"Nope." She shook her head. "I refuse to believe it. Wanna know why?"

"Not particularly, no, but saying no to you is like waving a red flag in front of a bull. Should I sit down for this?"

"No, but you can hold me."

"I'm already doing that."

"And you are sitting down, silly Italian."

"Such a good student."

She flicked my nose.

"I was your teacher first, smart ass."

"One day…" She sighed happily. "…you're going to fall in love, and it's going to be epic and beautiful and heartbreaking."

"I feel that way now." My words felt thick as I clenched her body tighter.

"I refuse it!" she said in a stern voice. "Because that makes our story too tragic, and I don't do tragic. I think we deserve a happy ending… so you and me? We're best friends. We have a lot of firsts together. But imagine us growing old, Sergio? You'd steal the remote. I'd bang you on the head with a baseball bat."

"Don't forget the pots and pans," I said, laughing.

"I mean, who does that?" Andi finished. "Imagine our children!"

"They'd be beautiful," I said reverently.

"They'd be American-born Sicilians with a slice of Russian — they'd be horrible."

I burst out laughing. It felt good to laugh. That was Andi; I knew what she was doing, even in her last moments — trying to cheer me up. Maybe she could sense my heart breaking. Maybe she could hear it. I knew I could.

"And don't even get me started on the way you steal all the covers, Sergio. Not very classy and, I mean, you do snore."

"I purr."

"You snore," she corrected. "And you sing like shit."

"Thanks."

"It's the truth."

"No sugarcoating, hmm, Russia?"

"No, Sicily, no sugarcoating."

"So where does that leave us?" I was almost afraid to ask.

"With goodbye." She shrugged then kissed me softly across the lips. "But it's going to be a hell of a goodbye… with kissing, hugging — no tears though. Don't go all soft on me. Russians don't cry."

"Even when Russians watch *Frozen?*"

"You were sworn to secrecy! You know that means I have to kill you."

"Do your worst." I held open my arms, but, instead of hitting me, she just leaned back, her head resting against my chest.

"Remember this moment, Sergio… when I'm gone… and please, for the love of God, smile don't go back to that place. Don't get angry, don't get resentful, just smile… because we had a chance. It was short, but we still had it. And that, my friend, is a beautiful ending, remember?"

I closed my eyes, blinking back tears. "Yes, I remember."

Andi kissed my cheek and sighed; her breathing sounded more laborious; her body felt cold, frigid.

"Andi…" My voice broke. "…I broke my promise."

She shifted in my lap and faced me. "What?"

"I cried… I cried over you."

Andi's eyes welled with tears as she cupped my face with her hands. "That's okay… I cried too."

I nodded, not trusting my voice.

"Will you hold me now?" She sighed. "So we can watch the sunrise together?" Her voice cracked.

"Yeah, Andi."

She relaxed against me. Her body felt so frail, so tiny.

"I love you, Italy."

"I love you too, Russia."

"For as long as we both live…" Andi whispered.

"As long as we both live," I repeated.

The sun rose over the horizon; it was bright, breathtaking. Andi gripped my hands tight and sighed happily.

My whole life I'd watched people die. After all, most of the time I'd been the one to offer death. I'd been on the other end of the gun, the fist, the knife.

I'd always thought of it as being something so indifferent, mechanical.

I was wrong.

So wrong.

Dying didn't have to be tragic.

It didn't have to be horrific.

Or dark.

It could be beautiful.

I'd known the minute I'd stepped out of our bedroom I wouldn't be walking back in with Andi in my arms.

I'd known it in my soul.

Yet I followed her.

I would follow that woman anywhere.

And she knew that.

It was a kindness — to pull me away from my family, from the house, from what the memory would be like to find her lifeless in our bed, in the room we'd shared.

"Andi," I whispered, "I love you… until we both shall live…"

She took her last breath.

I felt it like it was my own.

And I held her like my strength would somehow bring her back.

It wouldn't.

But I held her anyway.

For an hour I sat there with Andi in my arms. The sun shone across her face — it was bright, so beautiful — and I knew… death didn't have to be ugly.

It could be like Andi.

Absolutely perfect.

I kept my tears in.

At least I tried.

But I didn't last long.

Because after that hour was up, I felt a hand touch my shoulder. Tex sat down next to me and wrapped his arm around my body and held me…

While tears flowed freely down my face.

Nixon sat on the other side.

And then Ax.

Chase.

Frank.

Phoenix.

The mob bosses and two made men.

They didn't just hold me.

Every single one of them cried with me.

Andi hadn't just affected me. She'd affected all of us, brought us together, made something beautiful out of what had for so long been so dark.

And I had to, in that moment, smile…

Luca.

Damn the man.

He'd known what he was doing all along.

CHAPTER FORTY-NINE

Sergio

THE FUNERAL WAS SMALL, NOT LARGE.

The people invited?

Family — and only family — plus one Russian doctor and his ever-present scowl and wise eyes.

"Nicolai." I held out my hand.

He took it, his grip firm. Faint shadows beneath his eyes, he looked as exhausted as I felt. "Sergio, remember what I promised."

I smiled sadly. "I'd rather feel than forget."

He nodded his head. "I figured you'd say that."

A woman stood next to him, practically glued to his side, but something about her stance seemed cautious, like she was afraid I was going to pull a knife on her or something.

"Ah…" Nicolai stepped to the side. "…meet Maya."

I held out my hand.

She stared at it.

Nicolai nodded to her like it was okay for her to actually do something as simple as touch me. When her hand touched mine, a zap of familiarity hit me; my eyes narrowed as I took in her face, the features so similar to the woman I'd just buried.

"Maya," Nicolai said in a low voice. "Andi's sister."

I dropped her hand in shock. Where Andi had bright features, Maya's were much darker. She was slightly taller with an athletic build. But her lips, her nose — they were so similar it was scary.

"I'm—" Her voice cracked. "I never knew her." Tears welled in her eyes. "But from what Nicolai has told me, she had a good life. Because of you, she lived." She hung her head. "Thank you for protecting her from my father."

"It was my privilege," I said honestly, silently wondering if she was in the same predicament Andi had been in — or worse, still under her father's thumb.

My gaze flickered to Nicolai, but his expression gave nothing away. If anything, he'd completely shut down. Emotion, it seemed, still had no place in his life — not that I could blame him.

"Thank you for coming." I took a step back.

Nicolai wrapped an arm around Maya.

She flinched, not necessarily in fear, but almost like his touch had caused physical pain — maybe even emotional.

They walked off to a waiting limo.

And I was left by the gravestone.

The rest of my family stood close by. I told them I needed a minute alone, which, naturally, they interpreted as backing up at least twenty feet but not letting me out of their sight.

I couldn't blame them — not really. They were worried about me. They shouldn't be.

I was sad.

Devastated.

Alone.

Upset.

Angry.

I was all of those things — I'd be lying if I said I wasn't — but every time I wanted to yell or scream or shoot something, I thought of her face, I envisioned her smile, and suddenly it all seemed pointless.

Why would I respond in anger when I'd been given one of the most priceless gifts of my life?

I crouched down next to her simple grey gravestone and touched it with my fingertips. "You were right." I swallowed and closed my eyes. "You said I was dead inside, and you were right. I was so pissed at you for calling me out, for upsetting my carefully planned-out life, for making me feel when all I really wanted to do was throw a pity party and lock myself away with a gun." I opened my eyes and smiled, remembering the way she'd woken me up that first morning. "You said I was dead. I think because of what you were going through, you recognized death easily in others. You saw the signs in me, and, instead of allowing me to follow you, you healed me." I stood. "Thank you."

I took a step back and shoved my hands into my pockets.

"I'll love you… until we both shall live."

"Eat." Chase shoved a plate piled high with at least three different types of pastas, two sauces, and enough bread to feed a small country in my direction. "It helps."

"Eat my feelings?" I countered, picking up a piece of bread. "Don't know if that's such a good idea."

"Drink." Frank poured me a healthy glass of wine.

"I'm fine," I said, probably for the tenth time in the last three minutes. "Really, you guys don't have to stay."

Mo pulled out a chair next to me and scooted my wine closer.

I sighed in her direction then took it and sipped. The taste wasn't comforting; it was missing something. I frowned then got up from my chair.

The room was silent.

Swear, they were just waiting for me to snap.

I wasn't going to.

But no matter how many times I said that, they didn't believe me.

When I reached the edge of the kitchen, I reached up into the liquor cabinet and pulled out the giant bottle then turned to face everyone.

"Vodka?"

You'd thought I'd just agreed to give all my cars to the homeless and go on a *Lord-of-the-Rings*-style journey to find myself.

"Vodka?" Frank repeated, his voice just barely above a whisper.

I pulled out shot glasses, filled each to the rim, then nodded to the guys. Each of them grabbed one and handed the other to their significant other.

I held mine into the air and whispered, "To Andi."

"To Andi," they said in unison.

Italians drinking vodka at a funeral, never thought I'd see the day.

CHAPTER FIFTY

Sergio

A WEEK WENT BY AND THEN TWO, followed by three.

I counted them; it made me feel less like I was going insane and more like I was developing a serious case of OCD.

Everyone left a week after the funeral.

I was alone in my house again.

And it felt lonely — damn, did it feel lonely. I hadn't been able to focus on anything except actually making it through the day, eating three square meals and exercising to take my mind off the emotional pain that sliced through my chest every single time I went into the bedroom I'd shared with my wife.

Finally, during the third week…

I woke up.

And felt different.

I wasn't better, not by any stretch of the imagination, but I felt… okay, like the world wasn't crashing down around me. Like I could breathe, maybe, just a little bit deeper.

After breakfast I walked by my study and paused. The

door, the door I'd always had shut from the world, was ajar.

I scratched my head.

The last time I'd been in there had been months before. The guys knew not to go in on account that I was a private man, and there was a certain amount of respect between all of us and our offices; it was our domain, where we did the ugly, the dark… where we sat and contemplated our sins and begged for forgiveness.

Curious, I stepped inside.

Nothing looked out of place.

Except the black folder.

I'd placed it on the farthest side of my desk.

But now? It was propped up against the lamp — the only light flickering in the room.

Was Frank behind this?

His final way to get me to read it?

I walked closer.

There was a small pink sticky note attached to the bottom. I picked it up and smirked. "Read me or perish — Andi."

I burst out laughing. Of course she would. Threatening me even in her death, bloodthirsty Russian.

The folder had no power over me, I knew that, but I also knew I wouldn't like what was inside. It was the equivalent of seeing all the horrible sins you'd committed in black and white.

Impossible to erase.

Impossible to forget.

Slowly, I pulled out my chair; it rolled against the wood floor. The sound may as well have been a gun going off.

I was doing this.

Because Andi had left me a note.

And I could deny that girl nothing.

The folder was heavy — it would be, knowing what I'd done, the things I'd experienced in my short life.

With shaking fingers, I opened the first page.

A small rubber bracelet was taped to the inside with another pink sticky note attached. *"Wear me."*

What was this? *Alice in Wonderland?*

The bracelet was one of those *LiveStrong* ones, the ones that high-schoolers wore like crack on their wrists. I lifted it into the light and smirked.

From Russia With Love.

On the other side, it said...

Best Friends Forever.

My laugh soon turned into a silent sob as I put the bracelet on my right hand. It felt like she was there – in that room with me. Tears dripped down onto the pages of the black folder, staining them, making them appear less terrifying and more breakable, like I didn't have to let them define me.

Andi wouldn't have wanted that.

Hell, I didn't want that.

I closed my eyes and for a brief moment remembered her bright smile, her big brown eyes, and constant sarcasm. If she could see me crying, she'd kick my ass. I laughed at the idea of her scolding me.

I could do this. I took a deep breath and looked down at the next page. It was filled with everything I assumed it would be filled with.

Facts about me.

My age.

My birthday.

My social security number.

Known aliases.

The date of my first kill.

The person's name and organization.

Like I needed to be reminded of any of those things.

I turned the page and paused. A piece of notebook paper was taped to the inside. My name was scribbled across it.

Frowning, I peeled it from the page and opened the note.

Italy,

I'm only going to say this once. Stop crying, or so help me God, I'm going to rise from the ashes and haunt you for the rest of your life. I'm sure right now you're thinking that would be better than nothing. But believe me, nothing cool about being haunted. Imagine me hitting a pan with my baseball bat every hour of the day. You'd go crazy, and nobody wants to see you lose your shit.

You may be wondering why I wrote you a letter.

I was watching you sleep.

Ha, creepy, am I right?

I snorted back a laugh and wiped at the tears on my face and kept reading.

Did you know you have a scar on the back of your ear, left side. It's hardly noticeable, unless you have superhuman vision like yours truly, compliments of my Russian heritage.

I rolled my eyes.

Stop rolling your eyes, Italy.

I smiled.

Anyway, when I first met you, I was constantly trying to find a stupid flaw. I mean, how could a guy be so perfect? Naturally, that thought was short-lived the minute you offered to kill me — thanks by the way, super special moment. I was lying in bed staring at that stupid scar the minute this idea hit me.

I self-consciously touched the scar behind my ear, the one given to me by my brother when he'd tried to shoot an arrow into a tree, and it had veered hard right, nearly impaling me in the back of the head.

You're going to be lonely, which is expected. I mean, let's face it. I brought a lot of loudness into your life. I forced you to take me on a crazy honeymoon, forced you to have sex with me — ha ha, just kidding. That wasn't forced, and we both know it. Aw, my little Italian lover. The point is… a lot of these things had a purpose, one I wasn't even aware of until now.

She's really pretty. I think you'll like her. She's a bit quiet — okay, so a lot quiet, more quiet than I am, but sometimes opposites attract. Her eyes are this killer hazel that I know guys have the capacity to get lost in. Her name is Valentina. Pretty name, right? Oh, stop freaking out. It's an Italian name! You should be jumping for joy!

She's scared of heights — you'll have to help her with that. Terrified of traveling out of the country — so maybe she deserves to go to the places I never had a chance to.

Can't shoot a gun to save her life. Loves romance novels — especially ones with dukes and earls. I may have bought you a costume, just in case your flirting's shit, and you can't get her to talk to you. Ha, kidding.

But seriously. You will talk to her. You will try. See, it occurred to me that I married an old man. I mean, you're going to be thirty this year. You need to settle down, have a family, stop shooting things. You get the point. And I thought... what better way to encourage you to start dating than to pick out your very first date — and hopefully if she's as amazing as I've heard from Luca all these years — your last.

Have you put the pieces together yet? Get there faster. In the pages of this black folder you'll discover some things about yourself, things you never thought possible. It seems great minds think alike.

I was meant for Dante. Care to guess who you were meant for? Valentina. Luca handpicked his own daughter to marry you. Just like he handpicked his son to marry me. Yet, things got messed up, and in that mess, Luca, bless his heart, still planned for the worst. I think that was me — my sickness — you and yours.

Because let's not pretend you weren't sick — maybe more sick than I was. But now you're better, and honestly — so am I. Remember, you promised not to cry, so stop it! I'm happy. I can kick ass without getting dizzy, and, as you're reading this, I'm most likely watching you from above, drinking wine with Luca and cheering to our amazing planning. We probably could have taken over the world someday, me and Luca.

In this folder you'll find everything you need to know about the Nicolasi dynasty. So you see... the black folder? Though it has a lot of your information in it, Luca built it. He created it to give you a path to follow. He knew you needed guidance — guidance you never got from your father. He knew you'd one day need him — and he wasn't so sure he'd be able to do that if he was dead.

Funny that the thing you were most afraid of... most

disgusted with — is going to be your salvation. Then again, life is like that, isn't it?

Frank's going to ask you to go with him to find the twins. To find Luca's kids — to convince them to join the family. Go with him. Take a chance.

Smile at the girl. Don't frown. It makes you look scary. Help her. She's going to need you.

And know you have my blessing, even though I'm going to be as jealous as hell that another girl is going to experience what I got to experience. We were lovers. Best friends. Enemies. We were everything. But that doesn't have to be the end. You still have time for more story, and I'd like to think that God isn't cruel enough to give us only one soul mate. I'd like to believe he gave you two.

I love you more than you'll ever know. Thank you for making my last kiss with you, my last moment, my last laugh, my last tears feel like the first.

~Russia

Hands shaking, I placed the paper onto the table and looked down at the folder again.

The very next page had a picture of a girl.

She was laughing.

Her hair was a lush chestnut, darker on the top than the bottom, like she was growing it out. Her eyes were hazel, just as Andi described, and she was holding up her Kindle in triumph, like she'd just gotten it at as a present or maybe had just finished reading the best book of her life.

Her smile was easy.

I looked away as my heart clenched.

The next page was information about Valentina and Dante — their location and known aliases.

And on the page after that…

In Luca's handwriting was another note. It wasn't long like Andi's. Then again, he was easily a man of few words, used his fists and gun to talk.

> *Find my daughter. Protect her. Marry her. I know your secrets, and now she will too. If you're reading this, I'm long gone. Carry on my legacy for me. You must know Frank and I have talked. If Dante does not want to take over the Alfero family, it will fall to you.*
>
> *You are who I choose. Who Frank chooses. You will lead the Alferos if Dante does not. And you'll do a damn good job, son.*
>
> *~Luca*

Dumbfounded, I stared at the letter, reading it over and over again. No wonder Phoenix had wanted me to read the damn folder! And Frank. I stood. My chair slid backward and collided into the wall with a crash.

I swallowed as the walls of my throat threatened to close in.

"I knocked," Phoenix said from the door. "Funny I was just about to ask you if you'd read the folder."

I pointed at it. "You knew?"

"Shit, Sergio, you even need to ask?" Phoenix folded his arms. "I know everything. Luca made sure of that the minute I took over the family. I just didn't believe it at first, nor did I want to, all things considering. But…" He shrugged. "…she changed you."

"She changed all of us," I whispered.

"Yeah." Phoenix nodded. "She did."

"So…" I scratched the back of my head. "…it seems I'm going to New York."

Phoenix grinned. "I already booked your flight."

EPILOGUE

Sergio

"WHAT DOES IT MEAN?" THE WAITRESS inclined her head at my right forearm. "Your tattoo?"

I leaned back in the booth, my hand tapping against the ceramic mug. The smell of greasy food filled the air. A bell dinged as Frank made his way toward me from the door.

"The tally mark?" I asked politely.

She nodded her head. Damn, the girl just screamed innocence.

I had to fight to keep myself from scaring her. "It's for a friend." I said in a gruff voice then shrugged. "My best friend."

"Lucky girl." Her smile was warm.

"She died," I said slowly, "and I promised her I'd never forget — I told her I only marked things that were desperately important to me. And ink is forever, you know."

"Is that why you put the inscription underneath it?" She pointed.

I looked down. *Until we both shall live* had been scrawled

in cursive beneath a black tally mark with a rose drawn around it.

"Yeah," I croaked. "That's why."

"Again…" The waitress shrugged. "…lucky girl."

"No," I corrected, "I'm the lucky one."

Frank cleared his throat.

"Well, I'll just…" The waitress blushed and scurried away.

"So…" Frank folded his hands onto the table and leaned forward. "…I take it you've read your folder."

"We leave tomorrow," I said quietly.

"New York." Frank sighed. "Never thought I'd return to that godforsaken place. It's where we started, you know, but Chicago had been new, clean, unaffected by the crime families. We moved in, and everything changed."

"You think they know we're coming?"

Frank snorted. "Oh, they'll expect it. Our cousins have been protecting that boy and girl for the past ten years."

"Are these cousins… friendly?"

"Hell, no." Frank grinned. "But a little gunfire never hurt anyone."

"I thought your family was the least violent of the five," I muttered.

"Funny." Frank checked his watch. "I'd always believed them to be the most violent."

"Fantastic."

"Aw, where's your sense of adventure?"

The list burned a hole in my pocket. Somewhere on it was written: *Go to a Broadway show in New York and sing along even if it sounds horrible.*

"Oh, I've got it." I chuckled and patted my pocket. "Right here."

"Good to know." Frank grinned. "Shall we?"

I followed him out, my mind focused in on one thing.

Keeping my promise to Andi.

And fulfilling my destiny.
Funny how they ended up being the same damn thing.

The End.

PREVIEW
EMPIRE
Eagle Elite, Book 7

Empire: *Organization, Kingdom, Business. To rule or have power or authority. Command, control, dominate; e.g., He built an empire. He refused to see it crumble beneath his feet.*

PROLOGUE

Frank

THE DAY MATCHED MY DARK MOOD. I clenched the umbrella tight within my hand, the sensation getting more and more difficult to feel with my arthritis creeping in. Age, had never been a friend of mine. The clock, it seemed, never stopped ticking, the seconds going by faster than I could have ever imagined, the years disappearing like sand through an hour glass.

Rain pelted against my umbrella, pieces of grass stuck to my black Valentino loafers.

I kept walking.

My stride strong.

My purpose even stronger.

The grave was marked well, I'd been sure of it. After all, it seemed the least I could do—give my brother a proper burial, when it was me, his most feared enemy and in the end most trusted ally—who had a hand in watching him die.

It wasn't my fault.

I didn't pull the trigger.

But I knew the dangers in what we did.

I knew the cost of our chess match.

I just wish it would have been me—instead of him.

A few more feet and I was in front of the large grey stone. I knew Luca wouldn't want something elaborate—after all he made his way through the world on being the silent one, the death blow you never saw coming, until it was too late.

I licked my cracked lips and shook my head as I read the tombstone. "Loving brother, fearless leader…" My voice cracked. "Blessed father." I closed my eyes as the sting of tears burned against my eyes.

Father.

And only two people in the world knew.

Phoenix and myself.

"I'm so sorry brother…"

Would I have done things differently? All those years ago when I made Luca into the man hew as, when I forced him into the Nicolasi family, when I stole the woman he loved and turned him against the world.

Knowing what I knew now…would I do it all again?

"For what it's worth old man…" I pointed to the gravestone next to his. "I'd like to think…that at least in the afterlife---you'll have her."

I'd buried my wife next to him, where she belonged. Where she always belonged.

Every night I prayed that they were finally united in

heaven.

While I was cursed to roam the earth without my brother—without my wife, and in charge of four mafia bosses who were younger than I was when I took over.

The empire I had built was changing, morphing into something I no longer recognized.

With a sigh I made a cross over my chest and mumbled a prayer.

"Well this is depressing." Came a low voice behind me.

I didn't need to turn around to know it was Phoenix De Lange, newest boss to the Nicoalsi family—handpicked by Luca himself.

"Did you bring it?" I kept my eyes trained on the gravestone.

Phoenix let out a curse, "Yes."

I held out my hand.

"Are you sure you want to know?"

"Yes."

"Maybe we should talk to Tex about this before---"

"—give it over damn it, I'm your elder."

"Don't pull the age line old man, you could still take me down and you know it."

I smirked and kept my hand firmly in the air. The minute the folder touched my fingertips, I snatched it away and held it tightly against my chest.

"They aren't going to like this…" Phoenix growled.

"They don't get a say."

"The hell they don't." Phoenix let out a bark of laughter. "But sure if it helps you sleep at night." The rain started to pour down in sheets. "When do you leave?"

"As soon as possible."

"Safe travels."

"Always."

"Does anyone else know you'll be gone?"

I turned and offered him a sly wink. "Secrets, secrets,

secrets, what else do I build my family on?"

With a slight shake of his head Phoenix took a step back. "I can't protect you if this goes badly—especially if I don't know where you are…at least bring one of the men."

"No." I glanced at my watch. My flight would leave within the hour. "Don't think I will."

"Damn it Frank."

"Don't damn it Frank me…" I held out my hand. "Now, leave like a man before I have to remind you who's older…and more experienced."

Phoenix offered a sad smile and shook my hand, "Be well, Frank."

"Be well, Phoenix."

OTHER BOOKS BY RACHEL VAN DYKEN

The Bet Series

The Bet (Forever Romance)
The Wager (Forever Romance)
The Dare

Eagle Elite

Elite (Forever Romance)
Elect (Forever Romance)
Entice
Elicit
Ember
Elude

Seaside Series

Tear
Pull
Shatter
Forever
Fall
Strung
Eternal

Wallflower Trilogy

Waltzing with the Wallflower
Beguiling Bridget
Taming Wilde

London Fairy Tales

Upon a Midnight Dream
Whispered Music
The Wolf's Pursuit
When Ash Falls

Renwick House

The Ugly Duckling Debutante

The Seduction of Sebastian St. James

The Redemption of Lord Rawlings

An Unlikely Alliance

The Devil Duke Takes a Bride

Ruin Series

Ruin

Toxic

Fearless

Shame

The Consequence Series

The Consequence of Loving Colton

The Consequence of Revenge

Other Titles

The Parting Gift

Compromising Kessen

Savage Winter

Divine Uprising

Every Girl Does It

ABOUT THE AUTHOR

RACHEL VAN DYKEN is the *New York Times, Wall Street Journal,* and *USA Today* bestselling author of regency and contemporary romances. When she's not writing you can find her drinking coffee at Starbucks and plotting her next book while watching "The Bachelor".

She keeps her home in Idaho with her husband, adorable son, and two snoring boxers. She loves to hear from readers.

Want to be kept up to date on new releases? Text MAFIA to 66866!

You can connect with her on Facebook at http://www.facebook.com/rachelvandyken or join her fan group *Rachel's New Rockin Readers.* Her website is www.rachelvandykenauthor.com.

RACHEL VAN DYKEN *Books*

CPSIA information can be obtained
at www.ICGtesting.com
Printed in the USA
LVHW092154140319
610738LV00001B/225/P